R.H. Bishop

Cover design by A.M. Matakena

ISBN: 97809987260-4-5 Trade Paperback

Visit: rhbishopbooks.com

For Jeffrey

Upgrade to Exclusive Concierge Class Stateroom and enjoy expanded drink menu and free** laundry service*

** adds espresso coffee and premium soft drinks.*

*** up to 14 garments per laundry bag; additional restrictions apply.*

. . .

Being of service comes naturally to our award-winning staff, whose devotion is as sincere as their exuberant enthusiasm. It is their genuine pleasure to devote their complete attention to fulfilling your every need.

~Jamboree Cruises Brochure

1

Armando

Only Three More Hours

It was like a freaking archeological excavation of a tomb, only the mummy inside was still alive. Slim and I had forced the dusty, paint-peeling door open just far enough so we could start removing the piles of books and boxes that jammed it closed. A yip of concern came out of the garage every time we dislodged a book and it fell to the floor. Finally, the pile blocking the door was low enough for me to put my head inside.

Close-set blue eyes stared from under a fright wig of bleached hair. I gasped. It was my boss, in my worst anxiety nightmare. But, no. Trapped under a fallen bookcase, it had to be Elaine "Sandy" Sanders, nutty elder sister of my boss Lucy Sanders, looking up at me like a wounded zombie.

"I think I've sprained my ankle," she said.

Sandy's garage was filled with stacks of books, magazines, newspapers, furniture, old appliances, and bags and boxes of God knows what. The only floor space left was a coffin-sized clearing, where Ms. S. Sanders was trapped.

Sandy made a move towards me, and I heard something fall onto the ground behind her. The huge bookcase slid closer to her crouching body.

"Stay still!" I said. "We'll get you out of there."

Extracting my head back out into the bright sunlight, I squinted my eyes and took a deep breath.

"Slim," I whispered, "She's stuck under a bookcase that looks unstable. Lucy will kill me if something happens to her."

The trick was to clear a path to where Sandy was trapped without causing another avalanche. Junk was stacked like a giant Jenga game. We removed the rest of the pile of books out from the other side of the door. Slim maneuvered his body sideways through the two-foot opening.

"Don't move, lady," he said. "I'm gonna prop up that bookcase with some of this furniture, and then you should be able to come out safely."

"Be careful of my things," she said.

"Right. Armando, can you slide the stepladder in here? Thanks. I'll just get this chair down and use it.... Whoa! Watch out!"

There was a loud crashing sound, and Sandy screamed. I'd lost sight of Slim when he'd taken the ladder behind a pile of boxes. I could see Sandy, still crouching under the bookcase. She started to move again, and the bookcase slid a few inches lower, making a scraping sound against the cement floor.

"Don't move!!!" I yelled. "Slim, are you okay? She needs help. That shelf's gonna fall!"

I started to shove the door open, and heard Slim yell from right behind it. "No! Don't push on the door! You'll fucking bury me!"

"Okay. I'm coming in."

Sucking in my breath to flatten myself like an octopus, I slid sideways through the narrow opening of the door. After checking that Slim didn't need my help, I moved forward towards Sandy. There was a giant recliner chair in front of me, upside down and still quivering from the impact of its fall. It was going to be too big for me to lift by myself. I started pushing it forward, towards the bookcase that was trapping Sandy. There wasn't a wide enough path for the chair, and I had to reach around and move aside boxes and books to make space for it. It was hard to see ahead of me, with only the narrow shaft of sunlight coming from the doorway, illuminating clouds of dust in the air.

The weight of the chair got lighter, and I realized Slim had come up behind me and started pushing next to me. We were halfway to Sandy when the chair totally jammed against something. It blocked our way so I couldn't get in front of it to see where the problem was.

"This chair thing isn't working," I told Slim. "We should just make a stack of boxes and books to hold up the bookcase."

"No, we got to use the chair. That bookcase is huge, and really heavy. A bunch of junk landed on top of it, weighing it down. I'll climb over and see why this chair is stuck."

While we were talking, there was another scraping sound.

"Help! It's going to crush me!"

Slim and I scrambled over the top of the chair, over fallen books and boxes, to the bookcase trapping Sandy. It was almost on top of her now, and she was kneeling on the floor and leaning forward as if in prayer.

I lifted up the bookcase while Slim shoved boxes under it to prop it up. Finally, we got the bookcase to a height where Sandy could safely crawl out. I was holding out my hand to help her, when the boxes we'd inserted started to slide and the bookcase lowered several inches.

Slim jammed his body against the boxes, and I dropped Sandy's hand and went to join him. We pushed the boxes back.

"I can hold it, Slim," I said. "Get her out of here. I'll follow you."

Slim stepped across me, and I heard him guiding Sandy out of the garage, talking softly, "Can you walk at all?... good, take it slow. Watch your step there, just step around this box, there you go...."

"I can't hold this much longer," I yelled to Slim. "I might have to let this bookcase drop."

"No!" Sandy cried. "That was my grandfather's. I brought it here from Oklahoma. Don't break it!"

I wedged my feet against a stack of boxes behind me and leaned my body into the stack in front of me, pushing with my shoulders like Atlas holding up the earth. I could hold this position a while longer ‘til Slim came to help me. Recently, I’d ramped up my weight training, and my back and legs felt strong.

“Armando! Move your feet!”

Slim was back, straightening the boxes behind me, which had started to topple over from my feet wedging against them. A second later and they would’ve been on top of me, along with the oversized Sanders family heirloom bookcase. Slim and I were finally able to get the bookcase upright. It was stable on its tiny legs, the heavy glass in the doors miraculously unbroken. We made our way through the maze of junk and out of the garage to join Sandy, who was blinking in the bright sunlight.

Slim, Sandy, and I stood together in front of the house. Sandy’s spookiness was gone. She was just a chubby middle-aged woman in a pink velour warm-up suit. I knew she was in her mid-fifties, a few years older than my boss, but she looked younger than her sister because her plump face was still unlined and she’d bleached the grey out of her fluffy blonde hair.

“I feel so silly,” she said. “I shouldn’t have tried to put that box on the top of the case. I really need more shelves.”

Slim brushed the dust off of the seat of his pants. “You need to get rid of all that trash you got in there.”

“I have to go to the bathroom.” She limped up to the front door and went into the house.

Slim and I sat down on the steps.

“Are you okay?” he asked.

I was far from happy.

“Just shoot me,” I’d complained earlier, when we’d pulled up to the house in the heat of the July afternoon. “How can Lucy let her sister live in such a dump?”

In contrast to Lucy’s gorgeous Spanish-style home in an upscale section of Mission Hills, Sandy’s address was a run-down cottage in a not-yet-gentrified block of North Park. The whole dead-end block was stuck in time. People's idea of landscaping was covering everything with bricks, cement, and chain-link fences. There were a few dusty shrubs by some of the front doorways and yellowed weeds sprouting out of cracked driveways. People who lived here seemed hopelessly doomed to a life of poverty and ugliness. And, in some cases, insanity.

"This is a new low, even for her," I said, as we'd gotten out of Slim's truck. "I'm her paralegal, for Christ's sake. Why did she stick me with her stupid plan to deal with her whacked-out sister? This is so wrong."

"It's because she's mad you're going on the cruise," Slim said. "You're being punished, *amigo*. I would've told her 'no.'"

"Yeah, well, you don't have to work with her, day in, day out," I snarled.

"No, I just have to listen to you bitch about her, day in, day out. You're burned out right now, baby."

"How can I not bitch about her? Just because she's some kind of genius, she thinks she can walk all over me. You're right. I'm not gonna do this. Let's get out of here."

But before we could get back into the truck, we'd heard Sandy's voice calling from the garage and rushed in to rescue her.

Now, with the emergency rescue over, it was time to do what we'd come to do. I got out the clear, horn-rimmed glasses I'd brought along to make me look more bureaucratic. They just slid down the bridge of my nose on a stream of sweat. I jammed them back on, which only aggravated the throbbing in my sinuses.

"Ow!" The glasses slid back down again, and I snatched them off and stuffed them in my pocket. My hands were sweating. I wiped them off on my leg, making a big dark streak on my new Aiden slim-fit chinos, which had taken on a load of dust in Sandy's garage.

"'Mando, are you okay?" Slim repeated.

"I'm good."

"I know you're good, but are you okay?" Slim tilted his head about six inches from my face and looked into my eyes.

I crossed my eyes and acted like I was going to faint.

Slim punched my arm and jerked his head towards the front door of Sandy's cottage. "So whatchu wanna do?"

I looked at my watch. "Three more hours, *amigo*, and I'm officially on vacation. Let's go ahead with Lucy's plan."

I took the fake ID out of my pocket and hung it around my neck. I inspected my best buddy Chantico Rubí, a.k.a. Slim. He's twenty-two, with the wiry build of a long-distance runner and an exotic Aztec face: a long sloping forehead, its angle repeated in the large arched nose beneath it, high cheekbones and flaring eyebrows, enigmatic red lips that will suddenly break into a dimpled grin, and completely smooth dark skin that glows with health. Today, he looked like the kind of worker you can see anywhere and any day in San Diego: a slender, short, young Mexican in work boots, white painter's pants, and an oversized T-shirt. He had on the white baseball cap he wears for his work as a housepainter. I turned the cap around so it faced forward instead of backwards.

"You look real good, *amigo*. Here we go," I said.

I knocked and pressed the bell on Sandy's door several times, and announced myself as an investigator from the County. Sandy didn't respond.

"We can't make her let us in," I said.

"Why don't you call your boss?"

"She'll just get pissed and tell me to deal with it," I told him. "She's probably waiting for me to call just so she can give me shit."

"Then let's deal with it," Slim said. "We can at least haul away the piles we took out of the garage."

We loaded stacks of newspapers and books into the bed of Slim's pickup. There were only a few books I wasn't sure about trashing. Some of these appeared to be college textbooks that were relatively recent editions. I pulled one out of this pile and showed the title to Slim.

"*Invitation to French*," he read.

"Yeah."

"So, let's see, how would you act it out in charades?" The game was a favorite with Slim's large family, and I'd often joined them, especially at holiday parties.

Slim started trying to act it out. Then we thought of other titles with "Invitation to…" and certain other interesting activities, and acting them out. I laughed until my stomach hurt when Slim fell over trying to do one of the more acrobatic ones.

Finally, I said, "Okay, that was fun, but now this book goes bye-bye."

"No, give it to me. I'll put it in the front seat."

We added some broken appliances and furniture to weigh down the papers. The bed was over half full, and we'd barely cleared a pathway around the spot where Sandy had been trapped. My chinos were wrecked. I sighed and looked at the load.

"Hey, Slim, you know about furniture. Are you sure these aren't priceless antiques or vintage pieces?"

"No worries. This shit is like old Motel 6 rejects."

"Well, I hope they're not more precious heirlooms from Grandpa Sanders." I picked up a vintage shit-green blender. It appeared to have no lid, and I tossed it back on the pile. "Let's try again with her," I said, jerking my head towards the house. "Lucy wanted us to clear up her living space. Like her bedroom."

"'Mando, I got news for you, man."

"What?"

"Where do you think she's been living? Didn't you see the sleeping bag in the garage?"

"Shit!" I ran back up to the house and pounded on the front door. "Ms. Sanders! Please open the door! We need to be sure you're okay. Open the door, or we'll call the police for a safety check."

The door opened abruptly, just enough for her to look out at us. She was standing there, still favoring one leg, and looking at us with a puzzled expression in her close-set blue eyes.

"I'm sorry. I thought you'd left. Did I forget to thank you? Really, I'm fine."

"Ms. Sanders, can we please come in? We're from the, uh, Public Guardian's office." I waved the card that was hanging around my neck. "We had a report your home is unsafe."

"Public Guardian? Who called you?" She peered at the card, and opened the door.

The front hall had newspapers and magazines stacked along all the walls, over head height. There was barely space for the three of us to stand in a single-file formation. Sandy opened a door on the left and motioned for us to enter.

Sandy closed the lid on the toilet and sat down on the shaggy hot-pink seat cover. I perched on the edge of the bathtub, which was filled with magazines. Slim stood in the doorway, his black, almond-shaped eyes dancing as they met mine.

I looked away from him so I wouldn't laugh. "Um, Ms. Sanders, why are we sitting in your bathroom?"

"My house is a bit of a mess right now. I really am all right. See? My ankle doesn't even hurt anymore." She held out her foot to show me.

Slim slipped out the door. I could see the flash of his cell phone camera, taking pictures of the dark, cluttered hallway. Then he stuck his smooth brown hand holding the cell phone through the half-open door, and I raised my eyebrows as the phone flashed at me behind Sandy's back. Slim's hand disappeared, and I heard the front door open and close behind him.

I got Sandy talking, asking her about her work as a part-time college professor, how she got her meals, trying to think what a real social worker would want to know.

"What about your family?" I asked. "Do you have someone who can come check on you sometimes?"

"I have a sister who lives in town."

"Are you close to your sister?"

"Sometimes. Sometimes we fight, and then we stop speaking for a while. She got mad at me last night when I wouldn't let her into the house. Is she the one who called you?"

"Sorry. We can't disclose that."

"Probably it wasn't Lucy," Sandy mused. "She's so wrapped up in her own work.... Was it a man? If it was a man, it was my ex, Paul. You can tell him I'm doing fine without him."

Sandy was voluble, but rational, except when I brought up the idea of trashing the junk that was making her home uninhabitable. After about half an hour, Slim came back into the room.

"I got the truck as full as I can get it. I cleared a path to make it safer to walk into this bathroom, but the bedroom's hopeless. You wanna help me with the ropes?"

Sandy stood up. "What are you talking about?"

Slim turned to face her. "Ms. Sanders, you got a decorating problem. I'm going to be a decorator some day. All this garbage, it's giving you bad *feng shui.* The chi energy in your house is blocked. I just cleared a truckload of old newspapers outta your hallway."

"You took my newspaper collection? Put it back. Don't you understand? I have to have it. I might need them for my work." Sandy turned red and started to breathe in big heaving gasps.

I took her hands and sat her back down on the toilet seat. "It's okay," I said. "We're here to help you."

Sandy clutched her chest. "I can't survive this. Those things will be worth a fortune someday! My sister's a lawyer, she'll sue you!"

The room started to close in on me. I motioned to Slim to sit with Sandy. I ran out of the house and leaned against the front door, my chest heaving with stress and disgust.

This was so freaky and unfair. I didn't know how to deal with this. I pulled out my cell and dialed.

"*Hola, m'ijo.*"

"Ma? Thank god you picked up! Remember when you had that clutter problem?" I described Sandy's situation, including the safety issue with her home and my boss's idea I should fix the problem before I went on my much-needed vacation. With Ma on the line directing me, I went inside and told Sandy we still had her things and could put them back. Sandy started to calm down at once.

"Yes, please," she said. "I appreciate all your help, but I need my things. Put them all back where they were."

"Ma?" I said, my voice rising.

"Yes, I heard. Stay calm, *mi amor*. Tell her you understand. And then, here's something that might work."

Two hours later we dropped a happy Sandy back at her house. It was four-thirty, half an hour to quitting time. "Don't start the car yet," I told Slim. "Turn on the radio. Let's look at this."

I reached into my messenger bag and pulled out the oversized brochure I'd been carrying around all week. Troye Sivan's "*Dance to This*" came on the radio as Slim and I put our heads together over pictures of buffed men drinking, dancing, sunbathing....

"Now for the centerfold," I said. "*Eh, voila*!"

I spread the triple-folded center page across our laps, and there it was: enormous, thrusting, gleaming white against a background of turquoise sea and powder-blue sky.

"Oh, momma!"

"Yeah, Slim-ster, it's the Mother Ship, the *Jamboree Breeze,* our home for the next ten days. With a couple thousand other hot party animals and not a care in the world."

At four-fifty, I called Lucy. When I told her we'd taken Sandy to rent an extra-large storage locker, my *jefa* went ballistic.

"You let her rent *storage* space? So she can collect even more junk? Honestly, I try to delegate a simple problem.... What were you thinking?"

"What was *I* thinking? I was thinking you sent me into a fucking war zone. I was thinking we saved your sister's life."

"What about her ankle? It might be broken. I'm going to call 911."

"Go ahead, but I'm telling you, she's fine. She needs therapy for her mental problem, not a trip to the ER. Your sister's been sleeping in a rat hole in her garage."

There was a pause. I could see her close-set blue eyes narrowing as she processed this. "I didn't realize it had gotten that bad. Did you tell her the County would get a conservatorship if she didn't agree to have the place cleared out?"

"Hel-lo? Don't you get it? The thought of losing her things triggered a freaking panic attack. You should get her a shrink, *Abogada.* How was it my job to go along with your stupid and totally illegal scheme? Maybe you'd like to fix some of the problems in my fucked-up family. Teach my sister how to control her spoiled kids. Haul away her stacks of out-of-date glamour magazines. And that will be the easy one."

There was a short silence. "I'll go check on Sandy," she said. "See you tomorrow."

"No, you won't," I reminded her. "You'll see me in ten days. I'll be completely *incommunicado.*"

She hissed, and hung up. I laughed and dropped my cell phone on the car seat like it was burning my hand. "*Aí,* she is pi-i-issed," I told Slim. "Once again, she makes me ask: 'how can a genius be so fucking clueless?' She's not gonna change her sister."

"You got that right," Slim said.

As Slim drove, I borrowed his cell phone, and texted Lucy the pictures Slim had taken of Sandy's garage, hallway, bathroom, and kitchen. Then I sent her a separate text, attaching Slim's picture of me interviewing Sandy in her bathroom. With my eyebrows raised in concern, the fake social worker badge hanging around my neck, and Sandy's plump ankle resting on my knees, I looked like an aid worker called to some third-world disaster. I texted, "*Saint Armando administers comfort to avalanche victim, a day before leaving on friendship tour of Caribbean.*"

"Work's done, Slim-ster," I said. "It's ten days of nonstop partying, with 10,000 selfies to show for it. Nothing's gonna mess up this trip of a lifetime."

2

Four for Four

The limo driver closed the door behind me, and I was alone in the vast leather-covered interior. I started to open my window, and then thought, "Why?" The temperature inside was perfect, like a pocket of warm water in a cool ocean, and everything I wanted was right here, behind the smoked windows of the black stretch Humvee. Each of the six seats was like a first-class airplane seat, with its own music station and adjustable mirror, two empty cup holders, and a cup holder full of wrapped mints. There was a mini-bar and a pull-down movie screen.

"Are you comfortable, sir?" The driver's voice came through a speaker in the dark glass window between us.

"Oh, yeah," I told him.

"If there's anything you need, press the button below the speaker and let me know. We'll be picking up Mr. Rubí shortly."

I pulled down the mirror in front of me, and was surprised how good I looked. I'd been up 'til four a.m., packing, and had less than two hours to sleep, shower, and dress before the limo picked me up at six. But my brown eyes were shining, my black hair perfectly gelled into shiny spikes, and my aristocratic café latte features clear and handsome as ever. But was I still hot? I held my arm up to my face to admire the wide faux leopard band I'd gotten to wear with my Fossil sport watch.

"Oh, hi!" I said to my admiring self. "Yes, you're right, this is not my first cruise, how could you tell? Oh, you think I look rich? Come from Money? Well, okay, my Dad is what *some* people might call rich.... Did he spoil me? Baby, do I look spoiled? A little? Well, maybe I was spoiled just a little. Ma gave me a lot of love and attention and taught me to love books and art and shopping. Dad was working a lot. I mean, it's not like he kicked me out of the house when I was in the middle of high school. I didn't have to survive in the streets, couch surfing at my friends' homes, and sometimes having to eat out of trashcans and.... Nothing like that. I don't look like I ever had to do that, do I?"

The fine face in the mirror had gone sideways on me, and I quickly rearranged it. I was going to kick ass on this cruise, so fuck 'em all. The limo glided to a stop.

The door across from me opened, and Slim slid into the seat next to me.

"Dude, did you see the size of the trunk? Good thing, 'cause I brought a lot of shit with me. I told the driver I could load my own bags, but he didn't want no help."

"Get used to it, honey," I told him. "You're going to be treated like the leading lady in a billion-dollar movie."

Slim stretched out on the tan leather seat. "Oh, check it out! This thing reclines flat like a bed." His long black hair was gelled straight back from his forehead, and he wore a silky leopard-print T-shirt, black jeans, and tan flip-flops. He pulled a case from his pocket and put on a pair of wraparound sunnies with leopard-print frames. "Whoa, it just got dark in here."

Minutes later, the limo stopped in front of a Hillcrest condo complex. "Do you think he dressed?" Slim asked. "I bet you he didn't do it. He's probably rebelled, and he'll be wearing work clothes or something. He better not. I want everybody looking at us when we get on that ship."

I cracked my window open an inch and looked out. "I'll bet, but you'd lose."

"Well, then, he's just doin' it for you," Slim said, leaning across me to look out my window. "Lemme see. Oh, yeah. You better watch out, 'Mando."

We watched my buffed-out ex, Rodrigo Ocampo, roll one neat carry-on bag out the front door of his condo and hand it to the limo driver. We've stayed close friends since we split up, and not just because his job as an investigator at the DA's office sometimes gives me access to information Lucy and I can use in our cases. Rodrigo looked back at his home, straightened the hose on the tiny patio, and got busy with the locks on the inside door and then the heavy outer security door.

Rodrigo got into the seat across from me, and ruffled my hair.

"Nice boots," I told him, patting my hair back into place.

"Is that all your luggage?" Slim asked. "Did you know we'll be gone for ten days? Did you bring your camo and your white and your sparkle...?"

"Yeah, I did, and I packed real light, 'cause I don't plan on wearing much," said Rodrigo, surveying the interior, including Slim stretched out flat in his reclining seat. "Nice crib you got here."

"Yeah, we're thinking of spending our whole vacation in this limo," I said. "Fuck the Five-Star Caribbean cruise. What do you want to drink?"

We sipped rum and cokes and talked about our party agendas, as the limo glided on. When we rolled to a stop fifteen minutes later, Rodrigo asked, "Where are we? Shouldn't we be at Justin's place?"

I turned and rested my face against the window. It felt cool and soothing against my cheek.

"He ain't coming," Slim whispered. Like I couldn't hear.

"Oh, yeah? What happened?"

"It's no big deal." I turned to face Rodrigo, keeping my expression light. "He couldn't get away."

Rodrigo raised his eyebrows.

"It's okay, man. I got a great replacement."

Rodrigo's face fell, until the door opened and my friend Mary Solya bounced into the seat next to him. Rodrigo removed his foot from Slim's lap to make room for Mary's long legs.

"It's okay, Slim, you don't need to move. Wow, this limo is mighty spacious, boys. Nice boots, Rodrigo. You put your leg right back up there, honey." She took his leopard-skin ankle boot in her strong man-hands, and hefted it back onto Slim's lap, stroking the coarse fur. "What is this made of? Is it real leopard? Feels like horsehair or something. Why didn't I find these? What size are they?.... What? Rum and coke? .... And I would want the coke for... what? Yeah, just the rum, lots of ice.... I am so excited, 'Mando, thank you so much for inviting me. I've always wanted to go on a gay cruise. Lots of gorgeous guys to look at and no hetero dickheads to break my heart."

The year before, Mary'd hired Lucy and me to investigate the suspicious death of her sister, and we'd become friends. She had on her favorite six-inch spike-heel boots with toes as sharp as knife points, over tight leopard-print leggings and an oversized, low-cut black tee that exposed a lot of her large chest. A leopard-print sun hat flopped over her plain face and long hair, which are both pale strawberry in color. Usually she wears little makeup, but for the occasion she'd applied a load of clumpy black mascara.

"Great threads, girl," I said.

"Yeah, our team is four-for-four," Slim said, reaching back to touch Mary's hat. She handed it to him, and he put it on, adjusting the brim so it dipped over one eye. "We all look good. I was afraid Rodrigo wasn't gonna dress for the occasion."

"He definitely got the memo," Mary said, stroking Rodrigo's boots.

"Hey, 'Mando, I like the new look with your hair," Rodrigo said. "You're not using that gel to cover up any thinning on top, are you?"

I felt my hand fly to my head. Rodrigo was smirking at me, his blue-green eyes glowing in his dark face. I turned to the mirror and checked my hairline. At the age of twenty-four, I have started to be vigilant for the onset of physical aging on my body. And I'd been through a lot of stress lately, thanks to a boss who thrives on producing stress in others. What would I even do if it was starting to recede?

"Here's to Armando," Mary said, raising her glass. "Thank you for doing this."

Everyone toasted me, and I blushed. "Thanks to all of you, for being my good friends and coming with me," I said. "You guys *get* me, and that's... that's everything to me." It was true. These were the friends who immediately understood why, when I got a windfall of $50,000, I would choose to spend it all on a dream cruise for me and three of my besties. I'd taken a lot of shit from certain other people, including my boss Lucy Sanders and my now-possibly-ex-boyfriend Justin, whose reactions had been remarkably similar.

Lucy, who had been partly responsible for my getting the money, through a sort of irregular settlement of an auto accident, had been unprecedentedly speechless when I told her how I'd spent it. But not for long. I've learned to block out her rants, but the general thrust was: "Blah, blah.... Irresponsible... childish.... school.... no ambition.... stagnating... opportunity.... Blah,... disgusting.... floating incubator of disease... biosphere of class stratification and repression.... exploitation of third world workers ...Blah, ... tuition...undergraduate degree... your unexamined life... you can't leave the office for ten days... death penalty case, urgent deadlines... co-counsel bailed.... train someone new... no consideration... not a team player... Blah, blah, blah." And it went on like that, for the months leading up to my trip, culminating in her punishing me by sending me out to take care of her whack sister's trash-infested home. I'd spent two full days training a nice temp to fill in for me, but I gave it about a day before she would quit on Lucy.

When I'd told Justin, it had been the evening of the day I'd told Lucy, and I'd been looking forward to presenting him with this beautiful gift of a luxurious summer trip together. It was during a late-winter heat wave, and we'd been lying on the rumpled bed of his Hillcrest apartment, with the fan going on high and all the windows open. When I told him my plan, his dark-red eyebrows had gone halfway up his forehead in a cartoon character expression of surprise, and he'd just stared at me with his sherry-brown eyes all dark in his white face. "You're joking, right?"

I'd assured him I was not joking, and shared with him my dream of a magical life experience. Yeah, it doesn't last in the same way as a condo or a college degree, but it's a statement about grabbing onto life and doing fabulous things while you're still young and cute and in your prime. Right? I was expecting our memories to last a lifetime, I'd told him.

Justin had tried, and I'd tried, over the next few months, to work it out. He even gave me sympathy when I complained about Lucy ragging on me at work.

But he finally told me, "'Mando, I can't stomach this. I thought I could do it, but I can't. I can't go with you, because I think it's a really bad idea on so many levels. You know I love you the way you are, and I don't care if you never go back to school. But you could do so many other things with fifty grand: spend a year abroad, travel around the world, go learn another language, or take a couple years off and join a dance company like you've always wanted. Those would be real life experiences. Or save it for something you really want, a dream, once you know what it is. I've been busting my butt for the past two years working full time so I don't have a huge debt when I get out of law school and I can do the kind of law I want. I know I sound like a prig, but it shocks me how much money you're going to just blow in ten days. Whatever it is you're trying to prove by doing this, you really don't need to."

I sat up, covered myself with the sheet, and stared at him as he continued, "I'm not even going to start on the whole class thing. And you know I'm not really fussy about hygiene, but a lot of nasty things go around on those ships, especially the giant ones. Did you hear about the recent one where the people were stuck on the boat, and they had to be quarantined for norovirus and...."

"I've seen those stories," I interrupted him. "Hundreds of cruises go out every day, and everyone is fine."

My logic had not convinced Justin. At the last minute, I'd gotten my new friend Mary to come in his place, because I'd already booked four rooms in the Concierge Class Epitome Tower, the best place on the ship. Justin and I hadn't seen each other for over a week before I left. Probably it was for the best. I considered myself newly single and was ready for the experience of a lifetime.

Swallowing the rest of my drink, I said, "Tomorrow this time we'll be cruising. I'm gonna be poolside in my green Rufskin Eurocut speedo."

Mary was scrolling on her phone. "Did you guys look at Jamboree Cruises' website? I've been on a big job the last two weeks, and I didn't get a chance to look at it. There's a whole special section here about the Epitome Tower. It's not really a tower, but it's the highest deck on the ship, and it's like an amazing spa resort. Only eight rooms, plus one grand suite," Mary said.

"Lemme see," said Rodrigo.

She handed him her phone, and we all sipped our drinks and watched his face as he scrolled. He was looking extra fine, I had to admit, in his black sleeveless T-shirt and tight jeans. His head was freshly shaved, with only a tiny vertical goatee on his chin emulating a certain Cuban-American pop star.

"Oh, yeah!" he exclaimed. "We get butlers. I wonder if they're cute."

"They will be," I said. "This cruise is run by the premier gay cruise company, *Adonis Enterprises.* They rent the ship and the staff from Jamboree, but they'll make sure the personal service guys are hot." I closed my eyes. "Ummm. I'm expecting a butler with blond hair, blue eyes, about 6’2”, who’s into...um... massage. And exotic dance.”

“Yummy,” said Mary. “Oh, well, I guess I’ll just be there to enjoy the eye candy.”

Slim took out his copy of the cruise brochure.

“Listen,” he said. “Here’s what we can expect on the *Jamboree Breeze*: ‘An unparalleled experience of total pampering, where indulgence becomes easy and our elite staff ministers to your every desire. Dance away a wild night at one of our famous costume balls, or enjoy a laugh with your new friends at a world-class comic revue.... Your pleasure is our business.’”

Inside the limo got quiet as we provided our own visuals.

3

Lucy

Clutter Problem

"Ms. Sanders, I know you don't like to be bothered, but I have a personal call for you on line two. Oops, I guess it's on line three. Um, is that okay?"

I gritted my teeth and told myself not to take it out on her. The poor woman. It wasn't her fault Armando hadn't bothered to train her in the most basic tasks, before taking off to squander his fortune on ten days of selfish dissipation and exploitation. Yes, he'd had two full workdays just to train this temp, Nancy, to cover for him for two weeks. This was only Nancy's first morning. Already, I was wasting an inordinate amount of my valuable mental energy speculating about what she and Armando had been doing those two days. I'd spent those two days handling most of the office work in addition to all my court appearances and client meetings.

Armando told me he had chosen Nancy because she was a homemaker re-entering the workforce after twenty-some years, and aspired to put herself through court reporting school. As Armando well knows, I am the first to offer sisterly support to a woman of a certain age who wants (needs?) to attain financial independence. But it had been his job, not mine, to train her in the simple, basic tasks of running The Law Offices of Lucy Sanders.

Unfortunately, Nancy's lengthy hiatus from work outside the home had atrophied her self-confidence, and she was unable to do even the simplest task without supervision. Bless her heart. Nancy seemed not to know how anything worked, from how to make tea the way I like it, to which buttons to push to shift our copier into fax mode. She seemed to think it was perfectly acceptable to consult me about any minor detail, as long as she prefaced her request with, "I know you don't want to be bothered...," or "I'm sorry...."

"Nancy," I said, "I don't care if the caller says it's personal. Our procedure is for you to take a message, unless the caller has my extension, in which case the caller will access my line directly. Please take a message, dear."

Less than a minute later, she buzzed me back. "Um, I know you don't want to be bothered, Ms. Sanders, but it's from a Mr. O'Connor. He says it's urgent, it's about your sister."

Why hadn't she told me? I picked up the line. "Paul? What's going on?"

"Hi, Lucy, how are you? I haven't talked to you in quite a while."

"No, we have regretfully been denied that pleasure. What's up?"

"Ah, yes. Well, I was supposed to meet her for coffee this morning. I'm working on a new vision for an art project. She was interested to hear my new ideas, and see some sketches I've made. It's going to be a...."

"Where is Sandy?"

"That's the thing. She didn't show up. So I went over to her house, right around the corner from the coffee shop, and I found her. She's just sitting in the driver's seat of her car, in the driveway. The whole car is filled with books, up to the top. It's not safe to drive, because she can't see out the back. She said she packed up the books to take over to her new storage locker, and then she was afraid to take them off her property. Now I can't convince her to get out of the car. She started shaking, and she says she doesn't want to leave her things."

"Wait a minute," I said. "Doesn't she teach today?"

"Yeah, she's got a one-thirty lecture over at City College. I told her she needs to get some of the books out of the car so she can drive over there."

"Can't you drive her to her class? It'll be good for her to work."

Paul's voice lowered. "I really can't spend my whole afternoon driving her around, Lucy. I have my work to do. I can't be true to my art unless I honor my boundaries. You'd better get over here."

I looked at my desk calendar, which showed two early afternoon court appearances, a late afternoon client interview, in addition to the preparation I needed to do for several upcoming hearings. Not to mention the *pro bono* death penalty appeal for which I needed to file yet another extension request and quickly hire a competent contract attorney to make a dent in summarizing the twenty-two boxes of case files.

Mr. Paul O'Connor, by way of contrast, has not worked since he married my sister twenty-five years ago, when he was twenty years old and she was thirty. She supported him on her adjunct professor earnings until he left her for a woman who could buy him nicer toys. Paul does not work. He spends his time pretending to be an artist, something for which he has absolutely no talent, and he still hits Sandy up for praise and occasional financial infusions.

"Anyway," Paul was saying, "I don't think she's in any shape to give a lecture. You'd better get over here. Now she's holding her chest and saying she thinks she's dying. And I've got to go."

"For God's sake, you idiot, call an ambulance! I'll meet her at the hospital."

***

An hour later, I watched my sister being wheeled into the psychiatric ward at the UC Medical Center, while I sat with a steely-eyed intake specialist filling out several pages of paperwork. By the time I'd arrived, Sandy had been triaged and diagnosed with a severe panic attack.

I handed the clipboard with the last of the forms to the specialist. "Here you are," I told her. "All the insurance information is there. That's all you really care about. The medical history, you'll have to get from her. I need to get back to my office, but you can reach me on my cell. Do I leave her wallet and sweater with you, or...?" I got up, pulling my cell out of my purse so I could call the office as I walked back to my car. Before leaving, I'd given Nancy a list of appearances and appointments to reschedule, to which she'd responded with a deer-in-the headlights look. Maybe I could make it to court for that DUI arraignment at two-thirty....

"Wait here," the intake specialist ordered. "The doctor will be out to talk to you, when he has time."

I shook my head as I walked out, not wanting to alienate her with an appropriate verbal response. I had recently had occasion to see what my insurance company had been charged for a short hospital stay, at the same hospital but in a different ward. Of course, it did not surprise me they would try to provide a third-world level of service for astronomical first-world prices. If the hospital owners had it their way, families would be responsible for bringing in meals, providing bedding and laundry service, and assisting the underpaid and understaffed nursing team in caring for their loved ones. Why not? More profits for the investors and bigger salaries for the CEOs. I wasn't going to play that game. Furthermore, if my sister and I spent much time together, I would be joining her on the mental ward, and then who would take care of my clients? I called Nancy, and told her I would keep the rest of the afternoon's appointments.

***

When I returned to the office a few minutes before five o'clock, Nancy jumped out of her chair to greet me. "Oh, Ms.

Sanders, I'm so glad you're back. I didn't want to bother you while you were in court."

"You can always text me on my cell, if you have a true emergency," I told her. "Did you set up the interviews for the temporary attorney position?"

"Oh, no, I'm so sorry. I was trying to print the documents for your appointment this afternoon, and I'm afraid it's taking a little longer than I expected."

I sighed, walked over to the computer, pressed a few buttons, and the printer started humming. "That's how you do it," I told her. "Now, can you make those calls while I get ready for my client? Armando did tell you I'll be needing you to work overtime, I hope? You should be able to finish by six o'clock."

"Of course, Ms. Sanders. I have your instructions right here. What if I can't reach them all tonight? Should I just leave messages, or....?"

I walked into my office and shut the door. Nine more days, I thought. My phone buzzed.

"Ms. Sanders, your client is here. Oh, and I forgot to tell you, the hospital has been calling about your sister. They said you weren't answering your cell phone. She's ready to be discharged."

Thirty minutes later, after I escorted my client out, Nancy looked up at me with a proud smile.

"All done," she said. "You have four appointments tomorrow morning, back-to-back. They all sounded very eager. Oh, and the hospital called again, twice. They say they can't release your sister until someone picks her up and takes responsibility for her."

"Good," I told her. "Then they'll have to keep her overnight. I can't possibly take her."

"Oh. I understand." Nancy patted her poorly cut grey-brown hair and bit her lip. "But, I mean, do you trust them about that? Hospitals will try to make you come, but if they don't think insurance will cover it, they'll go ahead and dump a patient out on the streets, any time of night or day."

"Damn." This was one of my precious nights with my soul mate, Claude. Was I going to have to choose between him and Sandy? I walked back to my office, punching a number on my cell phone.

"Hey, Luce. We still on for later?"

"Yes, if you don't mind that maybe we'll have company, by which I mean my sister." I filled Claude in on my day's ordeal. "And now, apparently, the hospital won't even keep her overnight, and they'll throw her out in the street unless I come pick her up. I don't even know if her house is safe. I was going to send someone out there to haul off her stuff before she was discharged, but I've been too busy with work. Oh, Claude, I just can't have her in my home. I can't do it...."

"Whoa! Slow down, love. Sorry things finally hit the fan while you're so busy, but this is a good thing. She needs some treatment. You gotta maybe take her in for a while, though. She's family. You can do it. I can be there for a few hours tonight, if you need me."

"Yeah, and then you'll waltz back home, and I'll be stuck with her." I hadn't meant for those words to come out of my mouth. "Sorry," I said. "I'm having a bad day."

"No worries. Listen, I'm just goin' in to my meeting. Let's talk in an hour."

I walked back to the open door of my office and stared at the front room. The reception area was dim but cozy, the colors of the Persian rug and pale green couch saturated by the late sunlight filtering in through the front window. Maybe Sandy could have my house and I could sleep here. But what about my dogs...? Nancy had neglected to clear my tea tray off the table next to my leather recliner. She was sitting at Armando's desk, looking at me as if she wanted something.

"Yes?"

"Um, I don't want to interfere," she said, "but if you want me to, I could talk to the hospital for you. I'm... I'm pretty good at that kind of thing."

"I really don't see...." I began.

She interrupted me. "The hospital won't tell you this, especially not the psychiatric unit, but there are appeal procedures, and anti-dumping and discharge-planning requirements. I don't personally know the staff at the senior unit, where your sister is, but I'm happy to give it a try."

***

Much later that night, Claude was telling me how glad he was we'd had the evening alone together. I turned to face him. In the pale moonlight that filtered in through my bedroom window, his black skin looked rich and beautiful against the white sheets. I traced the side of his cheek where there was an old scar that gave him a look of wisdom and experience.

"We can both thank my lovely temp, Nancy," I said. "She saved our evening. Her son has schizophrenia, and she's learned how to play the game with these hospital chiselers. You won't hear a single complaint about her from me over the next nine days. Then, I'll have Armando back, and things can get back to normal. I blame him for this whole thing with Sandy. He didn't handle her right."

4

Armando

Bahamas

"Ahoy!" Water splashed out of the pool, pricking my legs and feet with cool droplets. My eyes flew open. I watched as the water beaded over my skin, which I'd slathered with coconut oil to bake in the morning sun. Too lazy to move or talk, I lay still and let my eyes close, entertained by the sounds around me.

"I give that one a four and a half, Blake!" Whose voice? One of the Dans, maybe.

"Point your toes, and go in with your body straight, dude." Slim's voice. Slim had been executing clean pikes off the diving board. Unlike Blake, one of the less athletic of our cruisemates, Slim slid splashless and soundless into the water. The curved, deep infinity pool was set on the edge of the Epitome Tower, home to the ten guests traveling Concierge Class on the tenth and highest deck. The side of the pool facing the inside of Deck Nine was clear glass, so the guests on the lower deck could see the diver enter the water and swim back to the top. The night before we'd re-named the ship, from the boring *Jamboree Breeze* to the more poetic *Adonis*, on account of it was being invaded by two thousand men of god-like beauty. We were planning to stand out as the most beautiful and desirable.

"Should we go to the midnight bash tonight at the skating rink?" Mary asked. "They've got a Sparkle on Ice theme, and they have skates."

"Are you kidding? I'm not getting out on the ice with a bunch of drunks. It's not safe," said Rodrigo, from the lounge next to me.

"You know what's good here," said the younger Dan, "what's good here, if you like to dress, is Casino Royale night. They open the space between the Poolside Casino and the Ice Bar. On one side of the Casino, there's the pool area done up in a '50's Lounge look. On the other side, you go out into the Ice Bar, and it's made to look like you're at the bottom of a ski slope, with real snow on the walls. And the place is all over James Bonds in tuxedos and Queens to die for. Last time, I was Xenia Onatopp in that peek-a-boo black dress. They've got a great costume collection if you didn't bring one."

Slim parked on the edge of my lounge chair to towel off. "How do they do the Lounge decor? Is it, like, mid-century modern?"

I tuned out. The morning of our first day, I was getting my groove on. The Epitome Tower featured a luxury based on space and light and deceptive simplicity. Below us, the lower classes with their discos, bright colored lights, strangely shaped pools, water slides, and mobs of humanity, were not visible except from the barstools that lined the balconies on either side of the pool.

At first, I'd been disappointed to be away from the action. Then Slim and I decorated the balcony on our side of the deck with silver garlands and colorful thongs he'd brought from home. That started to get us some attention from below. The attention increased when he and I stood up on the balcony rail, took off our shirts, and started dancing to the music from the tea dance below us on Deck Nine. Our balcony was a great spot for checking out the action before going to join it on the lower deck.

I'd awakened that morning in my single cabin to find Barron, my Greek God of a butler, bearing a double cappuccino, and pulling aside curtains to display a view of pure sea and sky. He looked exactly like what I'd wished for on our limo ride to the airport: a blonde Apollo with deep blue eyes and a body like a statue come alive. With a little talk and a big tip to the Concierge Class director, I had appropriated Barron's services for myself and my friends on the starboard side of the Epitome Tower.

"I apologize if this is early for you, sir," he'd said, placing the coffee next to my bed. "We like to nudge our guests into local time, on the first day. Today, we have a poolside champagne breakfast for our Concierge guests to get to know each other."

I'd rolled to my side and took my leopard-band watch off the side table. It was eight o'clock, Miami time. "How long do I have?"

"No worries, sir," he said. "We have an hour to get ready. I've unpacked your bags and can run you a bath or a shower. As I told you last night, just let me know whatever I can do for you." In the light of day, he was even more beautiful. Since I'd first seen him, I'd known exactly what I wanted him to do for me. But his smile had this professional look that made me think I shouldn't ask. At least, not yet.

Breakfast had started with eight of the nine Concierge Class VIPS. I was seated next to Rick Collins, an Aberzombie who had got his pre-vacation tan sprayed on at the last minute. In less than one minute of conversation, I'd learned he was a puffed-up Harvard MBA with ambitions of becoming a CEO by the age of thirty-five. Then what the hell was he doing on this pleasure cruise? I told him I was a low-paid paralegal [true] and high-school dropout [not true], and I expected never again to have enough money to go on a cruise like this. He immediately turned away to probe the credentials of the other guests.

I turned to the boy on the other side of me. Scott Barnes had a superficial resemblance to my [now probably ex]-boyfriend, Justin. He was slender and gawky but sort of graceful at the same time. Also like Justin, he would easily win the prize for worst dressed in the present company, or, indeed, in just about any company. For our semi-formal introductory brunch, he wore threadbare cutoff jeans that had never been Levi's, a faded Batman T-shirt, and these ugly rubber shoes that you would find at a drug store, the kind with one thick strap across the ball of the foot, that maybe he thought were like Nike slides but totally weren't. I ached to get him into some classier threads, and to get a barber busy on the shaggy light-brown hair that fell over his eyes.

"I get what Scottie Shower Sandals is trying to do," Slim said to me later. "But he's taken that grunge motif a step too far."

Like [my?] Justin, Scott Barnes had a shy sweet smile. It almost transcended his messy appearance. "I overheard you telling Rick you flunked out of high school," he said to me. "Were you bullshitting?"

"Don't tell," I said in a low voice. "I guess I was doing a kind of reverse snob thing. But it's true I'm poor, and this is a trip of a lifetime for me."

"Good for you," he nodded vigorously. "I know what you mean. Sometimes you have to splurge, even if you feel a little guilty about it."

"Oh, I don't feel guilty," I said. "The money came as a windfall to me, and I believe it was for a reason. I was *meant* to do this as an affirmation of life."

"I like that. An affirmation of life. Going for the balance, right?"

Balance with what? "I guess," I said. "Although... I mean, if I could, I'd probably be happy living like this all the time."

"Well, right now it's hard to argue with that." We surveyed the charms of the Epitome Tower, our home for the next ten days. Our dining table was set up next to the perfectly oval infinity pool. The pool made a mini horizon a shade bluer than the strip of turquoise sea beyond it. The movement of the few clouds in the pale sky was palpable in the soft breezes that caressed our faces.

"Want some of my orange?" Scott asked. He was carefully peeling an orange with a small Swiss Army knife. He handed me a section speared with the point of his knife. "They put these bowls of fruit in your room, and then they don't give you anything to cut it with."

Across from us were "The Dans," a couple from Los Angeles who seemed like promising cruise companions. Dan number one was a paunchy, fortyish entrepreneur who favored Hawaiian shirts and was permanently attached to his cell phone and his thermos of black coffee. When he wasn't dodging around the deck trying to find a spot with cell service for his business calls, or at the low end of a mood swing, he could be hilarious and was especially good at imitations. Dan number two ("call me 'Dan-Dan'"), was a talky twink about half his partner's age. The Dans had been on this cruise for their honeymoon, and were repeating it for their second anniversary. They owned a chain of gay-friendly resorts in California and Nevada, with Dan running the business and Dan-Dan in charge of the "creative aspects."

Dan-Dan appeared unnecessarily possessive of Dan, since I didn't see anyone in our group who would want to put up competition. Maybe one of the Epitome Tower butlers could be a threat, though. Barron was going to be mine, of course, but the other butler, Evans, was a very pretty young Filipino, short and slender, with soft manners and a graceful body.

Our two butlers were supervised by the Concierge Cruise Director, Nick Kronos, a swarthy black-haired man in his forties. He wore a fancy white uniform with a captain's hat, a jacket with epaulettes, and knife-edge creased white pants. His black eyes were suspicious and mean even as he went through the motions of fawning over the Epitome guests. He occasionally was seen with two or three frightened-looking assistants who were apparently allowed onto the Tower to work under his tight supervision. His jaw worked continuously on handfuls of sunflower seeds, which he kept in a bag in his pants pocket. He appeared to grind them up, shell and all, swallowing them whole, and occasionally spitting out fragments of shell for his minions to chase down and pick up.

The Dans happened to be behind me when we entered the deck that morning and were greeted by Nick Kronos.

"He's very, ah, crisp," I murmured to the Dans after we walked past him.

Dan-Dan laughed. "Good word!" he said. "What should we call him, honey? How about Krispy?"

"I was thinking Krunchy," said Dan, "On account of those sunflower seeds he spits all over the place, but I like Krispy better. Krispy Kronos." He put an arm around each of us and steered us to the dining table. The white tablecloth was as crisply ironed as Kronos's uniform and gleamed white in the sun against the deep blue of the sea and pale yellow-blue of the sky. Champagne flutes and oversized silverware glittered up at us as we took our seats.

Mary made a late entrance, working a dark green bikini and sheer "cover-up" she had pinned open so it covered nothing at all. Her strawberry blonde hair poured down her back, and her freckled face glowed with health and confidence.

"That's my friend, Mary," I told Barron, whose shining blonde head was bent over to top off my champagne glass. I leaned closer than necessary to whisper, "She's the best plumber in the United States."

He raised his eyebrows and turned his head. Champagne fizzed over the edge of my glass. "Sorry, sir," he said, turning back to me. "A plumber, you say? That's unusual. For a woman, I mean." He wiped the side of my glass clean.

"Please don't call me 'sir.' It's not that I don't love it. It's just, I don't want to get used to it." I gave him my best smile and wink.

"What shall I call you, then?"

"Call me Armando. Or 'Mando, that's what...."

I jumped. A loud noise had broken the morning air.

"No worries, sir, er, Armando. Someone's landing at the heliport. I believe it's the last Concierge guest."

Conversation had stalled while we watched the helicopter hover loudly and land on a distant pad at the other end of the ship. Guests milling around on the deck below us turned like a flock of birds to watch the landing. A couple of ant-sized figures stepped out and disappeared through a door off of the landing pad.

"My God, what an entrance. I thought we were under some kind of attack," Dan said.

"Who's the new guest, Barron?" Rodrigo asked.

Before our butler could answer, Kronos stepped forward, clasping his hands together.

"It is his personal helicopter, sir," Kronos told Rodrigo. "He prefers to arrive and leave at his own convenience. That is Lord Blake Copland, son of the twelfth Earl of Bath. His grandfather, August Floyd, is an American banking heir, who also owns many newspapers and television companies. You have heard of the 'Daily World'? 'AME news'?" Kronos's chest puffed out. "His family also owns part of Jamboree Cruise Lines."

"Ah, damn!" Dan had knocked over his thermos of coffee. Dan-Dan grabbed all the napkins around him and started mopping up the flow, and the staff converged to keep the spill from reaching any of the guests.

"What do you know," said Rick, the spray-tanned MBA. "Lord Blake L. Copland himself. We've got a genuine billionaire on board."

The billionaire joined us a few minutes later, and Nick Kronos performed introductions. Blake greeted you with a politician's smile and a light handshake, making good eye contact and repeating your name.

"Sorry to be late, chaps." He was in his early thirties, mid-height, a portly but well-proportioned dude with a moon-face, side-slicked black hair, and a classy British accent. He unwound a light cashmere scarf from his neck and gave it in a blind handoff to Evans. "Cheers, everyone." He took his champagne glass in a manicured hand and raised it in the air.

"Hip, hip, hurrah, our ship's at sea!"

Something sparked as we joined Blake's toast. Our tribe was complete.

The night before, we had checked out the amenities in our spacious cabins, which all opened onto a wide curving balcony that looked down on the pool and lower decks. Then Mary, Slim, and I had put on matching neon orange bike shorts and tank tops, and our leopard-frame sunglasses, and gone to check out the action on the lower decks. We joined the mobs strolling around the lower decks, scoping out the hot spots. We chose the Lucky Star for our first night out, and partied until Slim needed to be half-carried back to his stateroom before he passed out.

Now, lying by the pool, sun-heated, with the occasional warm breeze ruffling my hair and kissing my skin, I heard the chatter of my old and new friends like beautiful music. My head was filled with the memory of the masses of hot men strutting the decks with faces lit up by that first-night excitement. I thought about all the looks I'd get at the tea dance later that afternoon, in my combat boots and Vuthy Sim Squarecut Camo swimsuit with the perforated print. Slim was telling the Dans about our outfits for the Sparkle party: silver skintights with bowlers, gloves, and pink boas. I really did feel, in the words of Jamboree Cruises, like I was floating on air.

"What's the Terrible Tribe of Nine up to today, eh?" Blake asked. "Who's for the Bahamas?"

"After last night, I thought I was gonna stay in my room with my head over a bucket," Slim said. "But our butler,

Barron, he gave me somethin' that made me all shiny and new. I'd be up for the snorkeling trip."

We consulted with Barron and Evans. The Epitome catamaran would deliver us to an offshore reef, from where we could snorkel, dive, windsurf, or take a dinghy to the beach and go into town. All the guests but Mary decided to go.

Barron told Mary, "Let me know what I can arrange for your comfort today, madam."

Mary laughed. "Thank you, Barron," she said. "I'd really love to see how the ship works, if someone could show me that. I've never been on a cruise ship before."

Scott, the badly-dressed techie who reminded me of Justin, had planned to enter a ping-pong tournament with a guy he'd met on the plane to Miami, but when he heard there would be snorkeling he wavered.

"No worries, sir," said Evans. "Some of the other guests want to be back for the tea dance. We'll be back here by four o'clock. I'll call down and have them sign you up for the tournament. What is your partner's name?"

"Lu Jin," Scott said. "He's a physicist from China."

"Quick work, Scottie," Rodrigo said. "You got a date before you even got on the boat."

"What deck is your date staying on?" Rick asked.

"I didn't ask, and I don't care," Scott said.

"You can't invite him to the Epitome Tower, you know," Rick said. "The Tower is restricted."

"What the hell are you talking about?" Scott said, staring at him. Scott's hair had dried in strings after his morning swim. Rick, with his blow-dried hair, orange tan, and Lauren polo shirt with a popped-up collar, looked back with open distaste.

"It's true," said Dan. "I personally think it's fucked up, but it's a rule. Last time we took this trip, I talked to the Concierge Captain about it. Jamboree Cruises and Adonis Enterprises always restrict the Epitome Tower, to keep a more peaceful atmosphere. Before the restriction, some of the Concierge guests complained the Epitome Tower turned into a giant party scene."

"So we can't even invite a friend to visit us here?" Scott frowned.

"Nope," Dan said. "But if you want to hook up, you can always get one of the pavilions on Deck Nine. They're free for Concierge guests."

Scott started to say something, but was drowned out by the laughter and obscene comments around him.

"This restriction thing is messed up," said Rodrigo.

"I think it's a good idea," Rick said.

"I wouldn't take the restriction too seriously, chaps," Blake said. "These rules are made to be broken."

5

Catamaran

Once we loaded ourselves onto the forty-foot catamaran, Nick Kronos lost some of his puffed-up attitude. He showed us around the boat and then took charge of motoring us on the short trip to the reef, steering with two fingers and occasionally turning his head to spit a sunflower seed out towards the sea.

"'Dan-Dan dished some good gossip last night," Slim whispered, as we leaned over the back deck. The sea unrolled beneath us, like a turquoise-and-lapis-blue-dappled carpet fringed by our foamy white wake. Two dolphins were surfing the wakes, one on each side. The warmth here was different from the desert-y dry heat in San Diego—here, it was soft and intimate like a mother's embrace. The metal railing radiated in a comforting band across my bare stomach, and I leaned into its heat in anticipation of the gossip.

"Tell me," I said.

"That orange-painted snobby dude, Rick? He's unemployed. Dan read about it in a business magazine. A year ago, Rick was on their list of '20 Rising Stars in US business.' Then Rick's boss got arrested for some shady dealing. The company just booted Rick, along with a few other guys who worked with him."

"If he's out of work, what's he doing on this spendy cruise?"

"The Dans think he's here to 'network.' He knew Blake, or at least people like Blake, would be on board and might give him a line on a new job."

"Networking on a cruise? Really?"

"Well," said Slim, "Look at him. His first day on the cruise and he's already spending the afternoon sucking up to a billionaire."

"True. What do the Dans know about Blake?"

"I didn't ask," Slim said. "You know, 'Mando, I don't get why Blake is slumming it on this cruise. He must have his own personal mega-yacht."

"Maybe it's got something to do with his family owning part of Jamboree Cruise Lines," I said. "He could be checking up on the quality of the service, deciding whether to keep or sell the stock. That would explain why Concierge Captain Nick Kronos is so jumpy."

"Oh, yeah. Dan-Dan told me about him. Kronos is a real son-of-a-bitch to his staff. The Dans hired away a couple of Jamboree's best staff to work at their resorts. Those people had some stories to tell."

Before I could get details, Slim and I were joined by the Dans themselves.

"We had to get out of the cabin," said Dan-Dan. "Blake raided the bar, and he's mixing the most disgusting combinations of drinks. He keeps convincing everybody to try them, but after one sip you have to throw them out. What a waste."

Dan stood against the rail next to me. "Blake's on a manic jag," he said. "It's a good time to be where he's not." He glared into the churning water below.

"Dan, check out the dolphins," I told him. "They've been surfing our wake this whole time. The one on my side, he likes to twist sideways so I can see the smile on his face."

A few minutes later, Evans leapt to the deck and threw an anchor over the side of the boat.

"It's imperative you follow a buddy system out there," Kronos told the Tribe, as Evans handed out snorkel gear. "If you wish to dive and you've been certified, come talk to me."

Slim and I had agreed to snorkel together. I was trying on a face mask when I heard Blake's voice raised from the inside of the cabin. "I'll bloody well dive if I want to! You're forgetting your place, my man!"

The voices lowered as Evans handed me my fins. Then bumping sounds came from the cabin.

"Lord Blake, stop!"

"Excuse me, gentlemen." Evans dashed into the cabin. Rodrigo, who was about to put on diving gear, followed him.

I duck-walked in my fins to the door of the cabin. Blake was clutching a pair of air tanks to his chest, and Kronos had planted his body between Blake and the door. Rodrigo stood by Evans.

"What's up?" Rodrigo asked.

"This slimy bah-stahd Kronos is trying to prevent me from diving. I came out today to try diving. I'll do it now or I'll have you sacked. Evans, get Mr. Kronos out of my way."

"You haven't been certified, sir," said Evans. "He has to follow regulations."

"No, but I've done it before. All you do is breathe through the tank." Blake demonstrated. His large green eyes were shining as he breathed and stared at Kronos.

"You still can't dive, Blake," said Rodrigo. "It's a fundamental safety rule."

"Come on, Blake." Rick came up behind me and put his head through the door. "Snorkel with me. I need you to show me how."

"Verah well." Blake put down the air tank. "Kronos. Evans. I gave you fair warning. This is your last cruise with Jamboree. Or any other company."

Slim and I hit the water. We swam slowly along the reef, which ran like a shelf about five feet below the surface, and dropped off into an underwater canyon. I'd snorkeled and even dived a few times in San Diego and Mexico, but nothing had prepared me for what I was seeing: tropical fish in all sizes and colors and ridiculous shapes like cartoon drawings from my childhood. Finally, we came upon a pair of squids, shaped like long coffee cans with fringe along the bottom, floating in tandem to the gentle current along the edge of the reef.

Suddenly, I felt a tug on one of my feet, and swirled around to see someone behind me. I came to the surface and pulled the mask and snorkel onto my forehead.

"Baby, I lost you for a minute," Slim said. "I looked behind me and you were gone. It's been almost an hour already. We better get back."

The area had filled up with a few more boats, and dozens of anonymous snorkelers floated along the reef lost in the underwater kingdom I'd just left. We located our catamaran with the Jamboree logo about fifty yards away and swam back.

The Dans, Rick, and Scott were already on the rear platform. "Have you guys seen Blake?" Rick asked, as we pulled ourselves onto the boat.

"No. What's wrong?"

"Blake hasn't come back yet. The Captain wanted to take us to another site, a pretty little island we could swim around. Or lie out in the sun," Dan-Dan said. "Now everyone has to wait. Darn it! Honey, we aren't going to have enough time for shopping in town afterwards, at this rate."

"I thought Blake was with you," I told Rick.

"He was, for a few minutes. Then he said he was done, we came in, and I went back out with Dan."

"I never last very long in the water," Dan-Dan explained. "After ten minutes, I'm cold. Dan can stay out forever."

"True," Rick laughed. "And he's fast. He left me in the dust, and I do a lot of swimming. You would've been clocking fast laps, even for my master swim group."

"Yeah, and I could still be out there if I'd known we weren't leaving right away." Dan pushed his still-dripping hair back from his face. He was still panting from his swim.

Dan-Dan rubbed Dan's hair with a towel and took a neatly rolled Hawaiian print shirt out of his large backpack. "Here, put on your shirt, honey. Blake doesn't have to hold us up. Evans can take us to the beach on the dinghy, and we can catch the bus to the straw market to do our shopping. The ship is docked right there at the pier."

"I already asked Evans," said Dan, starting to button his shirt crookedly over his hairy, dripping chest. "He can't leave until Blake is located. He may need the dinghy to search. Damn. I wanted to get to that craft furniture store today."

Kronos was using binoculars to scan the waters. Evans leaned close to Kronos and said something I couldn't hear.

"What's he saying?" I asked.

Slim said, "He just said a set of scuba gear is missing. Blake must've gone diving, after all."

"Hah!" Dan barked. "Like a naughty child. He's got to make trouble for everyone. Maybe he'll be sorry."

Rick turned on him. "How can you talk like that? He could be drowning."

"There!" shouted Kronos.

We all turned to look where he was pointing. Twenty yards away, a figure in the water was splashing and waving.

Evans leaped into the dinghy and took off. Rick dove into the water and swam after him with a strong crawl stroke. We all watched as Blake struggled to keep his head out of the water. When the dinghy reached him, Evans jumped into the water and helped Blake hang his arms onto the puffy rubber side of the dingy. Rick swam up and helped pull Blake into the dinghy.

Kronos ran to the edge of the catamaran and secured the dinghy, while Evans helped Blake into the cabin. "Stand back, please!" Kronos shouted, and entered the cabin. Rick followed Kronos, while the rest of us waited outside.

After a few minutes, Kronos came out. "Sorry for the delay, gentlemen. Mr. Blake is fine. Unfortunately, we need to take him back to the ship so the ship's doctor can examine him."

"What happened?" I asked.

"He tried to go diving by himself, without certification, and without permission, and he put himself in an unsafe situation. I regret this will cut our trip short. For those of you who would like to remain, we can transport you to the beach."

Rodrigo walked over to the dinghy and took out Blake's scuba gear. "Unbelievable Blake would do something like this. Really asking for trouble. I wonder...." He bent his head to examine the tank, and then looked up at me, his blue-green eyes flashing.

"What?"

"Nothing. I'll go dump this in the cabin. You going back to the ship?"

"Haven't decided. Slim and I want to snorkel some more."

"Stay, then."

I went into the cabin with Rodrigo. While he was placing the scuba gear in the gearbox, I walked over to the couch where Blake was reclining, his round head propped up on a pile of life preservers. Rick knelt at his side.

"Are you all right, Blake?" I asked.

"Fine, old bean. Never felt better." He did look oddly triumphant. His eyes fixed on the top of my Kiniki Amalfi psychedelic tan-thru trunks. "Nice cozzie."

"You got good taste, *amigo*."

"Yes, I have. Especially in men." He reached towards me and ran a finger down my bare stomach. "Ah, Ar-man-do. I'm giving a very special dinner tomorrow night, for our Tower Tribe. You will be there? You must come." He looked like it would ruin his evening if I didn't show.

"Oh, yeah? You want me at your party?" I touched my stomach where his caress had left a hot, exciting buzz. I could feel just the right amount of smooth padding over my six-pack.

The ripped look doesn't work on me, though I don't mind it at all on someone like, say, Rodrigo. I gave Lord Blake my best hard stare.

"I know all about you, Armando," he said, meeting my stare and looking like he really did.

"Huh? What do you know? Are you reading me?" I took a step back.

He smiled. "Of course. I'm reading a man who knows how to have a fine time. I'd say... you've made an art of it. Am I wrong?"

Spray Tan was turning green--not from seasickness-- and Blake was enjoying it. I took a step closer to Blake.

"You're not wrong. I'm always up for something special."

"Ah, Gorgeous, you give me hope, reall-ah you do."

Rick moved his body between Blake and me. "He needs to rest now."

I leaned around Rick, winked at Blake, and retreated.

Everyone but Rick decided to stay at the beach. The Dans took a bus to the market to shop for furniture for their resorts. Rodrigo went windsurfing, and was soon whipping his board across the ocean like an expert. Scott, Slim, and I set ourselves up on the beach, where vendors approached us with everything from clothing and jewelry to a photogenic bright green iguana who would sit on your shoulder and take a picture with you for two dollars. A little boy with big brown eyes and soft black hair that stuck straight out from his head took our order for burgers from a nearby stand.

"This is so relaxing," Scott said. "I almost wish I hadn't made that date for the ping-pong tournament."

I was wondering if he would be offended if I swept the strings of hair off of his face. Before I could act, Slim did it for me. "Dude, you should comb your hair back. You got a good face."

"That's what my mom's always telling me," Scott said. "She says if I fix myself up I'll find a nice girl."

Slim laughed. "You'll find a nice boy."

"A nice boy won't care if I comb my hair."

Slim and I exchanged a look. "I get that," I said. "But there's ways of dressing where you express your respect for yourself, without being superficial. You don't have to zombie up like Mr. Spray Tan."

"I respect myself as I am."

"Cool," said Slim. "So, Scott, you got a boyfriend?"

"No. I don't get out much. I've been kinda married to my work for the last five years."

"What do you do?"

"I, um, work in game design. My partner and I developed a new technology for interfacing with online sales programs to enable secure real-time purchases of game enhancements. We license the technology to some of the biggest game designers."

Slim and I were all over him, and his face lit up as he told us how his technology was already being used in some of our favorite games. His talk became technical, and I tuned him out and watched the way he used his hands while he talked, so much like my [ex?] Justin. I sighed.

"Do you ever play the games you work on?" I finally asked.

"Of course, but not as much lately. I love creating even more than playing." He hesitated. "And that's saying a lot. My team and I won the GalXECraft tournament my senior year in high school."

"Get out!" Slim exclaimed. "Were you 'GeeMen?' I idolized you guys. You were innovative and fearless. I remember that match you won, just using rocks. How did you get so good?"

"We played all the time. I don't need much sleep," Scott said. "Seems like a long time ago, now. Hey, let's go look at some fish. We didn't get much time at the reef earlier."

"Right," I said. "Thanks to the antics of Butch Billionaire."

***

"What's that you're humming, Barron?" I asked my gorgeous butler, as he massaged Peppermint Shea butter into my back that evening.

"Was I humming, Armando? I do apologize.... No, you're not sunburned. You have that fine olive skin. .... Yes, now your legs? I'm so glad you enjoyed your snorkeling. You were lucky to see so many eagle rays."

"Oooh, can you work on my shoulders for just a minute.... yes, right there..... So, what about Mary? Has she come back from checking out the ship?"

"Yes, we got back just before you did. We only had time to see a fraction of the ship. Mary wanted to spend most of the time studying the engine rooms."

"Oh. It was nice of you to take her around."

"My pleasure, Armando. Now let's get you dressed for the Sparkle Party."

6

Lucy
Heavy Load

"It was a sorry crop," I told Nancy, late the following morning after the last candidate had left. "I only hope I've picked the best of them."

"I'm surprised, Ms. Sanders," Nancy said. "Their resumés were so distinguished, and they all looked very presentable. Mr. Snyder, the one you picked? Really, on paper, he seemed almost too good to be true. Isn't he a Yale graduate?"

"That's not why I selected him. I'm not that kind of snob. He's done twenty-plus years of criminal trial work, and another six years of appeals. With that kind of experience, he shouldn't need me to hold his hand to do this death penalty appeal. And I can give him other minor matters to handle. My main reservation is he could be a burnout. Why work for me, when he could be doing contract appeals at a higher hourly rate? I should have hired the young woman who'd managed the mega-class action with the Court of Appeal. She was a ball of fire, but weak on criminal law." I sighed.

Nancy said sympathetically, "It must be hard for you. Your workload is keeping you from spending time with your poor sister."

"No, my sister is making me get behind on my work. Thank God you negotiated another day for her. You think they'll keep her awhile now?"

"They'll probably try to release her today because they've stabilized her panic attacks. What are you going to do about her house?"

"The psychiatrist says if I have her house cleared out, it could make her decompensate again. She might do herself in. I guess I'll just let her go back to wallowing in her piles of garbage. Bless her heart. I wish I could understand what is going on in her head."

"How does she explain it? You must have talked about it."

"No, that's the problem, we haven't talked about it. She doesn't see anything is wrong. She calls the stuff her 'reference papers' and her 'book collection,' and says she can't let go of any of it. I have a meeting at the hospital this afternoon. They should know how to fix this."

"Ye-e-s," Nancy said. "Possibly they will." She brightened. "At least now you have an attorney to help you with your legal work."

"True. Well, today I'll be in court all afternoon and then go straight to the hospital. I'll try to be back from the hospital before five. Get these death penalty case files moved upstairs to the empty office, so Mr. Snyder can start on them next week. There's a dolly in the closet, and you can use the service elevator. At least we'll have those blasted boxes out of my sight."

"Good luck with the hospital," she said. "And I'm sure Mr. Snyder will do a great job."

While she ended up being 100 percent wrong about my new employee, Nancy's doubts about the hospital's effectiveness were unerring. My sister's psychiatrist was a calculating cynic who radiated boredom as he briefed me on her condition. He was interested only in getting her out of his impacted facility ASAP.

Their bottom line was, hoarding is a sad and intransigent disorder, essentially untreatable, and unrewarding fodder for psychiatric institutions. After the immediate gratification of medicating away Sandy's panic attack, there was no further progress to be made.

She is not going to get better, and as she ages, the physical danger of fires and falls caused by the clutter will only increase. The good news is, her condition probably bothers you more than it bothers her.

So, please take your sister home now. Oh, and by the way, she should not go back to her house yet, it will make her anxious, so you should take her to your house. She needs outpatient day care and then ongoing therapy to stabilize her anxiety and start to address her hoarding issues.

"We don't want you to feel your sister won't get better," said the cynic, when I pointed out the inconsistency of his positions. "It's definitely possible for hoarders to respond to appropriate therapy. It will take time. She's ready for discharge now, and can start outpatient treatment next week."

"Oh, I'm sorry. I thought you said, 'ready for discharge now.' Perhaps you aren't aware of the appeal I have pending of your threats to discharge my sister prematurely. You obviously haven't done your job for her. You will be keeping her here until the appeal is resolved."

"The most you can drag out the appeals is one more night. Hospitalization is not medically necessary. You might as well take her home now."

"We'll see about that," I said. "Now, I want to see my sister."

When I met her in the dayroom, I felt a shock as I thought, maybe, after all these years, I'd get my big sister back. We used to be quite attached. Sandy looked remarkably well. She had blossomed under the medication and the attention. In contrast to the wispy-haired seniors staring into space from their wheelchairs or shuffling aimlessly around the lobby, my sister looked vital and human. She was bright-eyed, well-coiffed and made up, ready to get home and back to her teaching schedule.

Yes, she was perfectly pleasant and rational, until I brought up the subject of her house not being safe. Then her eyes would glaze over, and my sister disappeared into this Blind Thing, beyond reason and having no relation to the unique and intelligent woman it was inhabiting.

This Blind Thing was not unknown to me. It's what my clients disappear into when faced with topics such as their substance abuse, or their bad relationship choices. And yes, I'd seen it in Sandy before, when I'd tried to get her to see the truth about her dysfunctional relationship with Paul, and, more recently, when I'd broached the subject of her hoarding.

"Pull yourself together, Sandy," I said. "Let me get a dump truck over there, so you'll have space to move around when you go home tomorrow. You've ended up in a mental hospital. Is this really how you want to live the rest of your life?"

"I just had a panic attack," she said. "It's a straightforward case of anxiety, manageable with medication. Don't you make this into an excuse to try to control my whole life."

"Where do you propose to live?" I asked. "Your house is uninhabitable. What are you going to do, keep buying new houses when your old ones fill up? You can't afford it. Even wild animals keep their homes habitable. The finches that nested in my backyard last year, I watched them take out the waste every day; they weren't just bringing in the food for their babies. Even rats have enough space to move around in. You're living worse than an animal."

Sandy's eyes sparked. "Who are you to talk, Luce? You couldn't manage your own affairs if you didn't make that poor nice boy Armando run everything for you. What were you thinking, making him lie and tell me he was from the government? Armando saw all I needed was some more storage for my resources, and he took care of it. Your life's more of a mess than mine, with your married boyfriend and your two glasses of wine every night, and no one willing to work for you because you're pathologically hypercritical. If you didn't have Armando, your whole life would fall apart."

"You're the one in the nut house, Sister," I said. "I'm done here. Go home to your pigsty and wallow in it."

***

Entering my office half an hour later, I felt a fresh wave of frustration when I saw the twenty-two boxes of *P. v. Johnson* still cluttering my front room. I took a deep breath, exhaled, and directed a questioning gaze at Nancy. She was hunched over Armando's desk, talking into her cell phone, her face a mask of concentration.

"I know, honey. I know the medicine makes your mouth feel funny. But you still need to take it. Do you have some of those Jolly Rancher candies we got you last weekend? You like those? Which color do you like the best? Why don't you take your medicine, and then have a nice green Jolly Rancher. Isn't tonight movie night? Yes? Go tell Mrs. Zelinsky you're ready to take your medicine now. Okay, honey. Call me back after you take it. I'll be right here. Yes, you can call me right back. I'll be here waiting. Yes. I love you, too. Bye-bye."

She hung up and looked at me. "I'm so sorry, Ms. Sanders."

"How old is he?" I asked.

"Twenty-seven."

"Ah."

"How did things go at the hospital?"

"As you predicted. I filed the second-level appeal to get her one more night."

"What are you going to do?"

"I don't know," I said.

"Well, I'll get started on those boxes now." Nancy stood up and smoothed the top of her skirt. Her cell phone rang, and she shot me a panicked glance as she turned back towards the desk to answer it.

I hung up my jacket and got the dolly out of the closet. Three boxes onto the dolly, the clanging of the service elevator as it crept slowly to the second floor, three boxes unloaded, clump, clump, clump. Heft the dolly, carry it back down the stairs to my office, Nancy's voice making waves of soothing sounds into the telephone, load three boxes.... As I worked, my mind started to clear, and I breathed more deeply.

Memories of the old Sandy started to replace the recent images I'd been carrying around, of the bloated, crazy-eyed creature that had gradually taken her over. When we were little, Sandy was the protective big sister, proud of the straight blonde hair that fell to her waist, and generous with her share of food when there wasn't enough to go around and I was a scrawny tomboy with a tapeworm metabolism. Then she decided I was the smart one, and she didn't want to be only the pretty one, and she eventually overachieved herself into a PhD in Sociology to trump my law degree. Bless her heart, I admired her for it, and many times stopped myself from questioning the practicality of her choice of field.

We kept in touch when she was still at Oklahoma State and I was living in California, finishing law school and starting to practice and teach. After she moved to San Diego and started teaching at the community college, we went out together all the time, sharing drinks and stimulating talks. Things started to go bad for her, and for us, when she met that bloodsucker Paul....

"Ugh!" I carried the dolly down the last step and dumped it on the ground.

With only a couple of loads to go, I took a break. I sat on a stack of books and looked at my feet. I'd taken off my pumps after the first load, and my nylons were shredded.

Nancy hung up the phone. "I'm so sorry."

"Don't tell me you're sorry, dear," I said. "Tell me how I'm going to get my big sister back."

7

Armando

At Sea

"This will set you right up, Armando." It was our second morning on the *Adonis.* Barron opened the curtains a crack, shooting a thin shaft of sun across the foot of my bed. The light triggered a painful blinding glare in the small scuzzy goldfish bowl that had gotten stuck around my head while I slept. He helped me sit up and handed me a glass of something fizzy.

"Bottoms up, sir!"

The goldfish bowl started to expand and dissolve. "What time is it?" I asked.

Last night's Sparkle Party had filled all of the main deck. Men in sparkles were everywhere: in the giant shallow clover-shaped swimming pool, posing on rope lattices draped with silver tinsel, on balconies, on the dance floor in the Lucky Star.

I lay in bed scrolling through the pictures I'd taken, hoping Rodrigo had some good ones of me climbing on a pole in my sparkle thong, silver headband, gloves, and white Puma Cell Surins (no laces), with a vape cigarette in one hand and a topaz-colored Manhattan in the other. Late last night, Billionaire Blake had invited Slim and me to a threesome in his cabin.

"Come on, chaps," he'd whispered. He had been eyeing me all night, and finally joined Slim and me on the dance floor of the Lucky Star and piloted us into a dark corner, a large shapely arm around each of our shoulders. "I can teach you boys some things. You'll never regret it."

We'd laughed it off, but later he got our attention across the table and moved his head sideways towards the exit in invitation. Slim and I retreated to the bathroom.

"What do you think?" I asked. "We could have some fun."

"He's not for me," Slim said. "Not at all my type."

"He sort of is, Slim. You've liked other super-rich guys."

"True. The rich do have something to offer. Not just the money. They're different. You know?"

"Yeah," I said. "I do know. He's not my type either, but there is something magnetic about him. I'm just not sure."

"We got a whole nine days to decide," Slim said.

"Right." But I wondered if Blake would get bored and take off in his private helicopter.

It was almost noon when the last of us staggered, hungover, to the breakfast table. No one seemed hungry except Blake, who put away a plate of Eggs Florentine and a scotch and water before leaning back and letting Evans light his cigar.

"Armando! Slim!" he called down the table. "Look up, my beauties. You don't want to miss this."

We turned to where he was pointing. Fifteen feet above the Epitome Tower's pool deck there was a set of ornamental white canvas sails. These could be unfurled and moved around to provide shade or shelter as needed by the Concierge guests. The airy installation was anchored by masts that rose from the deck and supported a series of triangular sheets.

Barron and Evans, under the direction of Nick Kronos, stripped down to white spandex thongs and demonstrated the operation of the overhead "sails." The men climbed a rope ladder to a small platform where a series of ropes was hooked into place. They gave a graceful show of sails opening and closing and moving across the sky above us. When fully deployed, the sails formed a dome over the whole deck.

As a final flourish, Evans unhooked a rope from the high center mast, and anchored his hands on top of a large knot. With a quick, light, jump he swung on the rope out over the pool. With a move of incredible gymnastic beauty, he was suddenly swinging upside down with his body arched into a graceful half-moon. You could hardly see his white thong, and I thought of the ancient Greeks performing nude in their Olympic games. Evans's small catlike body was gymnast-strong, but you barely saw the muscles or bones under his smooth, bronze skin.

"He must've been in a circus or somethin'," Slim whispered to Mary and me. "That's really hard to do."

"I'm liking our butlers," I said as we watched Evans, spotted by Kronos, dismount gracefully onto the platform. The men climbed down the rope ladder, took a bow, and went to put their uniforms back on. Barron's blonde hair gleamed in the sun, and his perfect white teeth flashed as he helped Evans step into his shoes. Evans went to stand at the side of Kronos, who put a fatherly hand on his shoulder.

"They're beautiful," Mary said. "And they get along so well."

Dan was standing behind us. "There's plenty of cattiness behind the scenes, believe me. But they are really well picked. Danny and I recently hired away a couple of Jamboree's best staff for our resorts. They're so good at taking care of things for us, we were able to get away on this cruise."

"Is Mr. Kronos also a butler?" Slim asked. "He and some guy who wasn't one of our butlers brought me my coffee this morning."

"That seems unfair," said Mary. "I sure wouldn't want that creepy Kronos bringing me breakfast in bed."

"Kronos is the boss. He sometimes brings staff up from Deck Nine for training," Dan told us. "He'll stand back and watch them work, then personally escort them out of the Tower. He runs a very tight ship."

Mary sighed. "Well, the staff here are certainly well trained." Her eyes rested on the shining blonde head of Barron, who was helping Evans roll back some of the sails to let more sunlight onto the pool deck.

Blake had gotten out of his seat and was talking with Nick Kronos and gesturing upwards towards the platform. Kronos called Evans and Barron to join them for a short conference.

Blake returned to the table with a smirk on his round face. "What are my Elite brothers up to today? Don't forget my dinner party tonight. Dinner at eight. Dress is formal. Or wear your birthday suit." He winked at me.

It was an "at sea" day. Most of the tribe lounged around the pool until it was time to get ready for the Neon tea dance. After the dance, I had time for a swim and a massage from Barron before Blake's dinner party. The vibe still hadn't been right for me to come on to Barron.

"What's been going on around here, while I was at the dance?" I asked him, as he massaged coconut oil into my shoulders.

"Let's see. Several of the gentlemen went to the Donna Frock matinee."

"Did Mary stay here?"

"No. She was interested in seeing the catalytic reduction equipment. I believe Lord Blake and Mr. Rick were the only ones in the Tower all afternoon. Lord Blake has been consulting with our chef about tonight's dinner, and has been making some other, ah, arrangements with Mr. Kronos."

"What kind of arrangements?"

"I don't know if I should say."

"Come on, Barron, what is it? A surprise? I won't tell."

"Lord Blake persuaded Mr. Kronos to cobble together a sort of rope swing over the Infinity Pool. I hope you'll resist the temptation to try it."

Half an hour later, I joined the Epitome Tower elites poolside, where a long dinner table had been set up. The sun had just set, and the bright orange and turquoise sky and clouds were quickly turning dark, smoky blue-grey. Scott hadn't appeared yet, but the rest of the tribe was dressed for the 'very special' dinner Blake had promised.

Mary's wardrobe didn't include any formal attire, and the Dans had taken her to their cabin. The three of them were in full-on made-up drag showgirl realness, with matching red feather boas. Dan-Dan had fashioned a silver cone to hold Mary's long hair up all retro-Madonna. Rodrigo and Rick wore well-cut tuxedos. Slim wore a pair of harem pants made out of colorful Guatemalan fabric, with his favorite faux-pearl choker, and a small tiara. My slim-fit satin Bar III tux with the shawl collar glowed blue under the soft lighting.

Blake, wearing a baggy bathing suit with the British flag printed on it, was playing on his new rope swing. He was obviously getting off on Kronos's agonized expression every time he climbed back up the rope ladder for more.

"Ha, ha, gentlemen, and, er, lady," Kronos said to us, "Lord Blake Copland, he bravely wishes to swing on the rope, and we try to make it safe. Please, I suggest you do not engage in this activity, it is not recommended. Ha-ha, yes, you know, 'do not try this at home,' okay?"

"Come on, Dan," Blake yelled. "Take that tight dress off your hairy ass and get on this rope!"

Dan walked away from the pool. "For this British whale I'm waiting around for my dinner? Why don't we all leave him to it and go get a big steak dinner at the Ice Bar?"

Rodrigo raised his eyebrows at Slim and me.

"I'm kinda ready to eat," Slim admitted. "Lunch was a long time ago, and I danced for hours at the tea dance. Whoa! Look at this table. Every setting's got seven forks."

"Hey, boys," Mary walked up and stroked my arm. "Love your suit, 'Mando. Barron just made me the best drink in the world. It's called a Beachside Bonfire. Isn't it pretty?"

"I want what you're having," Slim said. "You look... *no se... muy satisfecha.*"

"Yeah, if I didn't know better, I'd say you'd gotten laid," Rodrigo said.

The night sky got dark as we spent the long wait for Blake's seven-course banquet getting smashed on Beachside Bonfires.

"Omigod," I said. "Don't look now, but Spray Tan is stripping down. He's gonna go on Lord Billionaire's rope swing."

Rodrigo pulled out a chair and passed around a bowl of nuts from the dinner table. "Might as well get comfortable."

Slim brought his iPad from his room. "I thought of this video when we were snorkeling. Check out Pitbull with the dolphins. Look at that smile, man."

"I love this song." Mary started dancing with Slim, towering over him in her five-inch heels.

Barron came over with a tray of appetizers. "I took the liberty. Dinner is ready, but your host ah, isn't quite ready for us to serve." He held the tray for me and stared at Mary until she turned and smiled at him.

The Dans were dancing next to me. "Come with us tonight, Armando," said Dan-Dan. "We're going to see Frankini, the hypnotist. He can make you do anything."

"I don't know, brothers," I said. "What level would that be on?"

Dan-Dan laughed. "I wish Mister Billionaire would get this dinner underway. I don't want to miss Frankini. "

We looked over at Blake. He was crunked, and intensely focused on improving his rope swinging technique. The rope swing was anchored about five feet short of the pool. To drop into the pool from the rope, Blake had to get up enough momentum to swing out to a six-foot radius from the center. This was not hard to achieve if you took a running jump off the platform and dropped into the pool at the height of the swing.

But Blake was practicing staying on the rope and swinging like a pendulum, waiting until it almost stopped over the cement poolside. Then he would pump his body, like a kid on a swing set, to get the momentum back up, before letting the rope go and dropping into the pool. When he couldn't get the momentum, he had to shimmy down the rope and climb back up the platform to try again.

"I gotta admire his strength and his constitution," Dan said. "He's carrying almost as much weight as I am, and got quite a few toxic substances in him. There's no way I could do that."

"He's persistent, that's for sure," I said.

"That's the problem," Dan sighed. He took a swig from his coffee thermos, which he was alternating with small sips of a Beachside Bonfire. A loose red fluff from a feather boa was stuck on one of his eyebrows. His drag attire only magnified his stocky, hairy masculinity. My macho father, only... nice.

"What do you mean?" I asked.

He leaned closer to me and said in a low voice, "I mean, Lord Billionaire scares the shit out of me. He's got money that gives him almost infinite power, but without any of the self-discipline he'd have if he earned it himself. He needs to be gotten under control, man." Dan's drag makeup had started to melt in the heat.

We watched Blake cannonball into the center of the pool. Upon release, the end of the heavy rope buckled and flapped wildly above the lounge chairs.

"Not so close, Blake!" Rodrigo yelled, from his lounge chair. "This asshole is crazy," he muttered. "Those ropes aren't made to swing on. Someone's gonna get hurt."

From Dan-Dan, a murmur: "If Blake gets himself hurt, I'm not gonna be crying. He can fly away on his fine helicopter, and I'll be right here doing the happy dance."

Dan took Dan-Dan's arm and led him to the balcony, where Mary and Slim were scoping out the growing nightlife below. I went to a lounge chair to lie down and think. Blake didn't seem dangerous to me. He was like an engaging cartoon character, with his well-proportioned physique, round face, slicked black hair, and white skin, his British accent, and his wind-up toy energy.

I liked Dan, but in some ways his seriousness and inflated work ethic made me think of Lucy, and of Justin. I lay on my belly and felt a little sad. Maybe I needed some action. If it hadn't been for my promise to Barron, I would've taken a turn on the rope swing myself.

Like the Gods had heard my thoughts, a loud yell sounded above me. "I...am...im-mor-taaaal!!!" Wind rushed over my body. I cried out and covered my head with my hands.

"Goddammit, Blake," Rodrigo yelled. "You almost hit him!"

"I'm okay," I said.

Blake grinned down at me. Lit by the tiki lamps, his face was huge, a wicked white moon against the velvet sky. He pumped his body until the rope swung over the pool, and let go, splashing me with water. His face surfaced like a figurehead out of the water, and he hauled himself to the pool's edge next to my lounge chair.

"You're a real sport, Armando. I am all over that suit you've got on. It's the exact same color as the sky right now. Look up and see."

It was midnight blue along the horizon, gradually turning to almost black straight above. We were far out at sea, and the only artificial light was that generated by the *Adonis*. Our ship seemed suddenly small and isolated. I could see thousands of stars, milky galaxies, and constellations you could never see at home because of the city lights.

"There's the North Star, Sport. Find the Big Dipper, and draw a line from the tip." Blake sat next to me on my lounge chair. He took my chin between his hands and turned my head to the north. His hands were still damp and cool from the water, and he had a light touch.

"There, you've got it. That's the way you'd go if you were going home. But you're not. You're still headed south, to Honduras. Now, look this way." He took my shoulders and guided me in the other direction.

"That's our friend Orion, and you can follow the aim of his bow to the Pleiades:

'Many a night I saw the Pleiads, rising thro' the mellow shade/
Glitter like a swarm of fireflies tangled in a silver braid."

"That sounds like Tennyson," I said.

"Ver-rah good, Sport. I am impressed," he said aloud. Then he put his lips close to my ear and whispered, "I knew there was a reason I was hunting you."

He'd been in and out of the pool for hours, but he still had his distinctive scent that was like complex fresh pipe tobacco even though I was pretty sure he didn't smoke a pipe. He let go of my shoulders and bounded off to dress for dinner.

Blake's touch left my body humming and warm in the cooling night air. I lay back in my lounge chair and stared up at the stars, following the aim of Orion's bow until I saw the Pleiades huddled in their tiny cluster.

8

Lotos Eaters

Absorbed in stargazing, I took a while to notice people were gathering at the big table. Blake had on a tailor-made tux that would have cost at least a couple months of my salary. He was at the head of the table, attended on his right by Spray Tan, who looked smug. I did a double take at the young man Blake was ushering into the seat to his left. It was Scott, his shaggy hair combed to the side, exposing his high forehead and making him look more grown up. When he saw me, he smiled shyly and held out his arms to display his tuxedo. I winked my approval, although the tux was at least a size too large for current fashion.

Evans and Barron poured champagne and laid heavy linen napkins across our laps. Our noisy tribe fell silent as the first course was served. On plates the size of a tea saucer, we were each served five thin slices of raw fish, arranged like the petals of a flower, with black seeds of caviar in the center and a line of sauce making a stem and leaf. Each of the tiny courses was more beautiful than the last, and the wine got finer. The conversation mellowed, and focused mostly on the food and wine. Blake had stories about the foods, and the wines, that made the event like a work of art.

After the spicy seafood soup and the saffron couscous salad, we had tart sorbet on tiny ice sculptures shaped like lotus flowers. The sorbet was shaved into lime-colored petals, and in the center of the petals were several little round piles of black chia seeds, repeating the visual theme started by the first course.

"Wasn't there some island of people called the 'Lotus Eaters?'" I asked.

"Yeah," said Scott. "I read it in high school. It's in the Odyssey or the Iliad or something. Eating the lotus made the sailors who landed there become lazy, and they didn't want to work or do anything."

"I can relate to that," said Mary. "I honestly love my work, but I could get used to this lifestyle. No more digging ditches and crawling under houses."

"Armando, your fine sensibility has detected my theme for the evening," Blake said. He gave me a look that would have gotten me right into his bedroom, if we hadn't been otherwise occupied. "More Tennyson, for you, my beauty."

Barron, wearing white spandex shorts, a white bow tie, and white bowler hat, had come to stand next to Blake. He swept off his bowler, held it to his breast, and recited.

> *The Lotos blooms below the barren peak, The Lotos blows by every winding creek....*
>
> ...
>
> *...Round and round the spicy downs the yellow Lotos-dust is blown*
>
> *We have had enough of action, and of motion we,*
>
> *Roll'd to starboard, roll'd to larboard, when the surge was seething free,*
>
> *Where the wallowing monster spouted his foam-fountains in the sea.*
>
> *Let us swear an oath, and keep it with an equal mind,*
>
> *In the hollow Lotos-land to live and lie reclined*
>
> *On the hills like Gods together, careless of mankind....*

We ate our sorbet lotuses and listened to the poetry. It wasn't just his beauty and rich voice that made Barron's presentation so good. His face expressed wonder, and his voice projected through the night air, as artfully as the actors I'd seen at the summer Shakespeare festival in San Diego. Even the noises from the decks below subsided as if to catch the beautiful sound. I realized I'd been holding my breath when the final lines came: "*O, rest ye, brother mariners, we will not wander more.*"

Into the silence, Blake said, "There you have it, friends. Lord Tennyson, recited by our own Barron, the Sir Kenneth Branagh of Jamboree Cruises." He reached back and gave Barron a spank, so loud you could feel it sting. "Good work, my boy."

"We really are the lotus eaters," Rick exalted. His face was flushed. "Like kings high above the mass of suffering humanity."

"Well, Rick, I don't know," said Rodrigo, "the mass of humanity on the lower decks doesn't sound like it's exactly suffering."

The shouts, laughter, and pulse of dance music were getting louder.

"The mass of partying humanity," Dan said. "Sucking down cheap booze, overeating at the buffets, and gyrating to the Top 40's House Mix."

Slim laughed, and then got serious. "I feel so lucky to be here. What did I do to deserve this?" Slim waved his brown arm in a circle to indicate our table and the Epitome Tower and the excitement below and the sky and sea around. He looked very Aztec tonight, his dark eyes lit by the fine food and alcohol, and the tiara angled back on his head to emphasize the sloping lines of his nose and forehead, like a warrior's headdress. "I wonder if this is how super-rich people feel, like, all the time," he said.

"I don't think the super-rich feel guilty," Rodrigo said, holding his glass up to swirl his wine in front of the candlelight. "If you're born with all this, you believe you deserve it."

Dan laughed. "What about rich people who made their own money? Should they feel guilty? Anyway, the rich aren't always lucky. All the fine amenities don't insulate you from life's universal problems."

"Like your boyfriend dumps you," said Dan-Dan.

"Your skin breaks out," Mary said.

"You get a loathsome disease," Dan said. "Or become paralyzed by boredom because life seems meaningless."

"Or worse," I put in, "you go bald. You know those hair transplants? You can tell when someone has had one. There's nothing you can do."

Rick had been looking impatient. "It's hypocritical to say money isn't important. If you have money, you can develop your appreciation of the finer things. Art, poetry, culture. Sure, there are things money won't buy. But look at all this." He made the same circular gesture as Slim, but much narrower, implying a radius reaching just to the edge of the Epitome Tower. "All this, it refines you."

"I'm not super rich or anything," said Scott, "but I still feel like I need to give something back. You know, to charity and causes."

"Oh, I don't know," Blake said. He looked at me and his eyes pulsed, saying as clear as words, 'let's share some fun.' Then he leaned away from Rick to wrap his arm around Scott. "Scottie, you're too modest. Thanks to your cutthroat business practices, your tech firm, GamezOn, just went public and made you worth something in the high seven figures and generates large annual profits of which you receive a substantial share. Crying poor doesn't become you, dear boy."

Scott edged out from under Blake's arm. Rick reclaimed Blake's other arm. Blake smiled.

"Now Rick here, he was in, ah, let's call it a transitional stage, but has recently agreed to join one of my companies."

Rick, who wasn't holding his liquor as well as the rest of us, leaned into Blake, lurched up in an attempt to stand and fell back into his seat, and then held up his glass like he was going to propose a toast. But Scott stood up and spoke first.

"I don't appreciate your mischaracterizations of how I run my company, Blake."

"Here's to gentlemanly disagreements." Blake raised his glass. "And to the more serious business of enjoying our final three courses."

"You mean we're not done?" Slim asked. "I thought the ice cream was our dessert."

An hour and a half later, the staff cleared the table as the tribe savored Cuban cigars and balloon glasses of "Black Pearl" cognac, which Rick later informed us cost an amount more than twice my annual salary. Even Scott seemed to have forgiven Blake's insult and was questioning him about places to visit in England.

"This cognac," Mary said. "I feel helpless to describe it. It's so complex. It, it....it tastes like its color. Does that make sense?" She held the glass up to her eyes and looked through the dark amber liquid. "Blake, my darling, you have absolutely spoiled me. Thank you."

A chorus of thanks burst forth into the night air.

Blake waved his cigar. "My pleasure, chaps. No need to thank."

A silence fell at the table, bringing into focus the music and cries of the crowds below. It was after eleven o'clock. Dan, Scott, and Rodrigo started blowing smoke rings. Dan-Dan looked at his watch.

Blake said, "Who's up for hitting the lower decks? I'm ready to get reah-ly stupid."

***

I'm sure I made it to Dr. Frankini's hypnotism show that night. People told me so, later. But my memories of the rest of the evening start after that. The Terrible Tribe of Nine is still together, at the Tropicana on Level Seven, sipping Mai Tais with fierce little umbrellas. Blake has reserved a long table at the edge of the dance floor for us and some new friends, and bartenders are ignoring other customers to keep our drinks coming. Dan is talking intensely with Doctor Frankini. Dan-Dan is telling Slim and me how he and Dan have overextended themselves buying a new property in New Mexico. "It needs so much more work than we thought to get it running. We couldn't have afforded this cruise right now, but we got a special offer from Jamboree Cruises, half price for repeat Concierge customers, this week only. We couldn't resist."

Later, Blake, still in his posh tux, with his white tie hanging loose, a strand of black hair falling over his forehead, whispers something in Scott's ear. Scott stands and Rodrigo pulls him back, walking him away from our table.

"What did you say to him?" I ask Blake.

"Scott was whining about what I said about his business practices, calling me a liar. I told him perhaps we could test that, with an article published by one of my family's papers. Then, I suggested I could use one of our papers to 'out' him. Who does he think he is? Staying in the closet when he should be out and proud, a successful gay entrepreneur. I don't know why he was so upset. No one takes what we publish in our rags seriously, Sport. Ha! I told him we're going to publish pictures of him from this cruise."

"What's wrong with that?"

I wonder if I could get Blake to publish some pictures of me. Before leaving the Tower, I'd changed into my navy blue JQC faux leather shorts with the long zipper and wore them with just my tuxedo jacket and black combat boots. Slim had helped me put my hair into spikes, and I was getting a lot of attention.

Blake laughs his rich plummy laugh in a way that makes me feel like I'm the wittiest guy in the world. "Nothing wrong with it, Sport, nothing ah-tall." He leans close to my ear. "Come back to the Tower with me now, Beauty, and I'll take some pictures of you. I'm raw-thah good at it."

I hesitate, and Dan comes up and pulls me away. "I've got to have a dance with the best dancer on this ship," he says.

Later, back at the table, Dan is on a roll, talking up his resorts and telling us all he'll give us discounts and VIP treatment.

Dan-Dan says, "One of the features of our resorts is the staff treat you like family. You get to know the local hangouts."

"Sign me up," I say. "Do you have any in L.A.?"

Rick has taken my seat next to Blake. "I hear you're about to go bankrupt," he tells Dan. "Maybe that family-style business model isn't really working for you. Armando, I wouldn't advise you to make any sort of pre-payment to these guys. After blowing all your money on this trip, you aren't going to have a lot of money left to burn."

"You don't know what you're talking about, you pathetic bootlicker." Dan tells him. "At least I didn't get fired for unethical business practices. According to the Wall Street Journal, your ex-boss is headed for prison."

"I had nothing to do with that!" Sweat pops out on Rick's orange face. "What's wrong with you?"

"Dude, you started it," Slim says to Rick. "Come on Armando, let's dance."

Dan and Dan-Dan join us on the dance floor, leaving Blake and Rick laughing and high-fiving each other.

Later, Slim and I join the Dans at the bar.

"Rick was out of line," Slim says. "He was trying to impress Blake."

"Blake is the one who fed him all that bullshit about me," Dan says. "Blake's been on this cruise a few times. The staff hate him. He makes trouble."

"Blake does like to shake things up," I say. "But he's charming, too."

"Watch out, Armando," Dan says. "There are bad rumors. About Blake bringing young crew members up to the Tower, and one of the boys killing himself after."

"God. I wonder if it's true. I was starting to consider him."

"Well, don't."

"Thanks for the advice, papa."

"I'm just saying."

I come out of a bathroom stall and see Blake and Spray-Tan huddled over a sink doing lines of white powder.

Back at the bar, Mary looks at her watch and takes off.

"That slut Mary is screwing my butler," I whisper in Slim's ear. "And Rick is being so extra right now. What does Blake see in him?"

Slim is flashing his fake pearl choker. "These are going to be all over the clubs in a year." He rolls one of the oversized pearls between his dark fingers. The opalescent balls glow against his skin. "They're all Audrey Hepburn."

A guy with mohawked purple hair and a long white cape walks by, giving Slim a long stare.

"There's my 'catch of the day,'" Slim tells me, and disappears soon after.

I can't take my eyes off this giant in Samoan attire, working a totally ferocious grass skirt, doing his job as a plus-size chunk of eye candy and bouncer.

I'm back at the bar with some college bros from Louisiana. You just want to pour their voices over pancakes. We switch to tequila, so the bros can show me this "vampire shot" thing that's popular in New Orleans.

A RuPaul classic comes on and the dance floor fills up. The dance floor looks kind of far away, but I want to dance. In fact, I'm already dancing in my seat, upon which one of the bros has joined me. What would it be like to dance on a round bar stool, the kind that rotates? Someone's tongue is fastened to my neck, licking off Tabasco sauce, and I brush it away.

Standing on the bar stool feels good. My well-trained body is made to dance on high places. Oh, they're clearing a space on the bar. I take a step up, with no break in my gyrations. I'm young, I'm fierce. Bam!

Whoa! Two giant hams, I mean hands, lift me in the air like I'm a prima ballerina. My feet hit flat down on the garish Tropicana carpet with a bound, the hands lift me up again and I am staring straight ahead into big round eyes that regard me with contempt and boredom. My feet hit the carpet again and I am staring at a huge bare chest and the top of a grass skirt. I reach out my arms for a hug, but am denied.

"That's enough, buddy," a voice mutters from above, "time to go."

I am in the elevator with a new friend, one of the Southern bros who's been staring at me with hot eyes all night. Late the next morning, I regain consciousness in his room, a cramped crib on Level Five.

9

Grand Turk

The room I woke up in didn't have any windows, not even a measly porthole. The only light came from a bright, flickering night-light plugged into the wall near the door. The bed was attached to the wall at the top and along one side. I was practically pinned against the wall. The Louisiana bro from last night, a less-cute version of my faithless butler, was crashed out against me.

After a quick rinse in the miniature sink, I dressed and went to look for the elevators going up. The hallways on this level, like the rooms, were low and narrow and seemed to go on forever, trapping me in the dismal underbelly of the *Adonis*. I was starting to panic, when I turned a corner and saw Slim.

"*Amigo,* am I glad to see you! So you stayed down here last night, too? Where'd you get that uniform?"

"*Como?* Sorry, sir, may I help you, please?"

"Ha, ha. C'mon, how do we get back up to the Tower? Man, what a night. Let's spend the day walrusing at the Infinity pool."

"Ah, you go to the Epitome Tower? I will escort you, sir. It is not easy to give directions."

He led me to an elevator bank. "After you, sir."

I looked at him closely as the door closed behind us. "Dude! Do you know you have a double? You're the spitting image, man. What do they call it, a doppleganger? This is so freakin' spooky."

"Excuse me, sir, I don't understand. My English...."

"*Habla Espanol?*" I explained to him in Spanish he had a double, who happened to be my best friend.

His name was Carlos. He had grown up in Honduras, and he worked as a Stateroom Steward on Level Five of the *Adonis*.

The elevator opened, and I saw the familiar neon of the Lucky Star in the distance.

"Oh, I know where I am, now," I told Carlos.

"Then I will leave you here. Have a nice day, sir."

"No, wait. *Ven conmigo*. You have to meet my friend."

He looked around him nervously. "I regret I cannot, sir. We are not allowed. You would like me to call a butler to escort you?"

"Please, I insist. I won't let you get in trouble. Come to the Tower with me."

"I'm sorry...," he began again. Then he stopped and stared at me. A strange look came into his eyes. "Yes, sir. I will come with you to the Tower."

When we got off the elevator, Barron was there like he'd been waiting for us.

"Good morning, Armando, Mr. Slim. Did you have a pleasant evening?" His blond haire was tousled, and there was a glow in his deep blue eyes that wasn't fully masked by his professional demeanor.

"Looks like yours was very pleasant, at least," I said. "Is anyone else up yet?"

"The other guests have had breakfast, and people are getting ready to go ashore. Have you had a chance to consider the beach and kayaking tour?"

"Not yet. Can you bring a couple of those hangover drinks to Slim's cabin?"

As I passed the pool, Mary was floating on her back, her palms submitting to the sky, her hair streaming around her like a mermaid's. Scott was sitting at the edge of the pool, his feet dangling into the water, staring out to sea. At first, I thought they were alone, then I heard an "Ahoy!" and looked up to see Blake waving from his platform. As Barron, Carlos, and I watched, he made a running jump, grabbed the rope, and swung out and into the pool. Mary had to make a quick dodge to avoid the missile, pasting herself to the side of the pool.

"Blake," she yelled. "You almost hit me!"

"Nonsense, Athena. I knew you would haul that big ass if you needed to." He swam to the edge of the pool next to her and rested his arms on the cement.

Next to me, Barron made a quick movement forward and then stepped back. "I'll get your drinks, Armando." He disappeared in the direction of the kitchen.

"Good one, Blake," I remarked. "You are definitely improving, or at least the rest of us are learning to dodge. Thanks again for that fabulous dinner last night. Best meal of my life. Have you been in the pool all morning?"

"Not at all, Sport. I had my usual eight a.m. rope swing practice, and I just got back in again. Would you care for a go at the swing? Or join me in my room for a morning romp? Both of you?" He swam across the pool and leered at Carlos and me.

"We had a long night," I told him. "We're gonna go have our hangover drinks and shower."

I hustled Carlos around the corner to Slim's cabin, knocking and saying in a low tone, "Slim-ster, it's me, open up."

When Slim opened the door, I pushed my way in, dragging Carlos after me.

It was like one of those fairy tales where long lost brothers are united after living very different lives. Facing each other like mirror images, their jaws dropped, eyes rounded, and red lips parted just the same way. I pulled my cell phone out of my pocket and took a picture. They stared, frozen, for a few long seconds. Then Carlos reached out his hand and gently touched Slim's arm.

"Are you real?" he asked in Spanish.

Slim took Carlos's hand and walked him across the spacious cabin to sit on the bed. Slim turned to me. "Where did you find him?"

"He'll tell you about it," I said. "I'm gonna go take a shower."

As I closed Slim's door behind me, I ran into Barron, bearing hangover drinks. I took one and drank it on the spot, and took the other to finish in my room.

Twenty minutes later, I went back to Slim's room. He and Carlos were still sitting on Slim's bed, chattering rapidly in Spanish. When he saw me, Carlos jumped up.

"Oh, I must leave now, sir!" He put his Steward's hat back on and joined me at the door.

I walked him to the Epitome Tower elevator. "*Hasta luego*," I said.

"*Sí.* Yes, we will see each other again. Thank you, sir!" His long eyes, bright and clear but with the whites a little yellower than Slim's in the sunlight, glowed at me, and he disappeared into the elevator.

Back at the Infinity pool, I found my favorite lounge chair and started rubbing coconut oil on my face and body.

"Join the hangover crowd," Rodrigo said. He looked good in in his contour pouch Greek camo speedo and the Carrera aviator mirrored sunglasses I'd given him when we were dating.

Mary was lounging in a glittery purple bikini and displaying a new purple mani-pedi. A *Modern Plumbing* magazine sat unopened in her lap. "You must have had quite a night," she said. "Where'd Slim come up with that uniform?"

"I don't know," I said, turning my back on her. I turned to Dan. "Where the hell are we, anyway?"

"You see that big flat white landmass ahead of us? That's the Grand Turk. British Colony. Diving, fishing, salt, and offshore banking services. And serving cruisers—if you want to, and God knows why you would, you can spend your day hanging out at the giant pool at the Cruise Terminal."

I decided to join Rick and Rodrigo on a diving trip. Slim, who wasn't certified for diving, decided to join Mary and the Dans on a snorkeling excursion.

When Scott said he was going to find a place to take advantage of reliable phone and Internet services to get some work done, Blake offered his assistance.

"Join me at the Jamboree offices, mate. We have a well-equipped office at every port."

"I don't want to put you out," Scott said.

"No trouble, old bean. I have a few little matters to look into, myself."

"I'll miss you today, baby," I said to Slim as we walked back towards our cabins to get ready.

We stopped at the edge of the deck to look out. The *Adonis* was lumbering into port, dwarfing the small pier that stretched from the white sand to the pale turquoise water in front of us. On the shoreline, backed by swaying palm trees, were hundreds of blue-and-white striped beach chairs, all empty and facing towards us like an audience of invisible ghosts watching the spectacle of our arrival.

Slim put his hand on my arm. "'Mando, I'm in shock. Seeing Carlos made me feel so funny. We can't possibly be twins, but I already feel like he's my brother. I'm sure we're going to be close, for the rest of our lives. Do you think that's just because we look so much alike? But that's not a good reason to feel this intense connection. Is it? It's like... I don't know how to explain it. Like meeting him is a sign, or a test."

"What kind of a test, Slim?"

"I don't know. He has a hard life. How come I got to be me, born in a rich country, with a great family and opportunity, and friends like you? All I know is, I'm gonna see Carlos again, and I'm gonna pray to God to tell me why we met."

Our day of diving was totally worth being away from the action on the boat for five hours. I wore my royal blue Rufskin draw-cord short trunks with the white stripe along the top. Instead of the big catamaran, Nick Kronos sailed us out in a skiff that just held the four of us. Kronos skimmed easily along the clear water, sometimes tilting the boat to one side until I thought it would fall over, only to whip it expertly back after a quick command of "ready about."

I'd been nervous about diving, as I was only at the beginning level, but felt okay with Rodrigo, whom I'd long ago nicknamed "Mr. Safety," and who had a lot of diving experience. Rick, who was also a beginner, looked even more nervous than I felt, intently focusing as Kronos showed him how to run the checks of the oxygen tanks.

I forgot my fears as soon as we got into the water the first time, the four of us swimming as a group into the alien but welcoming universe of colored fish I was starting to know by name, like the rainbow-and-teal-green Parrotfish, and of coral, giant rays, and bubbles. We boated up the west coast from Cockburn Town, stopping at several spots along the Grand Turk wall, swimming under arches formed from coral, leaving the shallow sand by the reef to swim over the "dropoff" where the water got deep and dark and cool, and diving for conch shells off the little island of Gibbs Cay.

As we headed back to the ship, Kronos let Rodrigo practice sailing the skiff. Rick and I leaned over the back of the boat and watched the wake, like Slim and I had done on the catamaran trip our first day.

"If we just lie back here in the center, with our heads down, we won't have to keep ducking every time we 'come about,'" Rick whispered.

I laughed. Away from the personalities on the *Adonis*, and especially away from Blake who seemed to bring out his worst side, Rick's snobbishness had faded.

"How are you liking the cruise?" I asked him.

"I'm liking it a lot. It's amazing, really, like a dream. I almost didn't come, since I'm supposed to be looking for work and saving my money. But it was such a great offer, I couldn't resist. Talk about a good investment! I might get a job out of it, if things work out with Blake."

The boat tipped as Rodrigo tacked us into the wind, and I fell against Rick. He was soft and yielding at first, then pressed me back into my space with a firm elbow. "And today was pretty fun, too. It was a blast, actually," he said.

"Well, don't sound so surprised! You're hurting my feelings."

He turned to look at me. The sun and wind and water had toned down his orange spray tan and roughed up his short brown hair. "I didn't mean it that way," he said. "I guess I haven't let myself have pure fun for awhile. Today was just that. No worry, no work. Sorry, I'm being a drag now. How about you? Is this trip what you wanted? You're getting a lot of attention. I think your boyfriend's jealous."

"Who?" Did he know Justin? But Rick's eyes were directed at Rodrigo. Rodrigo had borrowed Kronos's captain's hat, which looked like it belonged on him. His teeth were white against his dark skin as he steered the skiff and threw back his head and laughed at something Kronos was saying.

I was about to tell him Rodrigo and me were a thing of the past, when the boat suddenly turned, and I grabbed a rail to keep from falling. The *Adonis* loomed before us, so close to shore it seemed to be beached on the white sands of Grand Turk.

As we joined the crowd loading back onto the *Adonis*, Rodrigo recognized a famous young Romanian soccer star, Marko Medeiros, and talked him into joining us for a drink at the Lucky Star. After we'd had a few drinks, people organized a spontaneous Indian wrestling competition. Rodrigo beat several guys with bigger muscles, falling only to Marko Medeiros's iron will and strength in an epic and much-photographed final match. Rodrigo and Rick left with Marko and some of his fans to have a late dinner at the Ice Bar. I decided to head back to the Tower.

Rodrigo pulled me aside before I left. "Why don't you come with us?"

"Why do you care, Mr. San Diego?"

"Are you seriously jealous 'cause I got a little attention this afternoon? You've been in the spotlight the last three days."

"You know," I said, "that guy Marko is into you. And I think Rick digs you, too."

"So, 'Mando, what do you care? I'll see you later, *amigo*."

Back at the Epitome Tower, Evans let me in. I showered and headed for the poolside. The deck was dark and quiet, and I gave a start when I saw Blake, sitting alone at a table, smoking one of his cigars.

"Hey. Where is everyone?" I asked.

"Oh, out and about. How was your diving?"

"Fun. Now I'm starving. Are there plans for dinner?"

"So glad you asked. You're going to join me for a romantic dinner in my cabin," he said. "Just the two of us." He took a puff on his cigar, which glowed and cast light on his face and hands. His black hair and eyebrows and dark full lips contrasted with his white skin, somehow untouched by the past days of intense sun. I drank in the scent of his cigar, and the look in his eyes that was far away and intimate at the same time. I sat down across from him.

Was I about to spend a long evening alone with a famous billionaire? I'd regret it if I missed out, and it would be a story to tell....

"I'm not sure," I said. "You scare me a little."

"Do something every day that scares you, Sport. You came on this trip for adventure, didn't you?"

"I've heard rumors about you. About... the young sailor."

He didn't flinch. "Ah. Well, rumors are rumors. I can tell you, I didn't do anything he didn't want me to do. People may have cultural hang-ups, but I can't take responsibility for that."

"No, I guess that's true."

I started to stand up, when he grabbed my wrist, hard. His large, well-shaped hands were even stronger than they looked.

"Ow!"

"Don't go," he said, yanking me towards him and talking into my ear. "I could make the rest of this cruise very unpleasant for you, Sport. A word from me, and my buddy Kronos will throw you in the brig. Why are you being so difficult? Do you want me to get rough?"

"Blake, stop it!" I yelled, pulling my hand away. "That's not funny! I actually was going to go with you. I just wanted to go to my cabin and change."

"Well, come along then. You've made me impatient, Beauty."

"Screw you. I'm leaving. Just because you're a billionaire doesn't mean I'm going to let you push me around."

"Oh, yes, you are."

"In your dreams, you asshole. You're not what I want."

As I turned away, Blake called out, "I'm dead serious, Armando. You have a day to think about what I said."

I headed towards my cabin, breathing hard. As I turned the corner, I almost bumped in to Slim, Mary, and Scott. At the same time, Evans came from the direction of the butlers' quarters.

"Did you need something, sir?"

"No, thanks, Evans."

Evans walked to the poolside, and returned a moment later with a frown on his face as he headed back to the butlers' quarters.

"Are you okay?" Scott asked. He had on a frayed T shirt that said "Byte Me." At least the olive green color brought out his hazel eyes, which were round with concern. "What was that yelling about?"

"Nothing," I said. "How was your day? Did you have fun working with Blake at the luxurious Jamboree Grand Turk office?"

His eyes narrowed for a second, and then he gave his sweet smile. "Work is work, right? How was your diving trip?"

"Amazing. You guys want to go to dinner?" I deliberately turned my back on Mary, and heard her sigh.

"Scott and I are on our way to the all-night video gaming marathon," Slim said. "We wanna get there early and check out the competition. Come on, we're gonna grab a bite first."

We all walked out together past the poolside. When Blake saw us, he threw his cigar into the swimming pool and walked towards his cabin without a word.

"He looks pissed. What happened?" Slim asked me.

"Forget it. Come on, let's go eat."

Over our burgers at the Players' Lounge, Mary made a couple unsuccessful attempts to engage me in conversation but finally took the hint and left, saying she wanted an early night. As soon as she left, I felt horrible for freezing her out. It wasn't her fault Barron liked her better than me.

I turned to tell Slim about my weird encounter with Blake, but he was listening to Scott describe his company's new projects.

"... a lot of people investing in this new way of having a stake on your favorite player. And there's this other amazing technology. Basically, you won't need a console anymore, you'll be able to use hand gestures to execute your plans. A lot of companies are working on this, but we've found a way of making the detectors unbelievably sensitive. You start with a 3-D camera, it's, like, focused on your hand, and...."

Slim's eyes were shining, and he was unconsciously wiggling his fingers as he mirrored Scott's enthusiastic presentation. I tried to follow what Scott was saying, but it got increasingly technical. Finally, even Slim's eyes started to glaze over.

"Hey, Scott," I interrupted. "What happened to that ping-pong guy you met? Is he coming to watch you play?"

"Oh!" He looked startled, but not really surprised or hurt, at the interruption. He gave me his good-natured smile. "What ping-pong guy? Oh, yeah, him. That was just a date. Like I told you before, I don't really have time for long-term relationships."

"You said the other day that your mom wants you to find a girlfriend. How come you don't come out to your parents?" I asked.

"I could," he said. "They wouldn't mind. But I prefer to keep my preferences on the down low. My family still lives in a conservative little Midwest town, where I already had to deal with being the geeky kid in school. Why should I have to justify, to anybody, one more way I'm different?"

"That's funny," said Slim. "You seem so confident, like you don't care what people think."

"I totally don't care what people think. I just don't have time for the distraction. That's kind of funny, actually. One reason I came on this cruise was to get my parents off my back. They think I'm working too hard. So I told them I'm on a relaxing cruise. They want me to send pictures." He grinned. "I think I better not do that."

I followed his gaze into the room behind us, which was filling up for the tournament. There were a few nerdy looking guys who, like Scott and Slim, were wearing casual shorts and tank tops. But most of the crowd had dressed for the occasion, with one couple rocking Viking costumes, another in butterfly wings and saran-wrapped bodies, and more than one group of X-rated cheerleaders.

"Better not," I laughed.

I was too restless to watch the tournament. I couldn't find Rodrigo at the Ice Bar, so I went by myself to catch the ten o'clock show of Dixie Longate, the Tupperware Queen.

After the show, I returned to the Tower. Evans met me at the elevator and followed me to my room.

"Where's Barron tonight?" I asked.

"Barron has the night off, sir. If there is anything at all I can do for you, please let me know. I'll be looking after you."

"Our diving trip tired me out. I'm gonna crash."

"I'll help you get ready, sir. I think you could use a drink before bed. A White Russian?"

Evans didn't have Barron's godlike beauty, but he was a better butler, with a soft manner, anticipating my needs like a geisha before I even knew I had them. It seemed clear he would have met the burning desire that Barron would not, if I'd just given him the signal. But I didn't. I was picturing Barron spending his night off with Mary, probably going to the engine room to watch the pistons running before a night of wild sex. It was so unfair, I thought. I was the one who'd paid for this trip.

As Evans slipped my watch off my arm, he murmured, "Would you like it here on the bedside table, or next to your other one?"

"What other one?" I followed his gaze to the dressing table and felt a jolt. It was a large platinum watch I'd last seen on Blake's wrist when he grabbed mine that evening. I put down my White Russian and went over to pick it up. Was this a gift, Blake's way of apologizing to me for his silly threat? I was too exhausted to think about it.

"Just put my watch on the table," I told Evans.

I finished my drink and handed the glass to Evans, who slipped out wishing me a good night. I burrowed into my pillow. So many thoughts floated on the edges of my mind: Dixie Longate, turquoise waters with sting rays circling, and conch shells just out of reach, new advances in Tupperware, laughing with Rick, Blake's hand grabbing my wrist. Finally, I fell into a deep sleep.

***

I was alone on a small deserted beach, looking at the *Adonis* anchored just a few feet offshore. I counted ten levels of decks, not counting the Epitome Tower, which looked like a castle turret with a round crenellated top, made of ancient gold-colored stones with deep narrow windows. It was not strange, but only natural, that it looked that way. I saw a rope hanging from one of the tower windows. The end of the rope went into a small porthole on the lowest level of the *Adonis*. A hairy, muscular pair of hands appeared out of the porthole. Then the hands became a man in a pirate hat and thigh-high boots with red heels. He pulled himself out of the porthole and swung out over the shallow sea. Strapped to his belt was a dagger in a jeweled sheath.

The man with the knife started climbing up the rope, hand over hand. I knew he was going up to the Epitome Tower, and I tried to yell out a warning to my Tribe. No sound came. The intruder reached the Tower and his heels started tapping like a tap dance on the ancient stone wall.

I woke to the sound of the shade flapping in the breeze against the open window behind me. Alternating with the taps were puffs of fresh sea air lit with pale sunlight. As I came back to reality, I unfroze my body and the fear melted away. I yawned and stretched out my muscles as I came to full consciousness. Relieved my nightmare had been only that, I reached for my watch. It was almost seven-thirty.

I took a quick shower, threw on my Mollusk surf trunks with the cutout stripe, and headed for the pool. Maybe I could get in a few laps before Blake started his eight-o'clock rope swing practice.

It was too late. As I rounded the corner to the Infinity pool deck, I saw Blake's distinctive silhouette poised on the back end of his swinging platform. Behind him the mist in the low morning sky was pink and red, a filter casting a golden glow on the sails, the platform, and the deck. The moon, high above Blake's head, was a white fuzz ball in the clear blue upper sky. The air crackled with the promise of heat to come.

I started to turn away, but he called out to me, like nothing had happened the night before.

"Top of the morning, Sport!" he called. "Watch me!"

Something prickled at the back of my neck, before he even made his running start. Like in my dream, my throat closed up. I froze as he ran across the platform, flung himself onto the rope, and fell, screaming, thirty feet onto the hard cement below.

10

Lucy
Sandy Comes to Stay

"I'm going to get Sandy through this, dammit! We had a fight at the hospital, but later I called and told her she can stay with me when she gets out of the hospital. She can beat this hoarding thing and be back home in a week or two. It's not like she's got a severe mental illness, for God's sake."

It was Friday night, and Claude and I were having our after-dinner tea on my deck. The dogs lay at our feet snoring lightly after their evening walk. The summer sunlight faded, and Claude was like part of the night with his dark skin and deep voice. His hand took mine, black fingers alternating with white, like piano keys.

For fifteen years, Claude has been my colleague and my best friend, and for the past ten years, something more. Like me, he was born in Oklahoma over fifty years ago. He joined the Marine Corps and worked his way up, specializing in criminal investigations, and opened his own investigations practice in San Diego after he retired from the military.

We met when my former law partner hired him to investigate a gang shooting case, and all of us bonded over late nights in the office and unwinding afterwards at the corner bar. The heavy after-work partying lifestyle eventually led to my having to break up with my partner, romantically and professionally.

My former partner later sobered up, retreated into a less stressful practice, and married his secretary. Around the same time, Claude quit drinking after he seriously injured another drunk in a bar fight. I continued on as a solo criminal practitioner, and hired Claude as needed to investigate my more complex cases. We're a pair of tough old survivors, "working smart," as Claude says, to stay in the game. We survived a tough patch about six months previously, when I made the mistake of branching out into investigative work. With that fiasco behind us, harmony and healthful stimulation again ruled in our relationship.

"Glad you decided to take your sister in," Claude said, giving my hand a squeeze. "Just don't expect much change in her anytime too soon."

Thurgood, the elder of my two standard poodles, grunted and rolled over in his sleep, leaning into my bare foot. His body, and Claude's hand over mine, were warm in the cool the night air.

"Of course not," I told Claude. "I don't."

"'Cause if you do, you'll just make yourself crazy."

The following night Claude was not available. I left a message on his cell phone.

"It's me. I just had to report how well our day went. I picked up Sandy this morning. We went to her place and she went in and got a few things. You know what she said when she came out? She said, 'I really need to do something about this house.' Then we went out to lunch, and we had such a nice visit. She's teaching a new class this semester, and it's really quite interesting....

"Then we went window shopping, and picked up a few things for dinner. She can't drink yet, or drive, because of the medication they gave her in the hospital, but they reduced the dose and she'll be safe to drive by Monday. We had a salad for dinner. I got her to go on a short walk with the dogs. She couldn't go very far. Her knees have gotten bad, but once she gets a little weight off I'm sure she'll be fine. I'm so glad she's here with me."

***

I left home early Monday morning, leaving a note to remind Sandy I would meet her for her intake appointment at the day treatment center later that afternoon. Sunday had been quiet and uneventful, with Sandy continuing to improve and make good choices.

"I've done a lot of thinking," she'd said, as we drove to her house to pick up some more books she needed. "Next week I'm going to focus on my outpatient treatment, and I'll find a substitute to cover my lectures."

"Sounds like a good plan," I told her, loading a box into my trunk. "I know you hate to miss your lectures, but you need to take care of yourself first. Oh, is there another? Here, I'll just move these over and there should be room...."

"Luce, thank you for everything," she said. "Yeah, just a couple more...okay, on the back seat, then. You are the best sister ever. Maybe we can walk the doggies again tonight?"

As I entered the empty office at seven a.m., I knew I would need the early morning quiet time to rearrange my schedule. Sandy's intake appointment would take a couple of hours of my afternoon. It would mean juggling some appointments and a court appearance, but I was fully committed to being there for my sister.

I pushed out of my mind all thoughts of Armando and his playboy buddies partying in a Caribbean paradise, while I had to cover my own work, run the office, and take care of my sister. I told myself it was not Armando's fault Nancy's son had a relapse, resulting in her spending most of her workdays out of the office managing his hospitalization. I didn't really expect to see her at all that day.

At least my new contract attorney, Arnie Snyder, would be starting today. He could help handle my day-to-day appearances and filings for the next two days.

By eight twenty-five, I'd drafted a manageable schedule, even allotting a generous hour and a half for the one o'clock orientation meeting with Sandy at the outpatient treatment center. I was optimistic about the meeting. The emergency intervention, the medication, and my sisterly attention had almost restored Sandy to her old self. The outpatient treatment would finish the job, and I would have my sister back.

I made myself a cup of tea, and was just sitting down at the coffee table to review a file, when I heard the office door opening. It was eight-thirty on the dot, a promising sign. Perhaps by the end of the week, I'd even have Snyder trained to get in a few minutes early. I hoped he'd had the good sense to dress for court.

"I'm so sorry, Ms. Sanders," Nancy said, bumping her foot as the door swung shut behind her. "I meant to come in early today to catch up, after missing most of Friday. But I was at the hospital late last night and, and I just... overslept. I'm so sorry. Well, anyway, now I'm here, ready to work. What should I do first?"

"Your first task every day is to check the office voice mail," I told her. "Then the email. I've already checked the master calendar and put it in my schedule. I won't have time to babysit you in your work today, as I have several court appearances. You should have a list of things to do, and prioritize them based on deadlines. Mr. Snyder will be here shortly, and I need to meet with him without interruption."

"Yes, yes, of course. Sorry. Office voice mail." She repeated it as if it were some foreign language she was trying to decipher, but then she smoothed her skirt, placed her purse in the desk drawer, and pulled out the phone message pad.

I turned back to my file and lost myself in preparing for my eleven o'clock hearing in *U.S. v. Mendez*. My client Hernan

Mendez, a Honduran national, had been convinced by the Honduran police not to contest the United States' request to extradite him on drug smuggling charges. Prodded by the US DEA, Honduran officers had incorrectly advised Mendez his sentence by Honduran courts would far exceed the maximum confinement in the US. This undue pressure to forego his right to trial under the laws of his home country was in itself grounds to deny the US. court's jurisdiction.

This case presented a new legal issue for me, and I was optimistic the district court would rule the method of extradition was unconscionable and dismiss the case against Mr. Mendez. Extradition authority was a patchwork of case law, treaty, and federal laws of two nations. My task was to convince the judge that the law required her to make what would be a politically unpopular decision.

"Sorry to bother you, Ms., um.... sorry." Nancy had left her desk and was standing next to my armchair. Her eyes had black rings of exhaustion under them, and her hair looked like she'd just gotten out of bed.

"Yes?"

"Um, you have a message. From Arnie Snyder? He's not coming in today. He's got the flu. I didn't know whether to interrupt you...."

I looked at the clock. It was nine o'clock. Why hadn't she told me I was due in court? I grabbed my jacket, stuffed files into my briefcase, and headed for the door. "Nancy, call Department 10 at the superior court and ask them to trail my nine-thirty. Without Mr. Snyder here, I may have to move some of my appearances. I'll call you later from the courthouse."

***

I was on a roll in court that day. First, I obtained three favorable motion rulings in the superior court. Then, I made it across the street to the federal courthouse at the stroke of eleven, and walked out of the courthouse an hour and forty-five minutes later with Mr. Mendez, a free man. With us was my client's entourage, which included an immigration attorney with his law clerk, and two muscular men in expensive suits who were not introduced to me.

The immigration attorney was Frank Slattery, a third-rate hack. Slattery's law clerk Justin, on the other hand, is a very bright and committed young law student. I would have loved to recruit him to my own office. Justin had been dating Armando for several months, but I'd gotten the sense things had not been going well between them.

"Awesome job, Ms. Sanders," Justin said. "That was a righteous case you made in there. That unconscionability angle was brilliant. I hope this ruling will have some effect on the DEA's tactics."

"Not half bad," Slattery said.

"Thank you, Sra. Sanders," Mendez said as we parted. "You come to Honduras, I show you my country. You keep my card, yes?"

I tossed the card in my purse and rushed off to meet Sandy at the outpatient treatment center. As I got to my car, Justin ran up behind me.

"Ms. Sanders!"

"Yes?"

"Um, have you, have you heard from Armando?" His young face, so animated after our victory, now looked white and tired under his shock of red hair. I had known Armando would get bored and drop him, but I still felt sorry. On the positive side, Justin would soon realize he would be happier with someone less superficial and apathetic.

"No, dear, I haven't," I told him. "Honestly, you know, I don't expect to. He'll be wrapped up in.... well, whatever people get wrapped up in on these luxury cruises."

His face fell. "Right. I know. It's just... well, this case made me think of him. His ship will be getting to Honduras in a few days. What a coincidence, right? Well, thanks. And congratulations, again."

The TakeWing Center was located in the heart of Hillcrest, which was a short drive from the downtown courthouse. Unfortunately, I had no time to pick up lunch, and arrived at the orientation meeting late and lightheaded from hunger. Sandy was already meeting with the intake coordinator and the psychologist.

The meeting was in a large conference room, just behind the reception area. It was pleasant and soothing. The room had a high ceiling and was painted and carpeted in cool tones of beige, lit by a line of skylights high on the outside wall. There were healthy-looking potted palms reaching almost to the ceiling. On the walls were well-framed original paintings and collages in various sizes and styles. The paintings were probably the work of the program's patients, but they had been nicely selected.

Sandy looked up at me. Her eyes were watering. "They just told me my insurance won't cover this," she said. "We should go."

"What are your rates?" I asked.

The intake coordinator, a heavyset young woman planted solidly in her chair at the head of the table, told me.

"Excuse me." I pulled my cell phone out of my purse and dialed my office. "Nancy," I said. "I'm at TakeWing, talking to Carolina. Her program is run by a private group called MegaCare. Do you know them? Yes? We're having some confusion about the payment issue. She says there are only 'private pay slots' available, although my sister qualifies.... Oh, really? Here, I'll put you on speaker, please hold...."

I turned to Carolina. "Our mental health advocate, Nancy Foster, is on the line. Please talk to her." I turned on the speaker and placed my phone in the center of the table between us. The psychologist, a casually dressed elderly man, looked ready for a nap.

Sandy and I sat back as Carolina engaged with Nancy. Their conversation became technical. I let my mind wander, planning how I would cover my appointments for the rest of the afternoon and the following day. Our new attorney, Mr. Snyder, should be over his flu by tomorrow, I thought. Nancy could call him after she finished with us....

"Ms. Sanders?" Nancy's voice came over the speaker. "Is that okay with you?"

"Sorry?"

"If you pay the private rate for the first three days, the program can take your sister right away. And they'll guarantee her a subsidized slot starting Monday. That will be good for at least a month, or six weeks if she needs it."

"But, that's...." I took a deep breath. "Fine. I'll pay the first three days. Thank you, Nancy. I'll call you back in a few minutes."

Carolina left the room with a large check from me fastened onto her clipboard. Dr. Fehvre, the elderly psychologist, shuffled through a sheaf of paperwork in front of him, before starting the interview.

"Now, you are Sandy," he looked at my sister. "Is that right? Yes. Well, Sandy, I see you've been in the, er, hospital. Why don't you tell me, in your own words, why you think you were there?"

"Excuse me," I said. "I have some appointments this afternoon. Do you need me for anything else?"

"Ah. You are Lucy, Sandy's sister. An attorney, I believe?"

"Yes, and I need to get back to work."

"Well, Lucy, I understand how important your work is to you. You must be a busy girl. But your sister is going through what we call a life crisis, and she's made a very important choice to seek treatment. With her type of condition, if I may now explain her diagnosis...."

"I know her diagnosis," I said. "And I've paid your extortion. What more do you need from me today?"

"Ahhhhh. You feel frustrated. Lucy, this two-hour appointment is what we call a family intake. Sandy's support team is included in the process. That means you, young lady. I have read Sandy's file, and I see she has a complex relationship with you. Her hospital doctor, I see, also met with you personally. Sandy's particular condition, as I was about to explain, is heavily influenced by her family dynamics, and family members are often, ah, intertwined, with the condition itself...."

***

When I got back to the office, I found Nancy gone, and my four o'clock client waiting outside my locked office door. After ushering out my last client at six, I found a note on Nancy's desk saying she had called Mr. Snyder and he would be out with the flu for at least another day. I took the files I would need for court the next day and headed home.

11

Claude
Calls For Help

It's just before midnight Monday night, when the vibration of my cell saves me from my restless bed. I grab the phone off of my bedside table, pull my pants off the floor, and try to pussyfoot it out of the room.

"Where you goin', baby?" A lazy, singsong voice, even when she's not half asleep.

"Can't sleep," I say. "Might take a little walk."

Five minutes later, I'm a block from my apartment, headed towards our neighborhood park. A man can do laps around its perimeter any time of night in relative safety. Just don't cross into the park itself, and if there's dudes on the southeast corner, do the lap so you take a little detour across the street.

I speed dial, and she starts in the middle of a sentence.

".... bags full of things she got we absolutely don't need. My kitchen table.... jumbo boxes of sandwich bags.... massive.... snack foods, ... perishable deli food the two of us can't begin to finish. ....another load of bags and boxes of her stuff. ....enough trouble making room for my own things. Armando should have cleared out her house as I instructed him, before abandoning me for that obscene cruise. None of this would be happening to me now. How am I going to find space for everything?"

"Whoa, slow down, Luce."

She takes a breath. "Yes, sorry. I just don't know what to do. She was so good all weekend. This afternoon, I literally had to bribe the outpatient center, but we got her into day treatment. Then, for two hours, I listened to their moron of a psychologist. He tried to tell me *I* should be in therapy... regret paying for this program.... bullshit...psychoanalytic approach... thoroughly de-bunked....

"I think Sandy's psychiatrist at the hospital hated me. He must have written something bad about me in her file. I could tell by the way the new psychologist treated me. It was so hurtful, Claude. Out of the blue, like Sandy's illness is my fault."

"Why would he hate you, Luce? You say somethin' to him?"

"Say to him? Nothing. Merely pointed out his unethical attempts to discharge her prematurely. Why would he take that personally?"

"Those shrinks are a touchy breed."

"You're right. They're pathetic, really. I shouldn't let them get to me. It's so good to talk to you. You reminded me Sandy is my only family, and you're right. But when I got home from work to find her spreading her clutter over my house, I felt so betrayed. She talks constantly. She's so needy, Claude.

"I can't take her dusty books and her restless body and her repetitive chatter. She ate a whole box of those disgusting cheap vanilla wafer cookies after dinner. They were on a two-for-one sale. Do you think I could get her ex, Paul, to take her in? I could pay him something, and maybe his new wife wouldn't mind...."

"Good luck with that." I reach the park and start my first lap.

"True. Paul won't lift a finger. And he's the one responsible for Sandy's problems. She started hoarding and putting on weight when he left her. Now I'm the one having to fix it. How do I stop her?"

"Honey, it don't work that way," I tell her. "You can't sit like a hen on a egg, waiting for her to be fixed. If you don't set yourself some boundaries, you're gonna get sucked down into her trip. So. Tell me about your day. Didn't you have that big federal hearing?"

Six laps later, I'm up to date on the laws of extradition between the USA and Honduras. My girl has calmed down and tells me she's ready for a good night's sleep.

We confirm our usual date for Wednesday night, and say our goodnights. After I hang up, I take another lap to clear my head. Then I take a lap to meditate on my attitude of gratitude. As I spin off towards my apartment, I'm being grateful for the two ladies in my life. One who needs nine hours sleep every night to function, and takes ten when she can get it. And then there's my brilliant, prickly, true-believing Luce, who, like me, does great with five hours a night. Luce and I got this biorhythmic connection, even when we're not together, like twin electrons movin' to the same vibration all the way across the city. That and our cell phones, they'll get us through the next two days 'til I see her again.

***

Tuesday evening, seven p.m., I take leave of my AA brothers and sisters. I'm feeling my attitude of gratitude again, for the balance I enjoy in this life. I've been sober for a lot of years now, but you won't see me givin' up my three to four meetings per week. Truth is, I'd be okay without them, sobriety-wise. To call AA my church doesn't exactly explain it, but maybe it comes close, if you're that kind of churchgoer. My other church is a Zen community, a haven of earnest introverts who share my beliefs about the big picture of things. We focus on our Oneness, in silence, side by side, in a way that doesn't threaten our solitude.

Now, the AA folks are a whole different side of things. We're a gang of tough warriors who fought the demon of addiction, and we want to share the Word out loud. We reacted to the barbs of life by enslaving ourselves to the shit that robs us of our humanity. Then we had to retrieve our spirits from a dark place, kick out the drunken monkeys inhabiting our bodies and our minds, and fight to put one foot in front of the other. Lots of stories, one story. You can't hear it too many times.

My cell vibrates before I reach my car.

"I'm ready to kill her," she says. "I told her last night, I said, 'I just can't make another trip to your house tonight. You have eight boxes of books here, already, to use to prepare for your lectures next week.' And she said, 'You're right, the books I have here are enough for this week. I see that now. I know you've got a lot on your plate, Luce. Thank you so much for helping me.' She said she didn't need more books! She thanked me, Claude! And then she turns around and pulls this stunt. I'm surprised she was able to carry so much by herself in just one day....

"My new attorney bailed again today. Does the flu really ever last more than a day? I wish I'd hired the other one, that young case-management woman.... ...healthy. Sandy's senile psychologist has already scheduled another 'family counseling session.' Can you believe it?

"How much more am I expected to do, here? Where is the limit? Honestly, she's my sister, but I have no idea where this is coming from. My kitchen table.... Living room...bags.... It's like watching pure out-of-control human greed, warped into acquisition for the sake of acquisition, undiscriminating. ...in my own home.... no sense of recycling... It's revolting...."

She is panting, and stops to take a breath.

"Hang in there, Luce. How about I come over tonight, instead of tomorrow? Just you and me, all right? Forget her for a while. I'll pick you up and take you out somewhere. You want Italian?"

"Really? Oh, Claude, I... Aieeee!!!!" Crashing sounds, and then silence.

"Luce? You there?" The connection is gone. I re-dial. No answer.

"This is so funny," Sandy says, as we hang out together in the Urgent Care waiting room. "A week after I sprain my right ankle, Lucy does the same thing. It's the same ankle, even. Isn't that funny? We've both always been kind of clumsy. I hope hers isn't broken. Do you think it's broken? They say if you can walk on it right after, it's not broken. I don't think it is, do you? Isn't it funny, the same injury, the same week?"

Yes, I think, and the same cause of harm. I'd gotten to Luce's house to find her sitting on the kitchen floor, holding a bag of ice to her ankle. A stack of magazines three feet high was in the middle of the doorway to her dining room, and dozens more magazines were dominoed across the floor like an earthquake had hit. Her poodles sat at her side like nurses on duty.

As I'd helped Lucy up, a door slammed and Sandy came through the garage door into the kitchen. She had several plastic grocery bags in her arms.

"Hi, Claude! Are you here for dinner tonight? I stopped on the way home and got some good food. There's more, out in the car. Oh, no! What happened to my magazines?"

"Your sister's foot got in their way. Why don't you move them, while I take her to the doctor."

But Sandy had insisted on coming to Urgent Care, leaving her load of bags on the kitchen table and following us in her own car. Now, with Lucy gone in to the doctor, we stare at each other. The walls of the reception area are painted a bright orange, lurid under the fluorescent lighting. We're on uncomfortable vinyl chairs of the same color. Sandy's eyes are the same color blue as her sister's, and dosed with a much heavier load of makeup, but they'll never have the same spark. Her fuzzy light purple warm-up suit, white skin, and teased blonde hair are all bleached out under the waiting room lights like an overexposed film. I give her a smile, and she gives a wry smile and rolls her eyes.

"This is going to be my fault, isn't it?" She looks down at her hands, frowning at the chips in her pale pink fingernail paint. "You know, my doctor says I don't have to stop treating myself to things. I'm not supposed get rid of any of my things right away. But I know my sister, the lawyer. But for my cooking magazines being temporarily on the kitchen floor, Luce wouldn't have tripped. The law of causation.

"Claude, I brought those magazines over for her. I know she likes to cook sometimes, and she told me once she thought she should become a better cook. She won't appreciate my gift. She'll just be mad at me."

"Luce ain't gonna play the blame game, here, Sandy."

"She won't need to, will she? I'm already blaming myself."

"You sayin' that's her fault? That you're blamin' yourself?"

"Of course not. I don't think all my problems are her fault. It's not her fault she was always so independent and hard edged. So I had to play the role of the pleaser all the time. Dr. Fehvre says if I want to get...better, I have to recognize how I developed certain patterns, early in my life."

"Does he?"

"You don't agree?"

I shrug. "I'm no expert, Sister. But in my opinion, blamin' Luce, or your ma, or your pa, or even your ex, it ain't gonna get your house cleaned out."

She's starin' at me, wondering how I mean it, when her sister limps out, a compression bandage wrapped around her right ankle.

"The good news is, it's only a sprain," says Lucy. "The other good news is, they gave me some samples of painkillers, so we don't have to stop at the drugstore. Claude, if you still want to take me for Italian, I'll hold off on taking a pill. I want a glass of Chianti with dinner."

"Oooh, Italian!" says Sandy. "Where are we going?"

Over dinner, Luce holds forth on the pleasures of a life unencumbered by excessive material possessions. Her case is full of reason and aesthetic appeal. Sandy agrees with everything she says.

"You're right, Sis. I need to get rid of some things. Got to go through my stuff and get organized. Can't wait to get started."

We get home and I put Luce into bed, with her foot up on a pillow and her ankle packed in ice. When I go in to the kitchen a little later, to get Luce some water to take her pills, Sandy has gone to her room. The full grocery bags are on the table, the knocked-over pile of magazines *status quo.* I clear the magazines off the floor and pile them against the closed door to Sandy's room. The grocery bags go outside, on top of Sandy's car. I wonder how this Sister thing is gonna mess with Luce and me.

"Tonight went well, don't you think, Claude?" Luce says, as I hand her the glass of water and a pill. "She really sounds like she's ready to make some changes."

I ease onto the bed and put my arm around her. "Yeah, that's what she's saying."

"She felt bad about leaving her magazines where I tripped on them. She said she'd move them right away."

Then I say somethin' I better don't. "Listen, they got a group downtown, I think it's Wednesday nights, for co-dependency. I'll go with you, if you want."

A silence. Then, "What? Why?"

"Just sayin', your sister's problem is something you ain't gonna fix. You can't let it get to you like this."

"Claude, I'm not the one with the mental problem."

"No, but...."

Her cell, at the side of the bed, starts to ring, and she ignores it. It starts to ring again, and she picks it up and looks at it. She frowns and puts it down. The third time, she answers.

"Yes? Armando? Sorry, I can't hear you. Who is? Slow down, I don't understand you. ... Greek? A frat party? I must say that doesn't sound consistent with... Are you drunk? Yes, but aren't you still on the cruise ship? Where are you?... There are lawyers in Honduras.... Really, dear, I don't see what I can do. That's ridiculous. .... Armando, even if I wanted to, which I don't, I couldn't help you. You're very likely outside of the United States' jurisdiction. I might be more willing to listen, if you hadn't left me in such a mess here at home, but right now I'm just too angry and exhausted...new attorney sick... your fault my sister... out of control.... Well, I'm sorry you think that. ... Don't use that kind of language with me." She hung up and looked at me.

"Armando's gotten into some kind of mess on that cruise ship, and he wants me to take care of it. For God's sake, they're out at sea, in the Caribbean somewhere. He became hysterical and abusive. I suspect he may have been drinking, or on something. What time is it anyway? Almost midnight. Thoughtless.... I could have been asleep. My ankle hurts. ...going to turn off my phone. I hope that pill kicks in soon."

12

Armando
Monday, Jamaica

Blake's hands clung to the useless piece of rope, and his legs made frantic paddling motions like he was trying to bicycle through the air, as he fell from the platform. The second he hit the ground my own body unfroze, and I ran to his side. "Help! Someone, call a doctor," I yelled.

He was lying on his back, six feet from the pool's edge, legs bent at odd angles, and arms flung out to the sides. His head had fallen to one side, and blood was pooling from his skull. I took my swimming towel and tried to stop the flow without moving his spine.

"I'll take that, sir." Barron was kneeling next to me. "Evans! Code Six on deck!" he yelled. "He's still breathing."

Evans ran out from the kitchen. "The medics are on the way. What happened?"

I told them what I'd seen.

"He's got a pulse," Barron said.

A small crowd had gathered around us. "Someone bring blankets," Rodrigo said. "He may go into shock."

I stepped back to stand beside Rodrigo. Mary, Dan-Dan, and Rick all dashed to their rooms and came back with the thin blankets from their beds. Evans used them to cover Blake's legs and trunk. Rodrigo took my hand and squeezed it. "I heard you call out," he said. "Are you all right? What happened?"

"He was going on his swing, and the rope broke."

"Did you see it?"

"Yeah." I looked over at Blake. He was unmoving, but Evans still held his wrist, which I took to mean there was a pulse. Barron sat at Blake's head, still pressing the towel. Rick's orange tan seemed to have disappeared. His face was white as he knelt to adjust the blankets over Blake's feet.

The Dans stood at a distance, holding hands and whispering to each other. Scott appeared with a towel around his waist, drying his hair off with another towel. Slim, still in his rumpled shorts and T-shirt from the night before, came to stand next to him.

Nick Kronos came from the direction of the kitchen, barking orders.

"Barron, unlock the front gate and prop it open. The team is coming through with a stretcher. Evans, collect his passport and travel documents in case we need to transport him. As soon as he is moved, I want this area cleaned up.

"Gentlemen and Lady, we regret this unfortunate accident. Our protocol requires us to clear the area while the medical team is arriving. I must ask you to exit the deck for a short time. Barron and Evans will see to your needs in the Epitome Lounge, or in your rooms."

We all followed Evans into a large open room that spanned the second floor above the port side cabins. I had checked it out briefly on my first day. Even though it had fab views, it wasn't a place any of us had chosen to hang out. It was nicer outside on the deck. By the time we all got into the lounge, the medical team had surrounded Blake, on the far side of the pool. Evans made a move to draw the blinds over the windows.

"Forget that, Evans," Mary said. "We want to see what's happening out there."

We crowded around the window to watch the action below. My head started to spin, and I sat down quickly on one of the sectionals.

I tried to see out the window, but sunk in the deep leather seat, I just saw the backs of my fellow passengers as they angled for a view of the drama. Rodrigo, wearing nothing but the shorts he must have pulled on when awakened by the shouting, was jiggling a muscular leg in frustration he couldn't be down with the action. The Dans, ghostly in the matching gauze caftans they always wore at breakfast, put their heads together and whispered softly. Mary stood by the window, tall and bright in a long T-shirt and platform flip-flops. Rick, standing at her side, pressed his hands against the glass. Scott was wearing a towel around his waist and still rubbing another towel vigorously over the top of his head. I wondered if he was going to keep rubbing until his hair started to come out. Slim, sleepy-eyed, turned away from the window and came to stand next to me. People were talking, asking questions, but I couldn't focus on the words.

I saw Blake poised at the top of the rope platform, calling me "Sport" in his plummy accent, the sun behind him emphasizing his round head, bullish shoulders, and well-developed calves. My head swam, and I put my head between my knees.

Someone sat down next to me. "Drink this water, sir." It was Evans's voice. "That's right, sit up slowly."

"I—I couldn't save him."

"No, sir. Don't talk yet. Okay, put your head back down." He took the back of my head in one hand and forced it not very gently down towards my knees. "Stay there. Breathe deep."

A couple minutes later, I was able to sit back, leaning my head against a sofa pillow. Rodrigo and Slim sat on either side of me. A few minutes later, the others turned away from the window, and came to sit in a circle.

"They took him away," Scott reported. "Why didn't they get him on his helicopter? If he's got a head injury, he needs to be in a hospital."

"They took him to the infirmary to stabilize him first," Evans said.

"Right," said Rodrigo. "He hit his head. They have to get a quick handle on the swelling."

Evans pulled the cords on the blinds, shutting out our view of the pool.

"How did it happen?" Slim asked. "Did he try to jump into the pool without using the rope?"

"The rope broke," I said.

"That's not possible," said Evans. His smooth forehead had creased into sharp lines between his eyes. "Barron and I checked the rope this morning. It was solid."

"Kronos never should've let him swing on those ropes," said Rodrigo. "They weren't made to hold a man's weight."

"Blake was used to getting his way," Dan said, "as we all saw that first day out on the catamaran."

"At least Kronos tried to stop him from diving, that time," Scott said. "I wonder why he let Blake push him into making the swing. Did something change?"

"What do you mean? What kind of change?" asked Rick.

"I'm just saying, Kronos held his ground on the diving thing, even though Blake threatened to have him fired. Rodrigo's right. Kronos was crazy to let Blake go swinging around on those ropes. Those ropes weren't strong enough. The cruise line's going to be looking at some serious liability if Blake's family sues them."

"Blake's family owns the damn cruise line, Scott," said Rick. "Or one of their companies does. They're not going to sue themselves, are they? Besides, the swing was Blake's idea, not Mr. Kronos's."

"Yeah, and from what I hear, Kronos's negligence may have done Blake's family a favor," Dan said. "He was often an embarrassment to them. I doubt anyone's gonna sue."

"If Blake survives, he might sue somebody," said Scott. "It was gross negligence, for sure."

Rodrigo frowned. "If Blake survives, I doubt he'll be in any shape to...."

He stopped talking at the sound of footsteps and the lounge door opening. Mr. Kronos entered, followed by Barron, looking like a Greek god bringing a message of tragedy.

"Is there any news, Kronos?" Dan asked.

"Mr. Blake is in surgery. As soon as he is stable, we will transfer him to the best hospital. His family has been informed and is already making arrangements for his follow-up care and recovery."

Tears of relief burned at the back of my eyes. "Oh, thank God. After he fell, I thought he was...." I broke off.

"Can you tell me what you saw, sir?"

I repeated my story for Mr. Kronos.

"Thank you, Mr. Armando. Our investigation will be continuing." He looked around the room at all of us, like one of us had caused the accident and was going to confess. When no one spoke up he said, "Mr. Blake was advised not to swing on the rope. We shall see. Thank you for your patience in this unfortunate situation. You may now return to your activities."

13

Jamaica to Grand Cayman

When I finished my shower, dressed, and walked back out to the deck, the gang was breakfasting at the poolside tables. The scene was strangely cheerful and domestic, and for a second I wondered if Blake's fall had been part of my bad dream. Pitchers of Beachside Bonfires circulated. The two butlers hovered. The Dans still had on their gauzy caftans, and their heads were bent over their copy of the day's schedule of events. Dan said something in a low voice, and Dan-Dan gave a hoot of laughter. But when I sat down at the table with Slim and Scott, things got quiet.

"Stop looking at me," I said. "I'm okay."

Slim put his hand on my shoulder.

"You watched him fall," Rick stated, like somehow I could have stopped it. He was pale, and his shoulders sagged. He sat alone at a small table, in front of an untouched plate of food.

"Armando doesn't want to talk about it, he's had a shock," Rodrigo said. "Lay off him."

"It's alright," I said. "There was nothing I could do, Rick. He was trying that dangerous new trick."

"What new trick?" Scott asked. His hair was still damp and hanging over his face, and his clothes were, as usual, rumpled like he'd slept in them and put them back on after his shower. Maybe he had, since they were the same ones he'd worn to the all-night video gaming. He motioned for Evans to refill his coffee mug.

"What I already told Mr. Kronos this morning," I said. "He let the rope hang out over the pool, then took a running jump from the platform to grab it, and swung right out and into the pool in one swing," I said. "Don't you remember? He was practicing it when you and Mary were at the pool yesterday morning."

"Oh. I forgot," Scott said. "I'm kinda punchy. Slim and I didn't get back from the gaming marathon until almost seven this morning. That was on Level Six, Brother," he raised his voice and looked behind him. "In case the Class Police are wondering."

"Screw you," Rick snarled.

"No thanks," said Scott.

Rick turned to the rest of us. "So how could the rope have broken, if the butlers tested it this morning like they said?"

"It doesn't make sense,...." Mary began.

Dan cleared his throat and interrupted her. "Let's don't talk about this now, folks. Let Krispy Kronos do his job, and let us get on with our lives. Armando needs some good distraction."

Scott turned back to me. "Hey, Armando, did Slim tell you we won the competition last night? You should've stayed, man, and watched us win. Not that we had much competition, but there was one team that put up a good fight at the end. It was a rush." He brushed his hair back from his forehead and his light eyes were glowing like a kid's.

"Yeah, 'Mando, you shoulda been there. I learned a lot from Scott. He's a real cutthroat," Slim said. He yawned. "So what's everyone doing today? Are we allowed to... can we go on shore?"

"I don't know," Mary said. "But if we can, I want to snorkel."

Rick looked behind him. The butlers were standing by the kitchen, just out of earshot. "Finally, Mary's getting off the boat," he said. "Mr. Barron must have other assignments today."

Mary blushed dark red and gripped her chair seat until her knuckles were white.

"That's mean and untrue," Dan told Rick. "You can tell just by looking at Barron, he's really gaga over her."

"What're you insinuating? I intended no insult. That's coming from you, man."

"Uh-uh," said Dan-Dan. "Don't you put it on him, Rick. You're just getting bitchy 'cause your new meal ticket's gone bye-bye. Blake's never gonna give you a job now. If he even survives."

"Right. You know all about meal tickets, don't you?"

Dan stood up, and Rodrigo jumped to stand between him and Rick.

"Let it go, people," said Rodrigo. "We're all on edge, and it doesn't help to fight. Let's get on with our day. Nobody's said we can't leave the ship."

I reached my arm out to Rodrigo, and he came to take my hand and stand behind me. I leaned my head against his stomach and felt a familiar buzz flow through my body. His abs were rock hard as ever, and his hand radiated a comforting coolness in the rising heat of the day. Maybe later today we could....

Dan-Dan handed Mary a piece of paper. "Here's the land schedule for today, boys and girls. You are in Ocho Rios, Jamaica. You got to be good at saying 'no' or you'll get back to the ship with your hair braided."

"There's a tour to something called the Blue Hole," Mary said.

Rodrigo made a crude remark and everyone, except Rick, laughed. I moved my hand up Rodrigo's arm, tracing the line of his muscles.

"But for tonight, there's one activity we all need to focus on. Casino Royale Night," Dan-Dan breathed. "Make your choices: Bond, Bond Girl, or Villain?"

***

Rodrigo had made a date to go ashore with Marko, the Romanian soccer star, so I spent the day with Slim, taking a tour called "Journey of the Slaves." I tried to convince him to go to the Blue Hole, this amazing-sounding limestone sinkhole fed by waterfalls, where he could show off his diving skills. But Slim really wanted to learn about the slaves, and no one else wanted to go with him. We walked in the hot sun from the Lodge Yard, a slave plantation, to Mile End, and learned about how the slaves had lived. It was totally depressing, which in a way was okay because it put into perspective my worry about Blake and the shock of seeing him fall.

I was glad to get back to the *Adonis*. Evans met us and told us Blake was stabilized, and was about to be helicoptered to a hospital. I felt a little better, and we went to take a dip in the pool. Poolside had been totally cleaned up by the butlers. There wasn't a trace of blood on the warm cement where Blake had fallen. I floated and looked at the sky and pretended that part of our trip hadn't happened. Then I heard a loud familiar noise and looked up to see Blake's helicopter flying away.

***

"There's gotta be a way I can make this tiara fit with the Bond theme." Slim and I sat cross-legged on his bed, early that evening. We were surrounded by costume materials. He pushed the tiara towards the back of his head. With his newly braided hair falling almost to his shoulders, he looked like an Aztec warrior in a headdress.

I laughed. "What?" Slim said.

"Rick and I were playing around with the snorkels yesterday, on the catamaran. We should do a costume with a snorkel. It would be creative and cruise appropriate. No one else will be doing it. I wonder if we could get that kind with the ping-pong ball in the top?"

"Bam! Yes! I'll ring for Evans. Don't you love having butlers?" Slim reached across the bed and pressed the bell.

There was a knock on the door. "That was fast," I said. But it was just Mary, looking relaxed in khaki shorts and a ribbed wifebeater that clung to her big chest and showcased her muscular arms. Her hair was scraped back into a ponytail, and she couldn't have looked more plain. How could Barron have picked her over me?

My face must have shown my feelings. Her smile faded. "I haven't talked to you all day, Armando. I just wanted to be sure you're doing okay."

"Oh."

Slim said, "He had a good distraction today, with the Journey of the Slaves tour. But he almost lost it when we saw Blake's helicopter take off."

"Wow. How awful for you, Armando. Worse for poor Blake, of course. I mean... sorry, I just don't know what to say. Let me know if I can do anything. Barron wanted me to ask if you want a massage before dinner. He can do it in your room, or poolside."

"Tell him in my room," I said. "Not that I'm expecting to get lucky with him now. Thanks to you."

When we got to my room, Barron was all business, and his business was my pleasure. Up to a point. He stripped down to a black thong, and I decided he must have been a professional dancer before he became a butler. Before I could ask him, he helped me onto the massage table and covered me with steam-filled towels scented with orange and eucalyptus. Then, he put on New Age background music with sounds of ocean waves, punctuated at irregular intervals with a long low gong, like the sound of a distant temple bell. The gong didn't startle you, but came on slowly, vibrated through your body, readjusted all your molecules, and faded back into nothing. At the first touch of his hands, I started to forget it all: Mary and Barron's betrayal, Blake falling, Rodrigo going off with the hot soccer star, what to wear to the Bond Ball....

Unfortunately, as Barron's warm, firm hands worked down my back, I felt an unwanted urge. It would be so-ooo good if....

"He doesn't want you," I told myself, reciting it over and over in my head. All my effort went into subduing my excitement. After a few minutes, I cut short the massage.

"That hit the spot," I told Barron, before he could approach the more sensitive parts of my body. "I'm good to go, now."

I sat on my bed and watched the muscles on his beautiful back work as he silently folded up the massage table. The man doesn't work out, I realized with a sudden shock. This was one of those bodies sculpted by Nature, where the body's own natural daily motions, working from a flawless framework of bone, muscle, and skin, were all that was needed to maintain a stunning balance of strength and fluidity. I adjusted the towel over my lap, ready to cry in frustration.

"Tell me, Barron," I said, "What did you do before you became a butler?"

"We're not supposed to talk about that, Armando."

"Well, you already have, haven't you?" I said, bitterly. "Mary told me you played music, or something. Come on, just pretend it's pillow talk." I picked up one of the pillows from my bed and threw it at him, hard.

He turned to look at me with an expression of guilt and laughter.

"*Touché*, Armando. I'll tell you, but it's not very exciting."

"I don't want exciting."

"I was in the ship's orchestra, played the bassoon and the tuba, or any wind instrument in a pinch. I'm a third-rate musician, but they liked me because I'm versatile and I'm good at fixing equipment, and can also work as a sound engineer when needed. Before that I did a little acting and modeling, but that never really took off."

"Why not?"

"To be honest, I didn't try that hard to market myself. That's stressful work. Being a butler suits my temperament. Someday, I'd like to do the same kind of work, but at a resort on land somewhere."

"I'm surprised the Dans haven't hired you away for one of their resorts."

His face darkened. "They wanted me. Unfortunately, there was a problem breaking my, ah, contract with Jamboree."

"Really?"

"Enough about me. Let's get you ready for Casino Royale night. Shall I bring you dinner in Mr. Slim's room, so you can keep working on your costumes?"

When I got back to Slim's cabin, he wasn't there. He came to my cabin a while later, his face shining with excitement. While I was having my aborted massage, he'd gone to Level Five where the entertainment crew were lending out costumes, and found himself a gold-colored full leotard and a blonde wig.

"While I was there, I visited my twin, Carlos," he told me. "He's gonna take me to visit his family when we get to Honduras. You know he's supporting his whole family, his mom and his sisters and his little brother? Baby, I can't even support myself. What an eye-opener. We had to talk in the dressing room, and we didn't have much time. He's not allowed to show me his room. The staff discipline here is kinda strict."

"Slim, if you're not doing our snorkel costume with me, what am I supposed to do? I'm not gonna do it alone."

It was after ten o'clock, and I was sitting on Slim's bed, scrolling on my phone looking at pictures from Bond movies, trying to get some inspiration. There was a knock on the door, and Mary, the Dans, Scott, and Rick all piled into the room.

"We heard a rumor there's another Goldfinger girl in here!" It was Dan, his hair slicked back and his face powdered to look all pale. He had on this light yellow suit and a big fake gold ring and carried a can of spray paint. He held the can over Slim's gold body, and Dan-Dan started taking pictures. Dan-Dan was also a Goldfinger girl, and unlike Slim's androgynous depiction, Dan-Dan had on full drag and totally passed. Mary was a generic Bond Girl, with foundation all over her body and nothing else but her cream-colored bikini and a wig of long brown hair with heavy bangs. Scott had put on the too-big tux he'd worn for Blake's dinner party and left it at that.

The big surprise was Rick, who'd somehow managed to look exactly like Jaws. His pastel preppy outfits and lightweight presence had somehow drawn attention away from his height, well over six feet, and very square jaw. Now, he wore a black suit with padded shoulders, chest, and arms, colored his light brown hair black and slicked it back, darkened his eyes, and rocked a dangerously sharp-looking array of metal over his upper and lower teeth. Scott pressed his finger to Rick's teeth.

"These are like razors, man. Did you cut up a can or something?"

"Yah. I can bite through anything." He grinned and wrapped his hands around Mary's neck while the rest of us took pictures.

I ended up wearing the tux Slim had brought, classic black and white with a crisp bow tie. His pants were too short for me, so I just wore the top half, over a black thong. I flattened my hair into an early Connery and mascara'd out my brows. I know it sounds boring, but I didn't have the creative energy to think of anything else. Actually, the problem wasn't that I didn't look amazing, it was that I knew I looked amazing, but that wasn't enough to put me in the party groove.

I realized I'd unconsciously been expecting to show off my costume to Blake and to see again that mix of hot desire and admiration in his eyes and hear the way he said my name and called me "Sport," and to feel that promise of something previously unattainable, totally mysterious and glamorous, very grown up, dangerous and frightening, and more real and compelling than anything I had left in my life. But Blake wasn't there. The violent reality of his fall sunk in and I knew if he survived at all he'd never be the same.

Feeling restless, I ditched my Epitome companions as soon as we took a few group pictures next to the dance floor. The growing throng of Bonds, Bond girls, and villains was entertaining, at first. Then the Goldfingers and the Jaws and the bald, scar-faced Blofelds with their fake-fur cats started to seem like they could really be plotting an assassination or act of mass destruction. There was only one thing that was going to make this dark feeling go away.

I walked out by shallow clover-shaped pool, leaned against the poolside tiki bar and shamelessly scanned the ripped bodies and lit-up faces circulating around me. Immediately, I got a lot of interest coming back at me, but I held out 'til I saw what I really wanted. He was a big *cholo* with silver earrings, allover black tattoos, heavy sculpted eyebrows, and a killer stare. We'd been checking each other out for a couple days, and as soon as he saw me, he came at me like a magnet. By midnight, we were in one of the luxurious Deck Nine pavilions.

When I woke up a few hours later, the partying outside had stopped, and you heard only the hot wind blowing gently against the canvas walls. I felt like a harem boy called to the Sultan's tent, the two of us alone in the vast empty desert. We stayed there 'til the light of dawn started to come through a crack in the pavilion drapes.

14

The Adonis at Grand Cayman

It was after noon the next day when the Tribe surfaced for a late poolside breakfast and shared pictures of Casino Royale night. There was no news of Blake, other than what I already knew, that he'd been taken by helicopter off the boat.

"Today, my friends," said Dan, "we're in the Cayman Islands. This is one of our favorite places. There's a ton of things to see and great snorkeling. Is anyone here into salt? The gourmet salt they produce there is the best. We're picking some up for our resorts, and some rum cakes, from the rum cake factory."

Scott came up to me. "I saw you go off with that gangster-looking guy last night. You going to see him again?"

"Probably not." I yawned.

"Guess you didn't get much sleep last night."

"Actually, I did. I mean, we went all night, but I slept like a rock, in between. You know?"

He laughed. "Well, I gotta say, you do look...." He stopped and blushed when I smiled at him.

I was toying with my French toast when Nick Kronos and two other stocky dudes came up to us. Kronos asked Slim to come to his office for an interview.

"What's this about?" Rodrigo asked.

"Nothing to worry about, gentlemen and, ah, lady," Kronos said. "This is a simple protocol, to finish our investigation. Please relax and enjoy your day."

"Is there any news of Blake?" I asked.

Kronos looked away briefly before meeting my eyes. "He was taken to the hospital in Jamaica where they have a level one trauma center. That's all I can tell you."

"I'll come with you," I told Slim.

"Nah," he said. "Go ashore and have fun. I'll catch up with you at the beach."

"Okay," I told him.

I ended up not going to the beach. Watching Slim's boyish frame, bouncing up and down on his toes as he walked away with his three bulky escorts, made me uneasy. While the others went off to enjoy the day on Grand Cayman, I parked myself in a lounge chair by the Infinity pool to wait for Slim.

I read Vogue and swam, liking the solitude for a change. Finally, I lay back on the lounger, closed my eyes, started to reminisce about last night with the *cholo* in the pavilion, and fell asleep.

When I woke up, Slim was standing over me, with Kronos and one of his minions. All three of them looked overheated and frustrated.

"Thank God you're here, 'Mando. I think I need a lawyer or something."

"What's going on?" I asked.

"Your friend is refusing to cooperate with our investigation," Kronos told me.

"I thought your investigation into Blake's accident was over," I said.

"We have some new information that relates to Mr. Slim's possible involvement. It would be negligent for us to ignore it."

"What information?" I asked. "Can I help?"

"Convince Mr. Slim to cooperate by tomorrow morning, or we'll detain him in the brig."

"You can't do that," I said. "He has the right to a lawyer."

"We are at sea, sir," he replied, his black eyes flashing. "The captain makes the rules, and I'm his representative."

Kronos signaled his assistant, and they got on the elevator and left the Tower.

I sat up, and Slim sat next to me on the lounge chair. He looked tired and his jaw was set.

"Slim, what information are they talking about? They can't think you have anything to do with Blake's fall. What do they want to know?"

"I'm not going to talk about it. I don't trust these guys, 'Mando. It's better if I just wait 'til we get back to the US and I can talk to a lawyer."

"But you haven't done anything! Kronos seems serious about arresting you. What do they want to know?"

Slim wouldn't tell me anything more. I knew his stubborn streak, so I finally gave up and agreed to go ashore to explore Grand Cayman with him.

The *Adonis* was anchored offshore so we caught a tender boat to Scott Town. There we went to Rackham's dock, 'cause the name reminded me of one of my favorite books as a child, *Red Rackham's Treasure.* From there, it turned out we could snorkel to the shipwreck of the Cali, a cargo ship that had cracked and was then blown up by the owners after it sank to the bottom of the shallow, murky bay. I'd expected it to look more like a boat, but it was just bits and pieces of rubble with no soul left to it. We swam back to shore and got in a couple more snorkels around Smith Cove, where the water was clear turquoise and we saw this amazing jellyfish all clear with orange rings inside it.

On the tender boat back to the *Adonis*, I was cheered at the sight of the Dans.

"Hi, baby!" Dan had to put down two armfuls of shopping bags to give us hugs. "How was your day in paradise?"

I started to tell him about the jellyfish, but Dan-Dan was already chattering about their day of shopping. "We got so much amazing stuff; it was such a blast! We couldn't carry it all.

Most of it's being shipped. You can try one of our rum cakes.... The best thing is this work of art. They're going to ship it to us after the exhibit closes next month. Here, look, I took a picture of it. You can't tell how big it is from this, but it's really ginormous. We're going to put it in the lounge of our new retreat. It's by a local artist...."

As Slim bent to look at the picture, Dan took my arm and pulled me aside. "How are you holding up, Armando? Are you still in shock from...yesterday?"

"Well, I was feeling better. But now I'm worried about Slim...."

Dan looked at me questioningly, but just then the boat lurched below us, and he had to gather up his packages as the passengers started to press against us and flow towards the *Adonis.*

"Come to dinner with us tonight," he said. "You can tell us what's going on."

We met the Dans at the Tiki Lounge, where they had found a quiet table in a corner edged with fake palm trees draped with gold tinsel garlands. Dan-Dan, wearing nothing but a blue speedo and what looked like genuine Armani leather flip-flops, was sucking a rum drink out of a giant pineapple. Dan's baggy orange-and-blue Hawaiian shirt was unbuttoned, exposing his hairy chest and stomach. He stood and waved us over. When we told him about Kronos's threat to put Slim in the brig, he looked genuinely shocked.

"This is bullshit," Dan said. "Those idiots. They damn well oughta leave this thing alone. Shit. They can't treat you like this. Armando, don't you work for a lawyer? You'd better call her."

I dialed in an international code for the US and called Lucy's cell phone. There was no service. I tried leaving the Tiki Lounge and calling from outside on the deck, with no luck. The embarkation from Grand Cayman had been completed, and we'd been out at sea for over an hour.

At Dan's suggestion, I went back to the Tower and found Kronos at the butlers' quarters. The bastard refused to give me access to the ship's emergency communication system so Slim could consult an attorney. He advised me there would be spotty cell service that night and all the next day, until we arrived in Honduras on Thursday.

"What evidence do you have on Slim?" I asked him.

He worked his jaw for a few seconds and spat a sunflower seed shell onto the carpet at his feet.

"Ask your friend. He knows. You better get him to start talking, or we'll put him in the brig until we get to Honduras."

"Why until then?" I asked. "Why Honduras?"

"Tell your friend to cooperate with us now," he said. "It'll be better for him. He has until six a.m. tomorrow."

I knew threats wouldn't sway Slim. I left and started trying my phone from different areas of the *Adonis*. I couldn't get service, so I finally gave up and agreed to go out to the Lucky Star with Slim and the Dans.

"Come on, 'Mando. If it's my last night of freedom, I want to have a little fun."

"Ha-ha. You seem strangely unconcerned about your legal problem, Slim-ster."

His face darkened. "I'm very concerned. But I'm not worried. Got it? There's no more I can do 'til I talk to a lawyer. What should we wear tonight?"

We managed to forget our troubles, getting dressed up and back into our cruise groove. This legal hiccup of Slim's would be resolved.

The Dans, Slim, and I joined the crowd dancing in the shallow water of the Lucky Star pool. When the full moon rose and brightened the sky, the neon lights were turned off, and there were "oohs" and "ahs" at the sudden sensual connection with the natural night. The experience became less about the glare and glitz and how you looked, and more about the thousands of buffed bodies interacting with each other in the moonlight in the middle of the ocean. Five days of cruising had lowered the inhibitions of our fellow cruisers. People brought Slim and me drinks as we gyrated on the small round island in the center of the pool in our fluorescent orange Andrew Christian chain thongs and matching feathered headdresses.

The Dans were going to a midnight show, but Slim wanted to go to visit Carlos. It was not much after midnight when I got back to the Tower. I wasn't tired, so I took off my headdress and went for a swim. Then I scrolled through the pictures of men who'd given me their numbers and had asked me to text them that night. I was still poolside, considering my options, when Rodrigo and Mary showed up. Barron materialized out of the butlers' quarters, and offered to bring us nightcaps.

We talked about our day for a while, and then I told them about Kronos's threat to arrest Slim.

"That sounds bad, 'Mando," said Rodrigo. "Shouldn't we get him to talk to a lawyer, so he'll cooperate and avoid arrest?"

I explained about there being no cell service to reach Lucy, and Kronos's refusal to let me use the ship's communications system.

"Should I try calling her again?" I was asking, when Scott and Rick got off the elevator and joined us. I updated them on the situation. Their shock and concern at the news was contagious, and I started to panic. I started dialing Lucy.

While I was dialing, Slim got off the elevator. He put his hands into a prayer position, put his head on his hands in an "I'm going to sleep" pose, then flapped his hand in a light wave, and started to head for his cabin. Rodrigo went and grabbed his arm, seating him on a lounge chair.

"You got to stay awake, buddy, in case we reach your lawyer."

"Fine. But you guys are worrying too much."

Everyone watched me as I kept dialing. Lucy's phone rang, but there was no answer. I hung up and dialed again. The third time, she finally picked up.

"Lucy, for God's sake, don't hang up!"

"Armando, do you know what time it is?"

"Listen! We need a lawyer. Slim's in trouble. They're threatening to arrest him. These Greek people are evil...."

"Greek? Are you at a frat party?"

"No-o-o! These people are out to get Slim, and he has to talk to a lawyer right away."

"Well, I thought you were still on the cruise. Is this some stupid party stunt? Are you drunk?"

"Please, just listen for a minute." I held myself together, and gave her a report, just like I do when I'm reporting on a witness interview at work.

"Where are you?"

"What do you mean, where am I? I'm on the ship."

She sighed. "Where is the ship, Armando?"

"On the way to Honduras."

"Really, Armando, I don't know what you expect me to do. I'm not licensed to practice there. There are lawyers in Honduras, and I'm sure you can arrange to hire one once your friend gets there. I've been carrying an enormous workload while you have been gone, and although I've had some very satisfying results I am really up to my ears...."

She went off, telling me about problems with the temp I'd hired, and some new attorney I'd never even heard of who kept getting sick, and all the work she had to do, and how it was my fault her sister was living with her and ruining her life. Then I got frustrated and called her a selfish bitch, and she hung up on me. Tears started to roll down my cheeks, and I put the phone down.

"What did she say, 'Mando?" Rodrigo asked.

"Something about US law not applying because we're out at sea. So she can't be his attorney, or he may not have a right to any attorney. I didn't understand." Too late, I became aware the drinks I'd had that evening, plus the Beachside Bonfires I'd been drinking as a nightcap, had made me dumb headed and slurred my speech.

"She's correct," Barron said. "Each cruise ship has a flag state. Working conditions, accidents, even crimes that occur on the ship, are all under that state's jurisdiction. This ship has the flag of Honduras."

"You mean Slim is now under the Honduran criminal justice system?"

"I'm no lawyer, Armando, but that is what I believe. We dock in Honduras the day after tomorrow. They could take him off the ship and put him into jail there."

While I was digesting this information, which was all too consistent with the veiled threats of Mr. Kronos, the Dans joined us.

"Were you able to make your call to your lawyer-boss?" Dan-Dan asked. I told them about the jurisdiction issue and Lucy not being able to help.

"She could at least give Slim some advice," said Dan. "You better try her again."

I tried calling again, but there was no service.

"Try more out in the open," someone said.

As I continued to redial Lucy's number, without success, the whole Tribe stayed gathered at the poolside tables. Rodrigo was doing push-ups on the cement rim of the pool. Scott and Rick were seated at one of the tables, and Slim and the Dans joined them. Barron and Mary stood together at the edge of the pool. Evans hovered between our group and the butlers' quarters.

I finally stopped calling.

"Is this about Blake's fall?" Scott said. "That was an accident. Slim hasn't done anything wrong. He was with me the whole night before Blake had his accident. Why would you need a lawyer, Slim?"

"I don't trust Mr. Kronos," Slim said. "I won't tell them anything until I consult my attorney."

"This is crazy," Dan said. He hadn't shaved that day, and the heavy stubble made him look dark and wild in the now-fading moonlight. "Blake's fall was an accident. Right, Barron?"

In contrast to Dan, Barron's face was well lit by a tiki lamp next to where he stood with Mary by the pool. His blonde hair was lit up, and the light whitened out the tan on his face. He blinked at Dan's question.

"Er, I couldn't say, sir. I believe the investigation is technically pending. Any time someone is injured, there's a lot of red tape."

My hand was still clamped on my phone, which had become slippery with my sweat. I set the phone down. We were only getting farther from shore, and I'd lost hope of getting service that night.

"Does anyone think it was not an accident?" I asked.

"Apparently, Mr. Kronos does," said Dan-Dan. "Why else would he be threatening Slim?"

"Kronos knows he screwed up letting Blake swing on that rope," Scott said. "That was a dumb move. He'll be worried about a negligence claim. He might be looking for someone to blame."

"I'm not so sure," said Dan. "There may be a problem. I mean, would the rope really have broken like that? I want to think this was an accident, but I wonder. If Slim is really under suspicion, and he didn't do it, then we should all tell the investigators what we know. Not to Kronos, but to the police. If it comes to that."

"The Honduran police?" Rodrigo said. His blue-green eyes were blazing with righteous concern. "Do you think they're any better? What kind of justice would Slim, or any of us, get? Blake's not worth it."

"I wouldn't go out of my way to help find out what happened to Blake," said Dan. "I wouldn't say anything, for example, if I saw something that morning, like someone throwing a knife off of the backside of the Tower. Unless it would help save Slim. I'm just saying." Dan leaned forward on his chair, put his chin on his hand, and stared at the ground in front of him.

Dan-Dan took his partner's arm and said, "Well, that just won't arise. We're all making too much of this. I'm off to bed."

Dan got up to join him. "Try your phone again in the morning," he advised me. "It's an 'at sea' day but we'll be cruising close to Honduras by midday. You'll get service by then."

15

Wednesday, At Sea

I went to bed feeling better. Dan-Dan was right: I'd overreacted to Kronos's threats. After Barron turned down my sheets and left my cabin, I noticed Blake's watch was still on the table across from me. The platinum Rolex glowed like an ad for the good life. I made a mental note to give it to Barron to return to Blake.

My mind at ease, and tired from the day's activities, I fell asleep quickly and slept hard until I heard a knocking on my door and a voice calling my name.

"'Mando, wake up! They've taken Slim!" It was Rodrigo's voice.

I opened the door, and Rodrigo and Mary surged into my cabin.

"They just took him away," said Mary. "We were having coffee by the pool, and Kronos showed up with two goons."

"They said they wanted to interview him again, but I think they're going to detain him, because he said he wouldn't talk to them without a lawyer, and they took him anyway." Rodrigo said.

I gave Rodrigo my cell, and he started calling Lucy while I got dressed.

"Try the balcony," Mary told him, when the first call didn't go through.

A few minutes later, we were joined by the Dans, Scott, and Rick.

"Have you talked to Slim?" Scott asked.

"No, we're trying to reach a lawyer," Mary told him.

Scott, Rick, and Dan pulled out their phones but none of them had service. They started to compare their service plans and argue about who would get service first.

"It doesn't matter," Dan said finally. "We'll all have service in a couple hours," Dan said. "You want to reach her before we get to Honduras tomorrow morning and they put him in jail there. They might even take him there tonight, 'cause we'll be right offshore."

"I'm afraid we have more bad news," Dan-Dan added. "Blake died last night, at the hospital in Jamaica."

I gasped.

"What happened?" Mary asked. "I thought he was stablilized."

"The medical staff knew he was dying, but they kept his condition hush-hush," said Dan. "They sent him to the hospital so he wouldn't die on the ship. There are a lot of rumors, so I can't tell you for sure this is all true. Word is, security staff think someone cut the rope swing. That's why it broke when Blake jumped on it. This may be a murder case."

I was trying my cell phone again, from the inside edge of the Epitome Tower, when Kronos and one of his men approached me from the direction of the butlers' quarters. "Mr. Armando, I need to talk to you."

"Great," I said. "You can tell me what you think you have on Slim. Slim would never hurt anyone. Let me clear up whatever questions you have."

"Yes. Come with us to my office, please."

I followed them into the butlers' quarters. At the end where we entered, there was a half door on our right, through which I could see a kitchen and the backs of Evans and Barron working at a counter. We turned left, into a narrow room, almost like a hall. There were two bunk beds on one side and a couple of small tables with chairs in the center. The beds were so short, I doubted Barron could stretch all the way out when he slept. Past the beds on one side was a small door labeled "bath," through which you'd have to duck your head on the way in. A couple of small round portholes on the ceiling had been opened to let in much-needed fresh air. The place was clean and slathered with thick clean white paint like the rest of the ship, but it still felt like a cross between a small submarine and a high school locker room. We walked the length of the room, which led to a small elevator.

Unlike the elegant glass elevator that guests used to enter the Tower, this staff elevator was a small cramped box like the one Slim's twin, Carlos, had taken me in when he'd brought me up to Level Seven from Level Five. Kronos's office was on Level Seven, a moderate-sized room with a small porthole behind his desk.

I threw myself into the seat across from him. "Thank God, you're finally being reasonable. What do I need to do to get Slim back?"

Kronos leaned back in his chair and steepled his hands together. "It's not your friend I'm concerned with at this moment, sir. We take theft very seriously on my ship. Especially theft from an esteemed guest who is now deceased."

"What?"

"Why did you have Lord Blake Copland's Rolex watch in your cabin? Did you and Mr. Slim kill him, to cover up the theft?"

My head started to spin. With the drama of the morning, I hadn't had time to turn in Blake's watch. How had it gotten to my room? And who'd told Kronos it was there? I started to form a statement in my mind, when I heard Lucy's voice saying, "Armando, no!"

"I want to talk to my attorney," I said. "You and your cruise line are going to be in a lot of trouble if you lock me up. I've done nothing wrong."

"I'm sure you haven't," he said smoothly. "You have a good explanation. No need for an attorney. Just tell me, and I'll let you on your way. You can even visit your friend, before we take him ashore tomorrow."

"After I talk to my attorney. Let me see Slim."

"Even if I don't have grounds to arrest you, sir, I have absolute authority to detain you. You don't want to spend the rest of the cruise in the brig, do you? Did you steal the watch, and then kill Lord Copland to keep him from turning you in?"

"I won't talk to you."

Kronos pushed a buzzer on his desk, and his two men came in.

"Put Mr. Felan in the brig," he said.

16

Lucy
Take off

I woke up with my ankle throbbing. I got out of bed and limped to the bathroom, wondering how I'd be able to get through the workday. While I ate my cereal, Thurgood and Ruth sat next to the table and wagged their pom-pom tails.

"Sorry, babies, mommy can't walk you today. You'll have your brekky, then I'll throw the ball for you before I have to go. Maybe your Auntie Sandy will walk you later."

I picked up my cell phone and pressed the button that takes me to my computer calendar, to check on my day. The calendar was completely blank. I remembered Nancy had tried to tell me she'd been having trouble entering a new appointment. Incredibly, Armando had failed to instruct the poor woman, whose technical skills, as he should have figured out after two days of training her, were almost non-existent. Now, she'd apparently deleted the entire month's entries and I didn't have time to figure out how to get them back. I wouldn't know what I had to do until I got into the office. I knew I didn't have early court that morning, but I'd still better get into the office by eight.

It was already seven-thirty. I washed my cereal bowl and put it in the drying rack, took the dogs out for a ten-minute romp, swept the kitchen floor, and went into my bedroom to get my suit jacket. My dress pumps weren't going to work today. I'd spend the day in one sneaker, with the big ace bandage over my other bare foot. Could anything be more unattractive and less professional?

On my bedside table, next to the empty water glass Claude had brought me, was the vial of pain pills. I thought about bringing them in my purse, and decided against it. The pain was now only a mild pulse, and I didn't want to feel doped up at work.

As I walked through the kitchen towards the garage, I heard Sandy come out of her room.

"Good morning!" she called out. "Don't go yet, wait a second."

"I'm running late," I told her, as she came into the kitchen.

"Oh, okay. I just wanted to know how you're feeling. How's your ankle?"

"Better today. I should be home around six. If you have time, can you walk the dogs?"

"Sure. I don't have to be at my day treatment 'til eight."

"What? Sandy, you'll have to get dressed and leave right away. It's a quarter of. You don't want to be late; these draconian programs will kick you out if you miss too much, and I'll have wasted...." I bit my tongue. I wasn't going to complain about how much I was spending on this treatment.

"I've got to run," I said, opening the door to the garage. "Have a good day."

"Oh, well, I'll walk the dogs when I get home. Don't worry about me. Tell you what. I'll pick up some stuff for dinner on my way home. How about Thai food?"

The throbbing in my ankle and foot got worse. "Don't buy anything!" I yelled back at her. "Okay? We have way too much food in the house already. See you tonight, Sandy."

I focused on my driving through a haze of pain, fighting away visions of trying to stuff big white cartons of more leftovers into my refrigerator. When I'd opened it to get out the milk for my cereal, plastic bags full of groceries had bulged out and slid onto the floor. I started to compose a lecture to Sandy, a simple explanation of the need to limit purchases until we consumed what we had, making space for any new items. She'd understand, and, if we organized the refrigerator together, it would be a good lesson for her recovery. Those doctors who were trying to blame me for all her problems would see that, on the contrary, I was going to be part of the solution.

When I arrived at the office and looked at my desk calendar, I saw I had no court appearances that day, and only one minor filing due and one appointment with a new client. It would be a good day to sit in my armchair, rest my ankle, and get ahead of things for a change. I made myself a cup of tea, got the files I needed and a fresh legal pad, and got seated with my bandaged foot up on the coffee table. Then I turned on my cell phone and placed it on the coffee table, and picked up my tea.

My phone immediately started to vibrate and scoot across the wood table, and a second later it began to ring.

"Well, Armando," I said, "are you calling to apologize for that drunken call last night?"

A voice I wasn't familiar with responded, "Ms. Sanders, Attorney Sanders, this is Rodrigo, Armando's friend. He was arrested this morning, and he asked me to call you. Can you get to Roatán, Honduras, by tomorrow?"

After I ascertained this was not in fact a humorless prank being perpetrated by Armando and his cruising friends, I got Rodrigo to give me details. A man named Blake Copland had fallen to his death while playing on a rope swing. While the fall first seemed to be an accident, investigators now suspected murder. Armando's friend Slim had been videotaped inside the victim's cabin the night before, was refusing to explain what he was doing there, and had therefore been arrested on suspicion of murder. Then, a watch belonging to the victim had been found in Armando's cabin. Armando, following his friend's example, had also refused to cooperate and had gotten himself detained on theft charges.

The arrests, or detentions, or whatever they were, would certainly not have been justified based on this evidence under the laws of this country. However, I didn't know what maritime law, or Honduran law, would justify. I had Rodrigo give me the name of the cruise line and the ship, and the name of the employee who'd detained Armando and his friend.

"Jamboree Cruises, *Jamboree Breeze*, Honduran flag, Concierge Director Nick Kronos, Epitome Tower...." I jotted notes onto my yellow pad.

"I'm willing to make a few calls, but I doubt I can do much before the cruise is over," I told Rodrigo. "When do you all arrive back in the US?"

"We get to Miami on Sunday," he said. "But tomorrow, Thursday, we dock in Honduras. Kronos told Armando he'll take Slim off the boat and put him in jail there. He might do the same thing with Armando. Ms. Sanders, can't you get to Honduras?"

"I don't know about that. If you don't hear from me in an hour, call me back."

Nancy walked in just as I was ending the call.

"Good morning," she said. "Oh, no, what happened to your foot?"

"A little fall, and a sprained ankle," I told her. I explained the hazards that had entered my home since Sandy had come to live with me.

"Oh, no. I'm so sorry, Ms. Sanders."

"Thank you. Nancy, I may need to make an emergency trip to Roatán, Honduras. Can you check the availability of flights for me? Leaving today or tomorrow."

As Nancy got on the computer, I called a former law school classmate who specialized in Maritime law. Fortunately, he was in and able to answer most of my questions. I must admit that by the time I hung up, my heart was pounding and I was forgetting to breathe. Armando's cruise ship was subject to

Honduran law, and there were few immediate legal protections for US citizens under its jurisdiction. My best option to ensure Armando and Slim's immediate safety and conditions of detention was to negotiate with the cruise line.

I found a number for Jamboree Cruises. It took me about twenty minutes to reach their legal department, and then I was told the staff were out of the office and I had to leave a message. They assured me someone would get back to me within twenty-four hours.

Nancy was still on the phone, but she appeared to be on hold.

"Any luck?" I asked her.

"Not yet," she said. "I couldn't find anything before this Friday. My friend, who's a travel agent, says there's a strike in El Salvador that has impacted the flights to Honduras. She's trying to find you something."

The office door opened and a man walked in. At first I didn't recognize him. He smiled and greeted me, and I recognized the lanky frame, short grey beard, and reddish cheeks. It was my new attorney, Arnie Snyder. He was suited up, and carried a rather worn briefcase and a canvas lunch box.

"Welcome," I said. "Excuse me for not rising, but I'm supposed to rest my ankle. Thank God you're here. Are you well now? I'm so glad. Have a seat. I need to brainstorm something with you."

He sat on the couch and listened as I explained Armando's situation.

"Have you any experience with Maritime law? International law? Any thoughts on this, Arnie?"

He yawned and scratched his chin. "Let me think. I don't really have any knowledge in this area. Anecdotally, of course, what I've heard about the legal systems in the less developed countries is that it helps if you either know somebody influential, or you have a lot of money to pay in bribes. That's a stereotype, of course. You know, the banana republic. I guess that's not very helpful."

"Oh! No, it is. Thank you!"

I looked at Nancy. She was just hanging up the phone.

"Any luck?" I asked her.

"I'm afraid not. There are no available commercial flights. My friend says you might be able to charter a plane but it would cost about, um, $30,000, and they still might not be able to take you on such short notice. Do you want her to look into that?"

"Seriously? Well, tell her to see what she can find. But first, bring me my purse."

I opened my purse and took out a card.

***

At nine o'clock that night I was in a private jet, about to take off from the small Montgomery Field airport located just twenty minutes from my house. Seated across from me was Kenny, a grizzled muscular man about my age, rugged like a cowboy or a gangster, one of which he probably was. When my Honduran client Hernan Mendez introduced him to me, I recognized him as one of the two bodyguards who'd accompanied Mendez to the federal court hearing.

"Kenny will keep you safe in Honduras," said Mr. Mendez. "He is my best man."

I told my client I didn't need a bodyguard, but he was insistent. "There is some instability in my country at this time. That is the reason I, unfortunately, cannot accompany you personally to return the great favor you have done for me. Kenny can also translate, and, ah, facilitate certain negotiations for you with the legal system."

When Mendez had offered me the use of his private plane to get to Honduras, I'd agreed to accept the ride as full payment for the balance of what he owed me for my legal services. When I saw the inside of his plane, I understood why he'd laughed as he agreed to the arrangement. This was more than a $30,000 ride, and more than what Mendez owed me. I'd been expecting a small rickety craft with tiny seats, like the little six-seater Claude and I had once flown on to nearby Catalina Island. As the young, smartly uniformed co-pilot told me, this plane was a Lineage 1000E, one of the "most comfortable" planes ever made. The inside was like a fine hotel suite, divided into several defined areas for dining, sleeping, and working or watching television. Kenny and I were the only passengers. The pilot, co-pilot, and steward stayed in a separate forward cabin when they weren't serving us.

I settled into one of the wide leather seats in the dining area, which the steward told me would have the best view during takeoff. I gave Kenny an annoyed glance as he sat in the aisle seat right next to me. Apparently, Kenny had been instructed to stay literally at my side. He pretended not to see my annoyance and settled his broad shoulders into the backrest. At least the seats were quite wide.

There was a smooth lift as the jet's wheels left the ground. The plane made a dashing sideways slant, and I could see right into the backyards of the homes below us. On this short flight, I would be experiencing more luxury than Armando would on his ten-day cruise. I laughed out loud at the idea.

"You like?" Kenny's tough expression had relaxed into a shy smile, revealing a gold-capped front incisor.

"Pardon me? Oh, yes, the airplane. Very nice, very luxurious."

The steward appeared at my elbow and asked me in perfect English what I wanted to drink. I ordered a martini, and he slipped behind the curtain to the front cabin to make it.

"Aren't you having a drink?" I asked my companion.

"No alcohol when I working," he said.

"Well, there's no work for you here for the next five hours," I told him. "But I certainly respect your restraint."

I picked up the martini that appeared on the table in front of me, and took a long sip. "Yes, Kenny, I admire your restraint, I really do. I don't ordinarily have hard liquor on a work night, but this is an unusual occasion. First of all, I worked myself half to death today to get my legal practice in order so I could leave at all. Fortunately, my new attorney, Arnie Snyder, can take care of the critical filings and appearances, and my temporary paralegal, Nancy, will reschedule my other appointments. Snyder seems competent enough, although his face was rather flushed. I hope his flu doesn't come back. And I really, really hope Nancy's ill son maintains stability, because if not, the whole office will go to hell.

"Then I had to go to war with the monolith that is Jamboree Cruise Lines. We'll know tomorrow morning whether my threats to their legal department paid off. I'm not holding my breath. Tomorrow may well find us visiting my assistant and his friend in a Honduran prison. Anyway, Kenny, I feel I deserve a drink for getting everything in order, and I also need something to take the edge off this blasted pain in my ankle. In retrospect, I should have brought my medication with me."

"How you hurt on-cle?" Kenny asked, pointing to my foot.

"Oh. Well. I'll tell you. My sister has this hoarding problem, and she recently had to go to the hospital for a panic attack...." I told him the sad story of the events leading up to my fall and ankle sprain. He expressed appropriate sympathy, although from the look on his face, I gathered he understood less than half of what I was saying.

The steward appeared and offered me another drink, but I declined.

"Very well, miss. You will advise me when you are ready to retire, and I shall prepare your room. Perhaps you would like to move to the entertainment room? It is customary, and you will be more comfortable."

I opened my mouth to say I was perfectly comfortable spending the rest of the flight in my lounge chair, which was much wider than any first class seat I'd ever seen and which, I had ascertained, reclined fully. Then I stopped myself. Why not enjoy the amenities? To do so would show proper appreciation and gratitude to my client, Mr. Mendez. I allowed the steward to lead me to the next room, which was more spacious, with thick cream-colored carpeting, mahogany cabinets and tables, and seating with maroon leather upholstery, including a circular arrangement of four wide leather seats like the one I'd taken off in, and a broad couch built into one of the side walls. I sighed with pleasure, feeling the restful effect of this clean, uncluttered space. When I got home, Sandy and I would do a good clearing out of unnecessary stuff. While I was at it, I'd have Armando move a couple of the large file cabinets out of our front office and put them upstairs in our storage area.

There was a slight lurch in the plane, and I felt a pressure in my sore ankle that made me gasp and grab onto the wall next to me. I felt a strong arm circle around my waist and take my other arm with an iron grip. Kenny led me to one of the chairs and helped me sit down. Then he stepped back, his face impassive.

The steward took a remote control from a cabinet and pressed a button, causing a television screen to rise up on the wall in front of me. He turned it on to a channel playing loud country music and scrolling annoyingly through an overwhelming number of prime viewing choices. He then placed the remote on the broad arm of my chair. I winced.

"Is your foot hurting?" the steward asked. "I'll get you some ice, yes?"

"Sure," I said.

Kenny said something in rapid Spanish to the steward, and a short exchange followed, of which I could understand nothing except several repetitions of the words, "no," and "La Señora."

The steward turned to me and asked, "Miss, do you wish me to retract the television?"

"Yes. And put away the remote."

He made the television disappear, stowed the remote, and went to get the ice for my ankle.

I looked at Kenny with a new respect. "Thank you for noticing," I said. "It's a shame to pollute this tasteful atmosphere with escapist television."

"You want music? We have... classico... old music?"

"Classic, huh?" I reclined my chair and rested my head on the headrest, closing my eyes for a moment. "Now, I wonder what you mean, Kenny, when you say 'classic.'"

I opened my eyes and was surprised by the look in his. Honestly, I'd not in the least meant to be flirtatious, only curious about his use of the word. I brushed my hair back from my forehead.

I hobbled across the cabin and got my cell phone out of my purse.

"Can we play this thing in here?" I asked.

***

When I arrived at the cruise terminal the next morning, and met with the captain and the Concierge Class director, Mr. Nick Kronos, we learned Armando's friend Slim had already been removed from the ship. The good news was Armando had been released from the ship's brig. My threats of legal action against Jamboree Cruises, a United States company operating under the patchy liability shield of the Honduran flag, had partially paid off. There were innocent explanations for Armando having the dead man's watch, so Jamboree's attorneys had ordered his release, on the condition he be confined to the Epitome Tower area of the ship.

Slim, having been caught on film breaking into the victim's cabin the night before he was killed, was a different matter. A hidden video camera installed in that room showed Slim entering the cabin a little after two o'clock in the morning, holding a knife, and leaving five minutes later. Slim's illegal entry, and his possession of a knife that might have been used to cut the rope swing used by the victim, suggested his involvement in the murder.

The captain offered to let me see Armando, but I asked to be taken directly to Slim at the jail. The ship was scheduled to leave Honduras that evening. I was going to do all I could to be sure Slim was back on board before then.

17

Armando
Thursday, Honduras

Hundreds of ripped, tanned, hot, half-naked male bodies swayed below us, the first wave of *Adonis* cruisers strolling onto the pier after a day of recreation in Honduras. Suddenly, cutting through the sinuous, bumping crowd like a razor, I saw a shining blonde helmet beelining along the dock between two gleaming white hats.

"Finally," I moaned. Rodrigo, Mary, and I were sitting on the balcony of my room in the Epitome Tower. It was almost four o'clock on Thursday, just two hours before embarkation, when we'd be abandoning Slim to his fate in Honduras.

I'd spent most of the preceding day in the brig with Slim. It was a cramped, hot, airless, windowless hole on one of the lowest decks, and the only thing that kept me from going into a full-scale screaming panic attack was my friend's company. That evening, a pair of guards, led by Kronos, came in and told me I was being released back to the Tower. I begged them to let Slim come with me, but they told us the Honduran police would be taking Slim off the boat in the morning "for questioning."

My bottled-up panic started to surface, and I yelled that I wouldn't leave without Slim. They started to get testy.

"Don't make things worse," Slim had told me. "Your boss must be on the job, or they wouldn't be letting you go. Wait for her, and tomorrow bring her to see me."

Early Thursday morning, after a restless night, I'd awakened to feel the *Adonis* lurching into port. From the Tower balcony, I saw Slim being escorted off the ship within minutes after we'd docked on the Bay Island of Roatán, Honduras.

Now, late Thursday afternoon, seeing Lucy disappear onto the deck of the *Adonis*, I was ready to rush out of the Tower, carrying my passport and a suitcase, in case we could not get Slim released before the ship embarked. But the Kronos minion discreetly stationed in front of the elevator stood in my way, trapping me in the Tower.

Rodrigo said, "I got this. I'll find her, and we'll take a cab to the jail and get Slim out. We'll be back before the ship leaves."

Mary and I watched from the edge of my balcony as Lucy approached the gangway and then stalled at the end of the long line to re-embark.

"Rodrigo better get down there before she gets on the ship, or he'll never find her," I said. "We don't have much time. Why hasn't she been answering her cell? How did it take her so long to get here? She told us she was flying out last night. Oh my God, what happened? Is she limping? What have they done to her?"

It seemed like forever, but was probably less than five minutes, when Mary cried, "There's Rodrigo!" She pointed below. "He's running down to the dock."

I turned and saw Rodrigo approach Lucy, gesturing towards the taxi he had waiting at the edge of the dock. Lucy shook her head, but stopped walking to talk to him. A minute later she looked up, spotted me, and waved. Then she, Rodrigo, and her escorts continued up the gangway and onto the *Adonis*.

A few minutes later, the elevator opened and Lucy came out.

"Boss! You have to get going!" I said. "You've got to get Slim out of jail before the ship leaves port. Barron has arranged a cab—it's waiting for you at the dock."

"You may let go of my arm, Armando."

"Why didn't you answer your cell? Slim isn't on the boat. They took him away, hours ago. He's waiting for you, for us. God knows what they're doing to him. They won't let me off the boat. Tell them to let me off!"

"Do you really think all this drama is going to help your friend? Honestly, I should have thought you would take this situation more seriously. Why am I surprised?"

Tears started to spill down my cheeks.

"Slim is on his way," Lucy said. "These gentlemen are taking me to see his friend, Carlos Aranda. So if you will excuse me, I'll...."

"Armando!" I turned and saw Slim stepping off the elevator. His eyes were shining, and he had on the grin I hadn't seen for a couple of days. He hugged me, and Rodrigo slapped him on the back.

"Slim-ster! Are you okay?"

"I'm fine, *amigo*. Your boss got me out. She's gonna take care of everything."

I looked back to see Lucy walking back to the elevator. In addition to the Kronos minions in their white uniforms and hats, her entourage included a craggy, buffed man in dress pants and a custom-tailored button-down shirt, with a gun in a holster at his waist.

"Come on, 'Mando," Slim said. "I want a shower and a swim."

***

Dan-Dan was on a roll, talking about his trip ashore. "'Magic Flying Beach Chair,' my ass! 'How about rusted-out third-rate ski lift to nowhere?' I said to Dan. I was so worried we weren't going to get back in time for the Drag Queen Bingo. The line was like a two-hour wait for a Disneyland ride, but then our Concierge Class cards got us moved up to the front."

"Go, VIP class," Dan said, clinking his beer bottle with Scott's beer and Rodrigo's mojito.

"Yeah, we got it good," Rick said, reaching around to join the toast. His spirits had improved considerably since the day before. Tonight, he'd shown animation and an unexpected knack for mimicry as he and Mary reported on their afternoon at Drag Queen Bingo.

"You have to trust me, Danny," said Dan. "Admit it, my little surprise was nice."

"My legs are all scraped up from the rust," said Dan-Dan, running his hands across the backs of his bare thighs. "But yeah, honey, we had a fabulous day on our jungle hike."

The whole Tribe was there, hanging out at the Epitome Tower pool, recovering from the day and re-grouping before evening activities. Everyone had been very warm in welcoming Slim back into the fold. When people asked him what had happened, he'd said simply, "They had me mistaken for someone else. My lawyer took care of it. It's over now."

Fresh from his shower, in his fluffy white terry-cloth bathrobe, with his long black hair wet and combed straight back, Slim looked tired, and was quieter than usual. Scott sat on the edge of Slim's lounge chair, an arm on his shoulder. His joy at seeing Slim had seemed a little out of proportion to me, but maybe he'd just been missing his gaming partner.

Dan-Dan gave Dan a big tongue kiss. "I love you, honey." Then he pulled down his shorts, displaying his tasty backside to the Tribe. "And I'm sure these mosquito bites on my ass will heal before Brazilian night tomorrow."

I was joining in the laughter, when I caught sight of my boss watching us from the elevator entrance. Her face was a mask of disapproval. Laughter faded as people turned to stare at her. I jumped up and ran over to her.

"*Jefa!* Thank you, so much, for saving Slim. Can I order you a drink before you go?"

"A drink would be helpful," she said, pulling off her black suit jacket. Her face was flushed from the heat and a strand of her straight grey-blonde hair had escaped and clung to her forehead in a wet dark wave. "Unfortunately, I'm not leaving quite yet."

She stepped aside. Behind her was the craggy well-dressed man with the gun at his waist who'd come up with her earlier. He was now holding a small carry-on suitcase. The door to the elevator opened, and Nick Kronos stepped out with two of his white-suited minions carrying what looked like my boss's black oversized J. Crew garment bag.

"Yes, Ms. Sanders, we have for you our best suite on the boat. Room for your associate, best Concierge Class. We'll take your bags, you order yourself a nice drink." Kronos moved his head half an inch, and Evans and Barron materialized at Lucy's side.

The minions took the luggage and headed towards the right side of the Epitome Tower. Lucy's "associate" followed them, carrying his suitcase.

"They're going to Blake's room," I heard Scott whisper to Slim.

"I'm going to shower and change," Lucy told me. "But first, you and I need to talk." She looked over at the Tribe assembled by the pool. "Privately."

I walked Lucy over to one of the seating areas on the far side of the Epitome Tower, past the lounge. Evans and Barron both followed us, their usual deadpan expressions replaced with unconcealed curiosity. Lucy ordered a gin martini, "so cold it hurts." After serving our drinks, the butlers faded away and we were alone.

"Thank you so-o-o much for coming, Boss. I'm confused, though. Why are you staying on the ship? Slim said you took care of his problem. Do you need him to sign something?"

"Nice to see you, too," she said. "Didn't Slim bring you up to date? I'm about talked out, and I'd really like to enjoy my martini and relax for a few minutes. I've been going all day. Didn't Slim tell you about our deal?"

"Um, he told me you got him out because that video of someone in Blake's room couldn't have been him. Slim was at the video-gaming conference when the video was taken. He saw the video and said it was that guy who looks like him. Carlos. Slim's in the clear. So why didn't he tell them that in the first place?"

"Why do you think? You should know your friend well enough to reason that out."

"I get that Slim didn't want to get Carlos in trouble. That's why he wouldn't even tell me what was going on before they arrested him. But he was going to have to come clean sometime, right? Carlos is going to have to explain himself, and if he has a good explanation, he'll be okay."

She sighed. "Just like any innocent person sucked into the justice system will be 'okay' if they tell the truth? Honestly, I wonder what you--."

"Slim barely knows Carlos," I said. "Why was he being so protective?"

"Slim feels a strong connection to Carlos. There is certainly a striking physical resemblance. That's why I'm still here. Slim wouldn't tell me anything until I promised him I would help his friend, who was going to be in trouble if he talked. If I'd known Slim had an alibi for the time the video was taken, I could have resolved the problem without telling the police Slim has a double. But Slim maneuvered me into making this deal with him. I'm now Carlos Aranda's attorney of record."

"I thought you said you couldn't practice law down here," I said.

"This is a somewhat irregular arrangement. It will take a long time to explain. I have a Honduran client I was able to help in a very interesting extradition case. The primary issue in that case was whether...."

It did take a really long time for her to explain, although it need not have. There were two ways to get Carlos released from jail without waiting a long time, maybe years, for a trial. The first was to pay a whole lot of money to some judge, who was well known to Lucy's Honduran client. The second was for Lucy to find out who did sabotage Blake's rope swing.

"To do that, I need to be on this boat. I threatened to sue Jamboree for kidnapping Slim, and they quickly agreed to let me on board for the rest of the cruise. The head of the Honduran Jamboree office was very impressed by my legal work for my Honduran client, Hernan Mendez. Ridiculous, of course, as this investigation is not really legal work at all. Honestly, I don't know how I'm supposed to find the person who committed this sabotage. I'll need a full report from you on everything you know about the people staying on this section of the boat. What is it called? 'The Epitome Tower?' Cute."

"Why just us? There's thousands of people on this boat who could have done it."

"True, but unlikely, given what I understand to be very limited access. I'm going to start with the people staying in the Tower, including the butlers and Mr. Kronos."

"Why do they suspect Carlos? Just because he was seen in Blake's room? Blake wasn't killed in his room."

"The video shows Carlos was in Blake's room the night before Blake died. Carlos had a knife in his hand. Fortunately, as you say, Blake wasn't in the room. But Carlos admits he saw Blake on the rope swing the day you brought him to meet Slim. He could easily have gone and cut the rope after he failed to find Blake in his room.

"Carlos has a good a motive, Armando. His older brother Jareth was a cabin steward on this ship. One year ago, Blake ordered Jareth to his cabin, and Jareth became Blake's, er, concubine. Blake had a practice of 'inspecting' the staff on the lower decks, and picking the ones he liked to provide him with sexual favors. These young men were told by Mr. Kronos that they didn't have to go, but if they didn't they would be fired as soon as the cruise was over. Jareth was supporting his family in Honduras with his salary, so he went with Blake.

"When the ship docked in Honduras, Jareth left the ship and went home to his family. He told Carlos what was happening and that he couldn't go back to the ship. The next morning, Jareth hanged himself from a strangler fig tree the two brothers used to climb when they were young boys. Carlos is the one who found Jareth. Carlos had just accepted a job with Jamboree Cruises, and he took it because his family needed the money."

"Uhhhh. So those rumors were true." I flushed. "This is all my fault for bringing Carlos up here to the Tower to meet Slim. I should have left him alone. Do you think he killed Blake?"

"We'll know more when we look at the evidence. The knife Carlos had was a box cutter he took from a tool chest on Deck Four. Experts should be able to tell if it was used to cut the rope. I think it's a bit far-fetched that Carlos would have known that only Blake used that rope swing, so that cutting the rope would kill his intended target. Did you tell him that?"

"I didn't. I don't see why Slim would have mentioned it to him, either."

"Slim says he did not," Lucy said. "But this will be a tough case to fight, if we can't find the real killer. We have a lot of work ahead."

A silence you could feel came over us. The silence was our friend, in that moment, with the horrible story of Carlos' s brother Jareth left behind it and the spectre of the work to be done to find justice for Carlos still in the realm of the future. It had gotten dark while Lucy and I sat at the porthole-sized table on the narrow side deck of the Epitome Tower. Below us, on the port side of Deck Nine, the white columns and rails started to flicker, reflecting the purple neon sign of the Lucky Star. The seductive rhythms of Acid Crew floated up on a current of warm air.

I got up and wandered over to the side rail, and Lucy followed me. A group of criminally sexy men in orange thongs and feather boas strolled by directly below us, shrieking with laughter. I glanced at Lucy. Her eyes were on the group but, of course, totally not appreciating it. Above the horizon the first night stars had come into focus in the dark blue sky.

"I'm going to shower and have dinner in my room," she said. "We'll meet back here. We'll work at this table out here; it should cool off soon. I'll want a full report from you on everything you know about the movements and interactions of every suspect, starting with the moment you got on the ship. Tell Kronos we'll need to interview the Tower staff tonight, and I want him to provide me their personnel files and their work schedules for the past week. I suppose we'll have to wait until tomorrow to interview the guests. No, wait, let's at least interview your San Diego friends. Schedule them for half-hour interviews, starting at ten o'clock. .... No, wait, let me think...."

I sighed.

18

Lucy
Thursday night, Honduras

It did not surprise me a murder had been committed here. I was glad I had the self-control to suppress the testiness and impatience the wet tropical heat was bringing out in me. The cooling effect of my shower had lasted all of two minutes.

My only consolation was seeing Armando squirming in his seat across from me. It had taken several hours for him to bring me fully up to speed on the circumstances surrounding Blake Copland's death. He was pining to join the dissipation on the lower decks now that his friend's liberty had been restored-- by me. He really seemed to think he was still on vacation and should be partying away, while I worked on without any support.

Before interviewing the other suspects, I reviewed what I had learned that day from Armando and from Nick Kronos, the Concierge Cruise director. Two of the staff, Robert Barron and Kidlat Evans, had made a routine check of the fatal rope swing at six a.m. They swore the rope was intact and bore the weight of a man securely at that time. At eight a.m., the rope had broken and the victim had fallen to his death. An examination of the rope showed it had been cut sharply and would have been hanging by only a few threads when Blake jumped onto it.

Mr. Kronos had given me a tour of the Epitome Tower. There were video cameras at all three of the entry points, which were a showy glass elevator for guests, a freight elevator entered through the butlers' quarters, and a small spiral staircase off the side deck. Only the side staircase had a security camera, which showed no activity that evening. While the butlers did not constantly monitor the two elevator entrances, they were supposed to be generally aware of which guests were in the Tower and to be sure no other passengers entered. The butler Evans had seen my client enter the Tower through the guest elevator shortly before two o'clock a.m., and leave the Tower about twenty minutes later. Because of the strong resemblance, Evans had assumed it was Slim, taking a break from his video-gaming tournament. That was certainly enough time for Carlos to go into Blake's room, find him not there, and climb the platform to cut the rope swing.

But butlers Evans and Barron had checked the rope *after* Carlos left the Tower. The only problem was how to prove Carlos had not come back and done the deed that morning. Carlos told me he'd returned to his own quarters and slept until he went back on duty at eight o'clock. Carlos's roommates had all been on earlier shifts and could only state he'd been there, asleep, when they left at six.

My first interview was with my own flighty paralegal. Armando seemed offended when I asked him about the circumstances surrounding his own arrest. I'd been able to convince Jamboree Cruises to release him based on a lack of evidence of any crime, but I needed him to tell me why the victim's watch had been found in his room.

"I'm not saying you stole the watch," I said patiently. "I need to know how it got into your room."

"That's the problem," he said. "I don't know how it got there."

"You must have some ideas. You had quite a few hours in the brig to think about it."

He lowered his voice. "Blake threatened me, Lucy. Okay? I came up to the Tower, the night before he died, after my diving trip. He was sitting there, by the pool, waiting for me. He wanted me to go to his room with him, and I said no. Then he grabbed my arm and said if I didn't go with him, he'd make the rest of the cruise a nightmare for me, and he'd get Kronos to throw me in the brig. He said I had until the next day to decide what to do. After Blake died, I didn't want to tell Kronos, or anyone, about his threat, because they'd think I had a motive to kill Blake."

"You think Blake planted the watch in your room so he could accuse you of stealing it?"

"I didn't suspect that at the time. If I had, I would've made Evans take the watch back to Blake as soon as I saw it that night. When I saw the watch, I thought it was more like a... a gift. Or, I guess, a bribe. I thought Blake was offering to give it to me if I would decide to go with him. It's a really nice watch."

"'A really nice watch?' Is that relevant? My God, do you know how much danger you were in? Were you... were you considering this, this offer of his?"

"Noo-o-o. Of course not. I mean, I admit I was attracted to him, at first, but after I heard the stories about him, and after he threatened me, I was pretty sure I wouldn't go with him."

At times I've wondered how Armando and I could both be human beings and still be so different. Simone de Beauvoir wrote she saw older people as "the dead whose legs still are moving," or something to that effect. To Armando, I'm an ancient, humorless crone, passionate about nothing but the practice of law (at which he incorrectly believes I'm a genius). To me, Armando is a vain, decorative, self-centered, ambitionless, sex-obsessed butterfly, who happens to be quite good at running my office. To tolerate our almost daily interaction, I'd convinced myself he was improving. His choosing Justin Bloom as a boyfriend, the genuine interest he sometimes takes in our work, and his seeming to learn from some of his worst mistakes, had led me to think he'd acquired some ambition, values, and the ability to project beyond his own immediate gratification. Perhaps I'd only wished myself into thinking he'd changed. Or, the unchecked hedonism of this cruise had temporarily suspended his judgment. I should have anticipated this and found a way to stop him from going.

The night got darker, but not much cooler. We started our interviews with Armando's friend, Rodrigo. Armando had occasionally mentioned Rodrigo to me, referring to him as "my contact in the DA's office." I believe they had a romantic connection at some time in the past.

"Rodrigo would never murder anyone. He's a hundred percent law and order, and he gets really upset when the police don't follow procedures. He's very idealistic," Armando said. "Sometimes I have to tell him to lighten up, 'cause, I mean, there's some things you can't really change."

"Not if you don't try or care," I murmured.

Rodrigo was a muscular man in his mid-thirties, with a shaved head and alert blue-green eyes that were startling next to his dark skin. Although casually dressed in a white T-shirt and loose drawstring pants, he had an air of professionalism. His poised demeanor, and clipped, formal speech, screamed, "law enforcement." The only time he looked uncomfortable was when I asked him where he'd been the night Blake died.

Rodrigo averted his eyes from Armando and looked at me. "I was down on Deck Nine, staying in the cabin of my friend, Marko Medeiros. I was out with Marko at the Ice Bar most of the evening until about one-thirty a.m. I stayed in his room and came back to the Tower in the early morning, around five-thirty. I went back to bed and slept until around eight o'clock, when I heard people yelling and came out to find Blake lying on the ground."

Armando let out a high, short whimper. "You stayed the night? But you never do that with someone new...."

"That's enough," I told him. I turned to Rodrigo. "Did you see anything, or hear anything, when you came back to the Tower in the early morning? Was anyone else up?"

Rodrigo frowned. "No, I didn't see anyone. When I came back I fell asleep quickly and slept hard."

"When did you last see Blake Copland?"

"That night, at the Ice Bar. Blake was all over Marko, talking about the soccer culture in England and Scotland and Ireland, and telling funny stories about the crazy fan clubs and gossip about the players. Rick was with him. Dan and I agreed they were both like different people. Dan said they were just trying to impress Marko, 'cause he's a sort of superstar."

"Dan was there?"

"He stopped by for a while. It was late. He came in without his boyfriend. I remember he said Dan-Dan needs a lot of sleep, so he was all on his own. Dan was still there, with Blake and Rick, when Marko and I left.

"Listen, there's something else I should tell you. Armando probably already told you Blake had to be rescued when he was diving off the Bahamas? Well, I looked at the tanks after he got back on the catamaran. The line to the tanks was pulled all the way out. I thought it could have been accidentally dislodged by rubbing against the edge of the tank, which could have happened if Blake had not checked the lines correctly. I decided not to say anything that might get the crew into trouble. It was Blake's fault for going diving when he was told not to. But it looked to me like the attachment must have been unscrewed most of the way, and come off as Blake swam around. When I heard about the rope swing being cut, I thought the same person might have done both things. Similar m.o., right?"

"Who had the opportunity to tamper with the tank?"

Rodrigo looked at Armando. "We were all on that trip, right? Except Mary, and the butler, Barron, who stayed behind. The diving equipment was in the inside cabin, and Blake was trying to grab those tanks and put them on, while we were still all together on the boat. He and Kronos got into an argument because Blake wasn't certified, so Kronos wouldn't let him dive. Blake threatened to have Kronos fired."

"Yeah," Armando added. "People were coming and going while we were getting ready. Probably anybody could have guessed Blake would go back and get the tanks, and someone unscrewed the line."

Rodrigo narrowed his eyes in an effort to remember. "Armando's right. There were a lot of us going in and out of the cabin, even after Blake's scene with Kronos."

"Yeah," Armando said. "We were all moving around, getting ready to go out. I remember the Dans came back early, when Dan-Dan got cold. Dan went out snorkeling again with Rick, before Blake went out diving on his own. I wonder if Dan-Dan tried to stop him. Probably not, he's not really confrontational, and he probably didn't care if Blake got hurt. Oooh, maybe Dan-Dan killed Blake because Blake was threatening Dan's business? You know, I totally get it now, what Dan-Dan sees in Dan. At first, I wasn't sure, you know, why he seemed so possessive. Dan is really hot for an old guy, especially his--"

The heat on the edge of the Epitome Tower balcony had not abated. It was almost eleven o'clock, and the dance music, which had started out loud, had escalated to a punishing, headache-feeding thump. I wondered whether the vibrations were harming the sensitive marine life below us. I signaled one of the butlers, who was hovering at a distance just beyond earshot, for another martini.

"Rodrigo," I asked, "did you ever possess a knife, or scissors, or anything of that nature, on board?"

Rodrigo denied having any sharp instruments that could have been used to cut the rope. I sent Armando off with him to bring back another interviewee.

I watched as Armando and Rodrigo walked together down the side deck, stopping to look over the rail at the spot where Armando and I had stood earlier for him to ogle a cluster of men scantily clad in orange. One of them had, I admit, been quite stunning, with ebony skin and good-humored features that had the soft blur of youth. A few decades would season that face with the greater beauties of character and mettle....

My assistant was in no rush, stroking his friend's back, pointing to the action below, and saying something that made Rodrigo laugh. Was he really going to just stay there all night, while we had so much work to do? I took a deep breath and fanned my face with my hands, which did little to abate the heat or my irritation.

Finally, Rodrigo nudged Armando, and gestured back towards me. They walked away, towards the front of the Tower. Yes, Rodrigo would always have been the responsible one in that relationship. He'd obviously been attracted by Armando's youth and good looks, because Armando certainly does not share Rodrigo's idealistic character. Could Rodrigo's rigid sense of justice have led him to execute Blake in order to protect or avenge someone else? Those with the greatest respect for the rules are often the ones who have the courage to break them for a greater moral purpose. In which case, was he trying to mislead me with this story about a sabotaged scuba tank?

Armando eventually returned with Mary Solya, who was already known to me as my former client and personal plumber. She looked astonishingly well, but then I'd last seen her when she was freshly grieving the death of her sister. She pumped my hand in her strong grip.

"Attorney Sanders—Lucy--, thank you so much for coming. You've done a great thing, saving Slim, getting him out of jail so quickly. I don't know what would have happened if you hadn't been able to come. Oh, wow. It's so good to see another woman on board. Did you bring a bathing suit? I know you packed quickly, and I can lend you stuff if you need it. Just let me know, okay?"

"Thank you, dear," I said. "However, I do not expect to require a bathing suit while I am here. Who had a motive to kill Blake Copland?"

She blushed and looked up, and she wasn't looking at the night sky. "Absolutely no idea," she told me. "I mean, Blake could be a dick, but I can't see any of us actually killing him. I'll bet it was an accident."

"What do you know about the butlers here in the Tower? Armando tells me you've gotten to know some of the staff here."

Mary looked at Armando with a hurt expression before turning back to me. "What do you want to know?"

"Well, what have they told you about the victim? Blake threatened to have Mr. Kronos fired for not allowing him to scuba dive. How did Mr. Kronos react to that?"

"I don't see much of Mr. Kronos," Mary said, "and I wasn't on that diving trip. My guess is Blake wasn't going to follow through on that threat. He was full of hot air. I don't think he was going to follow through on any of his...," she stopped. "Anyway, I doubt Kronos was worried. The staff are used to taking crap from guests, especially from Blake."

"Yes? What other threats did Blake make to the staff? I understand he may have abused other cruise ship staff in the past?"

"What if he did?" Mary said. "That doesn't have anything to do with Kronos, or Evans, or Barron. I didn't say he threatened any of them. He was going after the other guests, mostly. Talk to them. Everyone's going to try and blame one of the workers, aren't they? 'The butler did it.' Right? That's so unfair."

"When did you last see Blake?"

" I saw Rick and Blake coming back to the Tower really late, the night before Blake fell. Maybe Rick did it."

"What time was that?"

"Oh, it was after two-thirty a.m. Barron was getting off his shift at three, and I was going over to the butlers' quarters to meet him. Barron came back to my room with me and stayed in my cabin until a few minutes before six, when he had to go back to his quarters and start work. He only got away because Evans covered for him."

"Did you go with Barron back to the butlers' quarters that morning?"

Mary leaned forward and put a hand on my arm. "No, I stayed in bed and fell back asleep. But Barron didn't have anything to do with this, Lucy. Trust me."

"Well, dear, I didn't say he did." I withdrew my arm and looked her in the eye. "Is there something I should know about Barron?"

She stared back at me and then looked up at the sky. "No."

I couldn't get anything else out of her. Mary admitted to having a nail kit that had a file and small curved scissors, and she agreed to produce it for examination. I doubted the blades would be large enough to have made a flat incision through the thick rope.

When Mary left, I said to Armando, "Is everybody going to be protecting somebody else here? I should have known better, I suppose. I thought at least your friends would be able to give me some objective information. But no, of course not, they're all having sex with our other suspects. Why don't you go get me that fellow Rick? From what you've told me, nobody seems to like him much."

19

Thursday Night, Continued

Rick Collins was a tall, square-jawed young man who made good eye contact and shook my hand before he sank into the chair across from me. Armando had given me a withering portrayal of him as a sniping, cringing sycophant to the wealthy Blake. To the contrary, I found Rick's demeanor confident and appropriately respectful.

Armando told me Rick had an Ivy League education and had worked his way up to near the top of a large company, only to be put out of work after his employer was charged with some criminal practices. The details of this situation had been, of course, over Armando's head, or rather, not within his narrow sphere of interest, as he is certainly intelligent enough when he puts his mind to something. No matter. I'd ask Claude to get background on all the suspects.

Rick's strong chin went up, and his hazel eyes met mine again, intelligent and defiant.

"I appreciate you have a job to do, Ms. Sanders," he said. "But I'm not sure I should talk to you without my attorney present. On this ship, we're really in a Wild West of a legal system, aren't we?"

"Absolutely," I said. "Yes, we are. You don't have to talk to me at all, with or without counsel. I assume your attorney is not on this boat. You are free to leave. Go get some sleep. God knows that's what I'd like to do." I took a sip of my third martini and looked at my watch.

He leaned back in the small metal café chair, but kept his arms crossed over his chest.

"I'm not sleepy. I guess you can go ahead and ask me some questions. Is it true that Slim has a twin, named Carlos?"

"Yes, it's true there's a remarkable resemblance. They say everybody has a double, but I've never seen such a case until now, except in identical twins."

"And you're representing Carlos, and trying to prove he didn't kill Blake? I have to tell you, Attorney Sanders, Blake was my friend."

I raised my eyebrows. "I'm sorry. You'd met him before, then? Before this cruise?"

"No," he said. He leaned forward, putting his hands on his knees. His eyes had lost all trace of defensiveness, and his face was lit with enthusiasm. I noticed now the orange-ish tint of his skin that had earned him the nickname 'Spray Tan'. The color set off his short eyelashes, which were a whitish blond that looked unusual with his medium brown hair.

"Blake and I hadn't known each other that long, I admit, but we connected immediately. I know some people," he shot a glance at Armando, "some people thought I was kissing up to Blake because of his money and connections. That's not true. Blake was charismatic and cultured. He had this ease of manner, where he could talk comfortably about anything with anybody. The night before he died, we were at the Ice Bar talking with Rodrigo's friend, Marko, the soccer star? Blake knew so much about the worldwide soccer culture, and had all these great stories about soccer fans from England who travel all over the world to see their teams.

"Yes, Blake was born rich and privileged, but he made the best of it. He appreciated real quality. He made me feel valued, which is something I sorely needed at this point in my life. I felt lucky to spend time with him. I'm not going to help acquit the man who killed him."

"Ah. You believe Carlos killed Blake?"

"I heard he was in Blake's room, with a knife. People are saying Blake had something to do with Carlos's brother killing himself. I don't believe that."

"Did you talk to Blake about Carlos's brother?"

"No. I only heard the, uh, allegation, after Blake died. Some people say he had a dark side. I didn't see it. He just didn't like hypocrisy, and wasn't afraid to say what he thought."

"You're referring to his insulting and threatening some of your cruise mates?"

"Tch!" Rick waved a hand impatiently. "Look. Blake didn't like Dan's 'self-made man' smugness, or Dan-Dan's militant 'gay pride' flaming. He didn't like Scott's 'I don't care' facade. Yeah, maybe he shouldn't have threatened to ruin Dan's business, or take over Scott's company, but he was just poking holes in their hypocrisy. I doubt he really would have done anything like that, any more than he would have--" Rick stopped.

"Would have done what?" I asked. "Did he threaten you?"

The blonde eyelashes blinked and then opened into wide-eyed surprise.

"Threaten me? Why would he do that? He—he was going to give me a job. He said I deserved to have all my hard work pay off. What I meant was, Blake wouldn't have carried out those threats, any more than he would've, um, seduced one of his company's employees against his will."

I smiled.

"What?" he asked.

"Seduced," I said. "An old-fashioned word, from someone as young as you are. Well. Tell me what you and Blake did, the night before he died."

Rick's story was consistent with the rest of the timeline we'd put together. He'd had a late dinner with Blake in his cabin, then gone to the Ice Bar for drinks, where they'd mingled with Rodrigo and his friends for several hours. They'd returned to the Tower at around two-thirty, probably within minutes of the time my client, Carlos, had left Blake's room.

"When we got back to the Tower, I walked Blake back to his room, but I didn't go in. I left him at his door and went back to my room alone."

"Did you see anyone after you left Blake?"

"No. Wait. Yes, I did. I saw Mary, on the pool deck just outside the butlers' quarters. We just waved to each other, and I went to my room."

"What were you doing on the pool deck? Isn't your cabin on the same side of the Tower as Blake's room? You wouldn't need to cross the deck, would you?"

"No, you're right. I wanted some air before I went to sleep. I took a turn around the pool deck to clear my head. The next morning, I was asleep in my room until I heard the commotion on the deck. I came out and Blake, he was lying there, by the pool, with everyone around him."

"Why did you need to clear your head? Did something bad happen between you and Blake?"

"No! Why does everybody think that? I was groggy from a long night of drinking, that's all. Blake and I had a great evening, brainstorming about business ventures we could work on together. I was looking forward to working for him. Now I'm right back where I started: unemployed. I never should have come on this damn cruise. Serves me right for jumping at a great bargain."

"He's lying," Armando hissed, as we watched Rick's straight back receding down the side deck. "He was totally Blake's bitch. I bet Blake humiliated him, just to see how much he wanted a job. He probably made him do things...."

"That will do, Armando. Who's next?"

Armando couldn't find the young software tycoon, Scott Barnes, who was reportedly on a date with a passenger staying on the lower decks. Dan-Dan, the younger member of the couple known as "the Dans," was attending a late-late show of Reverend Cream [don't ask], but the elder Dan was in his cabin and willing to be interviewed.

Dan was middle aged, thickset and surprisingly paunchy, given the sculpted physiques of most of the other men on this cruise, even the older ones. He compensated for this flaw with his jovial, disarming personality, a handsome mane of iron-grey hair, and humorous dark eyes in a strong-featured face. When Armando introduced us, he shook my hand and immediately started talking.

"What a holy mess this is, right? The whole ship is talking about it now, especially the staff. One thing I just love about the *Adonis* cruises is how the staff and the guests get along. The staff all fight to get assigned to these cruises because gays are great tippers, and we're a lot of fun. I wouldn't have come this week, we got so much work to do right now on our new resort, but when I got the half-price offer, this week only, I couldn't refuse. So. Word is, this poor kid, Carlos, got thrown into Honduran prison (God help him) for killing Blake. I hope you can get him out. Blake deserved to be killed for what he did to Carlos's brother. I knew those rumors were true...."

"Well, Dan, if you truly want to help my client, Carlos, you can tell me who else might have killed Blake. What did you see that morning?"

"Nothing. That is, we didn't see Blake fall. Danny and I were still in our room when we heard the scream and shouting and came out to see what was going on."

I looked at the blueprint of the Epitome Tower labeled with the rooms of each guest. The cabin shared by Dan and his partner was on the same side as Blake's, but on the near end, towards the deck and the swimming pool.

"I see your cabin has a view of the deck, not far from the rope platform. Did you look outside, see or hear anything that morning, before Blake fell?"

"Oh, yeah, I did. That's right, I woke up early, like I always do, and opened the curtain to look out on the day. I saw Evans and Barron walk out towards my cabin, and at first I was hoping they were bringing my coffee. I have a standing order for coffee at six-fifteen, but I was up before that. They turned towards the platform, and I realized they must be there to check the rope swing. You know they had to do that, early every morning, on top of all their other work, once His Lordship decided he had to have this new toy? Anyway, I watched them check the swing. It seemed to check out okay, and then they left."

"Can you describe how they checked the swing?"

Dan squinted his eyes. "Let's see. Evans climbed up to the platform, and Barron stayed below. Evans dropped the rope down, and it hung about six feet off the ground. Barron's a tall guy, you know, about six-two, so it was easy for him to grab onto the rope. He grabbed the rope, pulled on it a little, and then lifted up his legs so he could hang from it. He hung there awhile, and the rope didn't break."

"Did Barron use the rope to swing over the swimming pool?"

"God, no. That so-called swing was only for billionaire entertainment. Nobody else was stupid or insane enough to actually use it. Barron just swung a little, side to side, maybe bounced a bit to make sure the rope was strong, and then let the rope go. Evans pulled the rope up and came back down the ladder. They walked away together towards the butlers' quarters, and a few minutes later Evans showed up with my coffee."

"I see. Could either of them have had time to cut the rope, after they tested it?"

"No. Wait. Well, it's possible Evans could have done something to the rope after he pulled it up. I couldn't actually see him up on the platform. But he came down quickly. I don't know."

"Did you see or hear anything else, before Blake fell?"

"Let's see. I got my coffee and got back into bed to go over some designs for our new resort. Later, I heard someone calling out, 'great job, Slim,' and I assume that was Scott, coming back from his all-night video tournament. Gaming is a giant sinkhole for time, don't you agree? Although I guess ol' Scott found a way to make a lot of money out of it, so good for him. Scott has the cabin next to us, and I heard his door open and close."

"What time was that?"

"I don't know. Later. Not long before Blake fell."

Dan denied Blake's allegations his business was in trouble. "My resorts are doing great. Yeah, I'm a little stretched right now 'cause I'm opening this new resort and we've invested a fortune to making it amazing. Blake envied me because I built my business all by myself. He never had to take a risk or work his butt off. I hate to say it, now that he's dead, but the poor guy was just a parasite on his family money, putting on this façade of a big man of business. I was sorry for him."

Dan denied having a knife or other cutting implement in his possession. He hesitated when I asked if he knew anything about the murder weapon, but if he knew anything he wasn't ready to tell me.

After Dan left, I said, "Well, he had a possible motive, and the opportunity to run out there and cut that rope himself, after the butlers checked the swing."

"No," said Armando. "Dan-Dan was there in the room with him. He was awake, so he would've seen Dan go out."

"So Dan says. Not an alibi I would trust. It also appears his neighbor, Scott, could have cut the rope after he returned from his tournament. That door opening and closing could've been a ruse."

"I don't think it's either of them. Dan is super cool, and I like Scott, too."

I closed my eyes and pinched the bridge of my nose. "You *like* them," I said. "And how does that help me right now? Is there anyone on this barge that you don't like, besides poor Rick?"

"Yeah, since you ask, I don't like that asshole, Krispy Kronos. Blake treated him like shit and threatened his job. He did it. I know! Blake's family paid Kronos to off Blake. You know, get rid of the embarrassing black sheep. You know if that story about Carlos's brother is true, and Carlos did it, I wouldn't blame him. Can't you get him off for, like, good cause, or something?"

"Good cause for murder? What are you on about?" I said. "Oh, wait, don't tell me. You've done some research on Honduran law and found an obscure and unique legal defense. Why don't you just take care of this mess, Armando, and I'll happily get the next flight back home."

"Don't start," he snapped.

It was three-thirty a.m., and my mind was overloaded. The pulsating music had subsided. The several martinis I'd had to drink to stay cool over the long evening had finally made me sleepy. I made a mental note to work out of my air-conditioned suite, instead of the outside deck, for the next two days. For tonight, I was done. Armando slumped in his chair, his eyes closed.

"Don't fall asleep yet, Armando," I said. "We really should re-interview Mr. Kronos about the security procedures before we turn in," I said. "You don't seem to understand we have only two days to crack this case. Once we get to Miami, the suspects will be free to leave the boat, and Carlos will be at the mercy of the Honduran courts."

"I wasn't asleep," he lied. "Go ahead, let's bring Kronos back. Serve the bastard right. Why should he get any more sleep than the rest of us?"

"On second thought," I said, "I think I'm done with interviews for tonight. We'll start in again tomorrow morning."

Armando started to say something, but cut himself off mid-word and walked away.

The air had finally started to cool down, and there was a faint breeze bringing in the scent of salt air. I looked up to stretch my neck and was taken aback by the dazzling array of stars, hundreds of them, and milky swirls of stardust against the black sky. The last time I'd seen such stars was at a retreat in Borrego Springs, a small desert community outside of San Diego that had been designated as a "dark sky" city and was a stargazing mecca.

When I took my eyes off the sky, I became aware of my bodyguard Kenny, still stationed in a chair against the wall of the deck. For such a large, striking-looking man, he'd managed to disappear well into the background while I was conducting my interviews. Now, he unfolded his arms and stood up, without taking his eyes off of me. I met his gaze and felt a low vibration spread through my body. I'd thought I was tired, and I was, but just in a nice way that made me feel I wasn't ready to sleep yet. The word "travelling" danced into my head, while at the same time the salty breeze and starlight and the slight motion of the boat made me feel like I was home.

"Thank you for staying up with me, Kenny. It really wasn't necessary. You must have been bored to death."

"It's not boring. You have power...."

"I'm sorry?"

"No, is my English."

We arrived at our cabin. After he unlocked the door, he put a gentle hand on my shoulder to hold me aside so he could enter before me. He checked the interior, then nodded for me to enter.

"Goodnight, *Señora*." His voice was soft now, almost musical, and I could still feel the warmth where his hand had touched me. As I walked through the doorway, he started to step back into the room to let me by.

"You don't need to...." I said. I reached up and put my hand on his chest.

He smiled and pulled me into his arms.

Later, I fell asleep to visions of gyrating muscular men in orange thongs. I woke up once in the night, not sure the pulsing disco beat I was feeling was real or in my head. A question came into my mind, about a pattern that couldn't be a coincidence.

20

Armando

Friday Morning, Cozumel

"If I may say so, Armando, your employer has a very forceful personality. I'm impressed. And Mr. Kronos is following her around like a faithful dog. That's a fine sight to see." Barron placed my double espresso on my bedside table, and opened the blinds halfway, letting in the soft sunlight of early morning.

"Yeah, I'd back Lucy against Kronos any day," I said. "Of course, right now she's got the clout of the Honduran mafia behind her."

His beautiful blue eyes widened. "Now I am scared. What has she said about me?"

"Nothing, yet. God. Last night is a blur. So many interviews. The woman doesn't need sleep. What time is it? I'm surprised she hasn't...."

A knock came on my door. Barron opened it to admit Kenny, the well-dressed thug who'd followed Lucy onto the ship and was apparently glued to her for the duration. He ignored Barron, and spoke to me in Spanish. "Armando? *La Abogada,* the boss, she says to come to her cabin now. She's ready to work."

"I'm on it," I told him. "Tell her I'll be there in half an hour," I said.

"That's no good. She told me to bring you now. No delays."

From the look in his eyes, I could see Kronos and Barron weren't the only ones who had gained a healthy respect for Lucy in the past day.

As I showered and dressed, while Kenny waited just inside the cabin door with his arms folded, I wondered if my boss could save Carlos. Carlos had a strong motive, and his resemblance to Slim gave him the opportunity to enter the Tower whenever he wanted to. My face flushed hot with shame. I'd thought I was doing a good thing bringing him up to meet Slim. He would have been better off staying in his place on Level Five. I'd dragged him up to the Tower when he didn't want to come, and he'd had to see the man who exploited and destroyed his brother.

I towel-dried my hair and quickly threw on some gel. Lucy would figure out how to prove Carlos was innocent. She'd interview all the other suspects, a.k.a., the rest of my fellow Tower guests and the butlers, and the puzzle pieces would fall together. I hurried to get dressed.

Kenny and I arrived to find Lucy on the telephone. Her cabin, formerly Blake's, was more spacious than the others on the Tower. Placed in the back corner of the starboard row of cabins, it was set to the edge of the back deck, with French doors leading to a wraparound balcony on the fore and starboard sides. It wasn't a studio like the rest of the cabins, but a full-on two-bedroom suite, including a separate living area the size of my whole cabin. Through the open door to the larger bedroom, I could see Lucy's luggage spilled open on top of the bed. The foot of the bed pointed towards the door, which Slim told me once is bad *feng shui*, because it's like you're going to be carried out the door feet first in a coffin. Behind the bed, also facing the door, was a double-sized round porthole with an unobstructed view of turquoise sea and cloudless baby blue sky.

As soon as he got me seated in the living room, Lucy's man Kenny wandered into the other bedroom and closed the door. There was an odd domestic vibe in this cabin. Could they possibly be...?

"Claude," Lucy was saying, "you're wonderful. If you can really check all those things by the end of the day, it'll be a miracle. Listen, I have one more favor. I just talked to Nancy, my temp. She says she'll be in late today, and she's afraid the new attorney, Snyder, is going to be out sick again. Can you go in and just.... What? You did? She didn't tell me... Nyquil? Is this some kind of a joke, Claude? Well, can you go back down there and... yes, several appointments, on the desk calendar.... Nancy's son having more problems... unreliable.... I know I've just given you a load of urgent work, but can you also go in and make sure these fires get put out? Thank you...."

Lucy's face got a look of relief, and then her brow tightened up as she listened. "What? Claude, I can't hear you very well. What about Sandy? ... You went by my house? A truck? But where is she...? Claude? Hello? Are you there? ...."

She hung up and glared at me. "Damn this spotty service. Things are a mess at the office. And, apparently, at my home, although I may have misheard what Claude was trying to tell me. I thought he said Sandy was moving boxes into my house, with a truck. Probably I misheard him. She was getting better when I left. Ahhhh. My ankle is killing me."

I opened my mouth to ask if I could get her some aspirin, but she spoke before I had a chance.

"Armando, did anyone, or any company, offer you or your friends some kind of a deal on this cruise?"

"Deal?"

"Yes, a special invitation, or a discount, a coupon, extra perks, or any other benefit, for choosing this particular cruise."

"No. I got a small discount for booking it early, but that was pretty much standard for the cruises I was looking at. My mom's friend, who's a travel agent, gave me a bunch of brochures from different lines, and I also asked some of my friends and did some online research. This cruise got great reviews."

"Nobody tried to encourage you to take this one?"

"No. Why?"

"Well, Armando, if you'd been paying attention last night, you would have noticed some of the other guests came on this cruise after being offered a big discount. What I also find odd is the number of people on this boat Blake had apparently 'messed with,' as you put it, before this ill-fated cruise even started. Are you sure this Epitome Club, or whatever it's called, wasn't some kind of invitational situation?"

My hand went to my cheek. "Right. Dan said they got a half-price deal, this week only. And Rick said the cruise was such a good deal, he couldn't pass it up. That doesn't make sense, business-wise. These cruises always get booked up."

"Was this cruise such a good deal?" Lucy asked.

"Not for me. Like I said, what I paid was comparable to similar cruises on other cruise lines this time of year. I wasn't looking for a 'deal,' Lucy. I just wanted a fabulous time."

"Don't get defensive, Armando. I'm just trying to find out...."

"I wonder if Scott got offered a deal," I said.

"All right, let's get him in here. No, wait. Do you think Mr. Kronos would know who was going around offering people these deals?"

"He might," I said. "He seems to micromanage everything about the Epitome Tower, and he was close with Blake. If Blake was behind these offers, I bet Kronos helped set it up."

"Let's talk with Kronos first. I asked him to create a log of what was on the video camera in Blake's room. The investigation focused on Carlos's entry into this cabin, but the tape may show other relevant comings and goings."

"You want me to get Kronos?" I squared my shoulders.

"Take Kenny with you," Lucy said. "And tell Kronos I want to talk to both of the butlers this morning, and to see the actual video footage from Blake's room. It's convenient Blake had a fetish for filming himself. There may be more useful information for us. How many staff members work on the Tower?"

"Well, just Barron and Evans, the butlers, and then Kronos comes up with some other staff to do some of the extra work, like serving and cleaning."

"All right. Kenny!"

Lucy had raised her voice only slightly, but the door to the small bedroom opened immediately and Kenny came out, adjusting his pant leg where it had ridden up to reveal the edge of a concealed holster.

"Get Kronos. Armando will go with you to his office."

Kenny hesitated. Lucy's face softened when she noted the conflict in his craggy face.

"I'll be fine," she said. "I'll lock the door, all right? Now, go. I have to call my sister in San Diego." She was picking up her cell as Kenny and I went out.

When we got back ten minutes later, with Kronos in tow, Lucy was talking on her cell phone, her helmet of grey-blonde hair shaking back and forth, and her shoulders bowed. She was standing next to a chair, leaning heavily against it with her free arm. The foot with the wrapped ankle was raised off the ground, and her face contracted in pain.

"Wait here," I said to Kronos. Kenny and I went into the cabin and closed the door behind us.

"Sandy, I know your doctor wants you to move carefully through your recovery. What I don't quite understand, dear, is why that requires you to expand your, ah, library, into my home. Claude tells me the refrigerator is getting too full of food, as well. Surely it would be therapeutic for you to clear that out, and have some nice empty space for some lovely, fresh groceries.... What?.... Ouch!... no, Sandy, I'm fine. No, my foot doesn't hurt. ...I understand it's stressful for you to discard things. Although frankly, rotting food-- never mind. How about this? As part of your therapy, why don't I hire a professional organizer for you? It would relieve you of the stress, and.... *Your doctor said what?*"

Holding the phone to her ear and grimacing, Lucy hissed, and hopped on her good leg to sit on the chair. Kenny and I rushed to her side and helped her lift her bad foot onto another chair, adding a pillow for support.

Lucy registered our presence with a blaze from her blue eyes. She turned back to the phone. "Sandy? Sandy? Yes, I realize I'm interrupting you, but I have a meeting. I'll call you back. Well, I'm sorry you feel that way. I have to go. Goodbye."

"Are you all right?" I asked.

"No. Do you have Kronos? Bring him in."

Kronos handed Lucy a written chronology of the events recorded on the concealed videotape in Blake's room, and she skimmed it.

"There are a lot of gaps in this list," she said. "During the times where no action is recorded, was the camera turned off, or was it on but nothing was happening?"

"Mr. Blake had a remote control he used to turn the camera on and off. If the camera was on, these notes record what the picture showed, even if it was just the empty bed, or people sleeping. If you look at this part of the list, you'll see when the camera was turned off and on."

"I see." Lucy flipped through the pages again. "Well. I certainly appreciate your not wanting to provide details of some of these recorded events. I'm going to need copies of some of these tapes." She marked several sections of the log, and then put it down. "Do you keep a log of which guests are present in the Tower, at any given time?"

"We have a chart in the butlers' quarters which notes which guests have gone ashore, and which tours or activities, if any, they have joined. As I've told you, they try to keep track, informally of which guests are in the Tower. We do chart the standing orders, or special orders, for services for each guest. For example, Mr. Dan has coffee at six-fifteen a.m., and Mr. Scott Barnes has what he calls his 'green drink,' a health tonic, prepared and taken to his room every morning at eight-fifteen. Evans was starting to prepare it when Mr. Blake had his fall."

I laughed. "Junk Food Scotty, sneaking a daily infusion of vita-minos. I love it!"

Lucy frowned. "Mr. Kronos, have you interviewed the staff about the movements of the guests, between the time the butlers checked the rope swing and Blake's fall?"

"Yes. No guest has been completely accounted for during those two hours, madam."

"Are any knives missing from the butlers' kitchen?"

"No, madam."

"Well, Mr. Kronos, you've certainly made my job easier with these initial inquiries. Jamboree Cruise Lines is fortunate to have you on board. You've worked for Jamboree for quite some time?"

"Yes, madam. Thank you."

"Blake Copland sounds like the sort of man who had exacting standards. You went out of your way to meet his every need, didn't you?"

Kronos nodded, but his smile started to fade. "I hope so, madam."

"Mr. Blake had Jamboree Cruises extend special discount offers to entice some of the guests to join this cruise. That was part of your job, correct?"

"No, not at all."

"No, it wasn't part of your job? But you knew about it, didn't you?"

"I—yes, madam. I knew about it."

"Blake instructed your colleagues in the marketing department to extend these offers?"

"Yes. Well, not exactly. Jamboree technically leases this ship, the *Jamboree Breeze*, to Adonis Enterprises for this particular, ah, type of cruise. Mr. Blake was going to join the cruise himself at this time. He wanted, ah, compatible company on the Epitome Tower, so he pre-booked several rooms on the Tower through Adonis, and then provided our marketing director with a list."

"Was Armando Felan on that list? He wasn't offered any discount."

"I believe Mr. Armando booked himself and his companions on the cruise several months in advance, before Mr. Blake decided to join. In fact, I understand Mr. Blake--" Kronos stopped.

"Mr. Blake had investigated Armando, and decided he might be compatible company?"

"I didn't say that, madam."

"But that's what you were going to say."

"Well, yes."

Mr. Kronos was excused a few minutes later, with instructions to bring back the videotapes Lucy wanted. She also asked for a piece of the kind of rope that was used for Blake's rope swing. Kronos left, sweating profusely.

21

The Butlers

Lucy wanted to interview the butlers next, so I told her I'd bring Barron. I found him in the butlers' quarters, and we walked together back to Lucy's cabin.

Before we got there, he said in a low voice, "Armando, I'm so sorry about Mary and me. We feel terrible."

I stopped in my tracks, surprised at his directness.

"Well," I said. "*You* don't need to be sorry. You don't owe me anything.

"Mary told me you invited her on this cruise. She thinks she's distracted me from giving you, um, the best service. She knows how important this cruise was to you. And with all the other things that have happened.... Anyhow, she's so upset she's thinking about leaving the cruise and flying home."

His blue eyes showed nothing but kindness and concern, and the combination of that goodness and his unearthly beauty almost knocked me over. I felt a wave of desire I had no control over, and that was totally, unbelievably, not reciprocated.

"Why should Mary fly home?" I asked. "What good would that do anyone?"

"That's what I told her, Armando. I don't want her to go; she's the only good thing that's happened to me for a long time. Listen. If you'll really forgive her, and make her stay on the cruise, I'll, I mean, it's not, it's never been part of my job before, but I'll give you what you want. One time."

"One time." I stared at him. I could have him. Wasn't that all I wanted, really? I knew the desire I had for Barron was nothing like the kind of love I had for Justin, or even the kind of sick love I could have had for Blake, if I'd let him seduce me. With Barron, it would be enough, to experience making love with a Greek god on the *Adonis*, one time. But not this way.

Barron put his hand on my arm, gently. "I really don't mind, Armando. You're a nice guy. It would be my pleasure. Full on."

I jumped at that last phrase. "God, you make this difficult, Barron. Right now I don't feel like such a nice guy. How could I have been such a bitch to my friend Mary? Or even be considering your kind offer?"

Mary had told me stories of her past bad relationship choices: abusers or losers or both. Though I'd only known her a few months, I'd met one of them: a crude slackass she'd dumped, fortunately, before coming on the cruise. In Barron, she'd finally picked someone who seemed to have his shit together. Maybe it was a shipboard thing, like she didn't have to worry about commitment because the romance was time limited. But still, how could I not be happy for her?

I told Barron I'd forgive Mary, and stop being such a jerk. Without the distraction of wanting Barron, I could focus on helping Lucy save Carlos.

A few seconds later, we entered Lucy's cabin.

"Sit down, Mr. Barron," Lucy said, an offer she'd not made to Kronos.

Barron had been with Mary, in her cabin, the night before Blake's death, and had left her just before six a.m. to go back to work. His account of checking the rope swing was consistent with what Dan had observed from his cabin that morning.

Between the time he checked the rope, at six, and eight o'clock when Blake fell, he was in the butlers' quarters, folding laundry, checking supplies, preparing trays for morning coffee, and setting the tables for breakfast. He hadn't seen anyone near the rope swing platform.

"Did you hear Blake talking with anyone that morning before he fell?"

"I heard him call out to Armando, right before he jumped," said Barron. "He said something like, 'good morning,' and then 'watch me,' or 'look at me.'"

"I understand you wanted to take a job with Mr. Dan's resort chain, but you had some trouble trying to break your contract with Jamboree. Did Blake do anything to keep you from leaving Jamboree?"

"He threatened to sue Mr. Dan. A couple other staff had already left to take jobs with him. Mr. Blake was angry when he heard about it. Mr. Dan's attorney said he didn't think Mr. Blake's lawsuit would win, but it would cost a lot to defend it. Mr. Dan didn't want to risk it. He told me he'd hire me if he still had an opening when my contract expires."

"You must have been disappointed."

"I got over it. Now my contract's almost over."

"Is Mr. Dan going to hire you?"

"I couldn't say, madam."

"But.... Never mind. I'll ask him. What did Mr. Blake really have against Mr. Dan? This hiring away of staff doesn't seem like enough for Blake to threaten to sue him. Blake was on this cruise, along with the Dans, a year ago. Did something happen between them on that cruise?"

Barron's face reddened. "There was the usual, ah, shipboard banter Mr. Blake liked to engage in with the other guests."

"Barron, if there was something, a business dispute or some other personal dispute, I'm going to learn about it. I can understand your loyalty to your prospective employer, but you may as well tell me now."

"I can't tell you anything more. To be honest, I think Mr. Dan poached some of the Jamboree butlers partly to annoy Mr. Blake. That might be why Mr. Blake made those threats."

"Armando tells me you have a gift for reciting poetry."

"Thank you, madam. It was just part of my job."

"Really? It seems to me to be above and beyond a butler's duties, to provide such entertainment. Did Blake Copland provide additional compensation for your performance?"

Barron broke into an easy laughter. "What do you think, madam?"

"What do I think? From what I've heard of Blake, he was more inclined to get what he wanted using a stick rather than a carrot."

"A stick? Mr. Blake didn't have anything on me, if that's what you're suggesting."

"I hope he didn't. If he did, we'll find out, of course. Good luck to you, sir. Oh, one more thing. When you checked the rope swing that morning, could you see Evans putting the rope back, from where you were standing?" Lucy asked.

"Yes. No. I could see just his legs. If you go stand next to the platform on the pool side, you'll see what I mean. But he wouldn't have had time to cut the rope before he put it back. He came down right away."

"I was there this morning at six a.m. There are several ropes fastened near the top of the platform. I assume those were there before Blake's accident? Could Evans have lowered one of the other ropes down for you to test, and then replaced the cut rope for Blake to use?"

Barron wouldn't admit Evans could have substituted the ropes, but he also couldn't explain why it wasn't possible. This was the first I'd heard Lucy had gotten up at six to check out the crime scene. Why hadn't I thought of that?

Barron had been on the cruise a year earlier, with Blake, the Dans, and Carlos's brother Jareth. He'd observed Jareth going to Blake's room and had heard rumors from other staff that Blake, with Kronos's cooperation, had coerced him into doing so. Barron did not own a knife but did have a straight razor he used for shaving. He agreed to provide the razor for

Lucy's inspection. When Lucy asked him whether Blake had made threats against anyone else, Barron glanced quickly at me. Then he looked straight at Lucy and said, "No, madam."

As soon as Barron left, promising to send in Evans, Lucy got on the phone to Claude. Apparently, the attorney she'd hired to cover for her had passed out drunk in our office. Nancy, the temp I'd spent so much time training, kept having family emergencies, and she wasn't getting the work done. Claude was handling those messes, plus now Lucy was asking him to take care of Sandy.

When she hung up, I said, "Lucy, I know you're worried about your nutty sister, but Claude's priority should be investigating this case, not cleaning up after her. Weren't you going to have him look into all the suspects? If he nails down evidence some of them had motives to kill Blake, that will be enough for reasonable doubt, and we can get Carlos freed. Right?"

She'd been gazing out through the oversized porthole at the blue half circles of sea and sky. She turned to me and rolled her eyes.

"Wrong, Armando. Remember, Carlos won't be tried in the United States. We'll need more than reasonable doubt. I really don't see how we're going to solve this case in two days. But I'm confident Claude will have the time to do the research I've asked for and also check on my poor sister." She sighed. "This problem of yours really could not have come at a worse time."

Evans appeared cool and relaxed, his eyes sparkling with interest at the proceedings. His account of the rope check procedure was the same as Barron's. He admitted Barron could not see him when he hung the rope swing back up on the platform.

"But I wouldn't have had time to cut the rope, while Barron was waiting there for me. I had to hurry back to get Mr. Dan his coffee. He usually wants it right at six-fifteen. Even though it turned out that morning I didn't need to rush, I still was right on time and left it outside his door. I didn't have time to cut the rope, madam. It would take too long. Those ropes are tough."

"I'm sure they are. We'll be testing them to see how tough. Well, Evans, quite a few people on this cruise had run-ins with Blake. How did you get along with him?"

Evans smiled. "I got no problems with Mr. Blake. I know how to handle customers like him. He's the big boss, so I keep him happy."

"Oh? And how do you do that?"

His jaw hardened, but his eyes were still clear and dancing. "Good service. Sex the way he likes. If you watch the videos he took this week, you'll see exactly how I pleased him. I knew what activities he liked on the cruise. I knew Mr. Blake for many years, since I started working for Jamboree Cruises. He promoted me to Concierge Class butler."

"Did your duties include finding him other men to have sex with? Did you bring Carlos's brother, Jareth, to Blake's cabin, last year?"

"No. I wasn't on that cruise."

"Do you believe Blake assaulted Jareth on that cruise?"

Evans clenched his hands into fists. "Does it matter what I believe? Okay, yeah, yes, I'm sure he did. It wouldn't be the first time."

"Thank you, Evans." Lucy's voice got softer. "All right. Can you take me through Blake's activities, starting when he came onto the cruise?"

"Let me think. Friday, he arrived by helicopter from Miami. We were already out at sea. He went on the snorkeling trip with the rest of the guests. After dinner, he had me, in his room, for most of the night. Saturday afternoon, Mr. Blake spent mostly with the chef in the kitchen, planning the menu and the drinks for that evening's dinner party. Mr. Rick was with him, following him around like a puppy. Later, he received a massage from Mr. Barron, and then took a nap. After that, he swam and played on his rope swing. After the big dinner, Mr. Blake and the other guests went downstairs to the hypnotist show and then to the Tropicana."

Lucy looked at the videotape log. "There's no videotape on Saturday night. Does that mean Mr. Blake didn't have, ah, company that night?"

Evans smiled. "You're right, that's what the camera was for. He liked to watch the tapes later. Mr. Blake could have slept alone, or had company somewhere else on the ship, though."

Lucy raised her eyebrows. "Is that likely?"

"There are lots of places to hook up, all over the ship."

"All right. The next day, Sunday, was Blake's last full day before his fall. What did he do?"

I picked up the log, which Lucy had put down on the table in front of us. Sunday was the night I'd refused Blake's dinner invitation, the night he'd threatened to get me thrown in the brig if I didn't change my mind. The log showed the video camera had been turned on at eight p.m. He must have turned the camera on shortly before he went out to the poolside table to wait for me, like a spider waiting for a fly. I put down the log, because Evans had started talking.

"Mr. Blake and Mr. Scott disembarked to spend their day working at Mr. Blake's office on Grand Turk. I let them back into the Tower around seven."

"It was just the two of them?" Lucy asked.

"Yes. Mr. Scott needed to do some office work, so Mr. Blake invited him."

"What did they do next?"

"Mr. Scott thanked Mr. Blake. Then Mr. Blake started laughing, like Mr. Scott had said something funny. Mr. Scott said, 'whatever,' and went to his cabin. Mr. Blake asked me for a Manhattan, so I made one and took it to him in his cabin. I asked if he would be wanting my services that evening, and he told me he had other plans."

"Did he say what those plans were?"

Evans looked at me. There was malice, and something else, almost like anger, in his eyes.

"Yes. Mr. Blake planned to have dinner in his cabin with Mr. Armando. Those plans changed. Mr. Rick was there when I delivered the dinner to Mr. Blake's cabin. After dinner, Mr. Blake and Mr. Rick went out to the Tropicana, and I saw them both come back to the Tower at about two-thirty that night. I didn't see Mr. Blake again until the next morning, after he, uh, fell."

Evans's voice shook as he said those last words. He denied having a knife or a razor in his possession. He hadn't seen anyone go onto the platform that morning.

"Mr. Evans, did you put Mr. Blake's watch in Armando's cabin?"

He didn't look surprised at the question. "Oh, no, madam. I don't know how that watch got there. When I saw it, I thought...."

"Yes?"

"I thought Mr. Blake had given it to Mr. Armando. He could be very generous."

"He's lying," I said, a few minutes later, after Evans had left us. "He for sure put that watch in my room. He was jealous Blake liked me, so he wanted to mess with me. No, wait, Blake probably made him do it, so Blake could accuse me of theft and get me thrown in the brig like he threatened. I bet Evans was the one who told Kronos he saw the watch in my room. He was under Blake's thumb. I bet Evans killed Blake, Lucy."

"Evans's relationship with Blake certainly appears to have been a complicated one. Evans had the opportunity to cut the rope while he was up on the platform that morning. He's clever, though, and careful. If he did it, we're not going to trick a confession out of him. Let's look at the log again. I can't remember the exact chronology the night before Blake's fall."

The log showed the camera started rolling at eight p.m., but all the tape showed was the empty bedroom, until nine twenty-five p.m., when Blake and Rick entered, were served dinner by Evans, then got into the bed, and "engaged in sexual acts." At eleven forty-two, the two men dressed and left the room.

At four minutes after two, someone else entered the bedroom. The name "Slim Rubi" was crossed out, and the name "Carlos Aranda" was written in. The log stated Carlos entered the room, holding a knife. He walked over to the empty bed, made a stabbing motion with his knife, and then left the room, at five after two.

Finally, the log recorded Blake returning, alone, to the room, at two thirty-seven, and the video was turned off.

"At least we're starting to get a picture of what Blake was up to that last night," said Lucy. "I have a hunch this was an act of desperation, something that wasn't planned very far ahead. Something happened that day, or that night, to make the killer take a great risk. If the butlers are telling the truth, the swing was intact at six a.m. Whoever cut the rope was out there, exposed, on the deck, in the early morning where anyone could have walked by and seen them."

"What about the scuba tank being sabotaged?" I objected. "That happened on our first day. The person must have already wanted to kill Blake."

"That's possible, but really that was a much more half-hearted attempt. It was a long shot Blake would really drown. The rope sabotage, however, was more likely to do serious, if not fatal, damage. From the angle he would have grabbed onto the rope, Blake could be expected not to land on his feet, but to fall onto his back and head. A fall of fifteen feet onto hard cement...."

The blood rushed out of my head. "Okay, I get it, Boss."

"So the question is, what happened that day, or that night, to make the killer cut Blake's rope swing? Blake spent that day onshore at his company's office. Was he still having his cruise mates investigated? Did he get more damaging information on somebody? Scott Barnes went onshore with him, and Evans hinted Scott seemed irritated when he parted from Blake. Then that evening, Blake made advances to you, Armando. Could that have set someone off? Jealousy, possibly?

"Blake spent the whole day at the Jamboree offices with Scott, and quite a bit of time at the Ice Bar that night, with Rick, Rodrigo, and later with Dan. It's interesting Blake returned to his room just a few minutes after Carlos left it. Could that be significant? Why didn't Rick go back to Blake's room with him? I'm missing something, something I heard today, that doesn't fit. One of the butlers...." She frowned.

"Maybe Rick and Blake had a fight when they got back to the Tower," I said.

"We need those videotapes," said Lucy. "In the meantime, who do we have left?"

"You haven't interviewed Scott or Dan-Dan."

"All right. Get them. But give me fifteen minutes. I should call my sister."

As I left, I had to walk around Kenny. Despite his bulk, I'd almost forgotten he was there. He'd been sitting on the edge of the chair that propped up Lucy's foot, like a guard dog keeping his body between her and the suspects.

The wet, hot air hit me as soon as I left Lucy's air- conditioned cabin. It was high noon, and the sun was blazing. The Epitome pool came into view, sparkling clean, with dark sleek heads bobbing in the water.

Slim and Scott waved to me from the pool. Rodrigo was doing tricep push-ups on the deck, Mary was sunbathing on a lounge chair, and Rick was drinking coffee and reading the daily activity sheet at one of the shaded café tables.

"Hey," I said. "Everyone's here but the Dans."

"The Absent Dans," said Scott. "They had a late night. As we all did. Not surprising it's after noon and the Dans are still in their cabin."

"What did everyone do last night while I was working my ass off?" I asked. "How was the black-and-white party?"

People started to tell me about the party. Slim got out of the pool to get his phone and show me pictures.

"How's Lucy's investigation going?" he asked. "Is she gonna get Carlos out?"

"Too soon to tell," I said. "Scott, Lucy wants to talk to you in a few minutes. And then I guess I'll have to wake up the Dans."

"Let me know when," said Scott.

I kicked off my flip-flops and dangled my legs in the pool. "Oh my god," I said. "I really want to go in."

"I'll swim with you later," said Slim. "I'm gonna stay on the *Adonis* today. Kronos gave me permission to visit Carlos in the brig. I'll be down there if you need me for anything."

Rodrigo came and sat next to me. "Do you want me to stay on board? Just tell me what I can do."

"Me, too." Mary sat up in her lounge chair, wrapping her arms around her knees. "I want to help," she said in a small voice. She looked at me hopefully. Barron must have told her I was going to forgive her. I gave her a smile, and her plain, healthy face lit up with a big grin.

"You guys should all go on shore and have fun," I said. "Where the hell are we, anyway?"

"Cozumel," said Rick. "We have to wait 'til the Dans get up so they can give us their recommendations. They're always dialed in to what's going on, on and off the ship."

"No, they're not," said Scott. "They just act like they are. Come on, Rick. You've been staring at that paper for long enough. Give it a shot. What do you recommend?"

Rick was looking more cool and relaxed than usual, even in an unbelievably ugly Kelly-green polo shirt with the collar popped up over the back of his neck. He looked at the activity sheet.

"All right. The Dans told me last night they're going to the Taste of Cozumel cooking class. Me, I want to go swim with the dolphins. For Rodrigo, there's a diving and jeep tour, or Xtreme zip-lining. Mary, I recommend the history walking tour, where you can learn about the goddess Ixchel. Scott.... Ah, yes! There's a Mayan laser tag adventure for you. You'll be at least ten years older than anyone else on the adventure, but other than that, you'll fit right in."

"Fuck you," said Scott. "Actually, I think I'll join you and swim with the dolphins. The poor animals will need a cool dude like me to balance out your nervous energy. But I won't be seen with you if you're wearing that hideous shirt. Go change it. I'll be ready to go as soon as Armando's boss is done with me."

When I entered the cabin a few minutes later, Lucy and Kenny were seated next to each other, their chairs pulled side by side, staring at the screen of an iPad. Lucy looked up. Her eyes were shining. Her bodyguard also had a pleased expression, which on him looked like he'd just successfully completed a tricky assassination.

"Armando, Kenny and I have made some progress!"

22

Voodoo

"That's great!" I cried. "Thank god. Did you figure out what happened? Can we get Carlos out of the brig? What should I tell Scott? He's waiting outside."

"I'll see him in a minute," she said. "We got the footage from Blake's room. Look at this." She turned on her iPad, clicked, scrolled, and clicked again, and handed it to me.

The film showed a semi-aerial view encompassing the far side of the bedroom of the cabin we were now in. It revealed a large, empty, unmade bed, both bedside tables, and a the space between the bed and the door into the room. The back of a man in shorts and T-shirt came into view, lit only by the pale moonlight coming through the porthole behind the bed. He came to the foot of the bed and made a full turn, like an animal that circles a spot before lying down. It was clearly Slim's face and body, but I knew it wasn't Slim; it was Carlos.

Carlos stood at the foot of the bed for a minute with his back to the camera, still for so long I wondered if he was waiting for his eyes to adjust to the dim lighting. Then he sat on the edge of the bed, his face now fully exposed to the camera.

Carlos reached under his shirt to pull out a utility knife and placed it on the bed next to him. He lifted his hands and put them together, thumbs and index fingers touching, to form a triangle, and twisted his body to face the head of the bed. Then he turned back, and picked up the knife. I felt like I was watching my friend Slim in a play, wearing clothes that were not his clothes and an expression on his face that was not one of his expressions. It was the face of a killer in action. Carlos's beautiful flaring dark eyebrows that are Slim's eyebrows too, were pressed together so they almost touched as he retracted the knife blade, raised the knife in his fist behind his head, and brought the knife down to stab the blade into the mattress. The motion twisted his body so at the end of the arc, his head was almost touching the bed.

Lucy, who'd been watching over my shoulder, took the iPad and stopped the video.

"Did you see that triangle he made with his hands? Kenny informs me that's a common symbol for a curse in Honduran voodoo."

"I don't know about voodoo signs, but from the look on Carlos's face when he stabbed Blake's bed, yeah, I'd guess it was a curse and not a love spell. So Carlos came looking for Blake to kill him, and when he couldn't find him, he did this curse and then went and cut the rope swing. No?"

Lucy looked at Kenny, whose own face bore the intent expression of someone trying to follow a conversation in a foreign language. He was shaking his head in answer to my question.

Kenny told me, "Man not try to kill the man cursed. He--" he stopped. He switched to his soft Spanish, with an accent similar to the one I'd heard from Carlos except with cleaner pronunciation and a larger vocabulary. "Some people in my country, especially those in a desperate emotional state, go to voodoo practitioners. Voodoo practice has been somewhat integrated with Catholic rituals, and made more familiar, and more compelling, to the Catholic population. Everyone knows you don't make a voodoo curse and then try to take the, ah, matter into your own hands. That would make the curse come back onto you. If Carlos was cursing that man Blake, which I think he was, he would not have gone on to kill him."

"*Y el cuchillo?*" I asked him. "Is a box-cutter knife part of the voodoo hex ritual?"

The look Kenny shot me reminded me of the killer stare of Lucy's boyfriend, Claude. But he just shrugged and didn't say anything more.

I translated Kenny's explanations to Lucy, and she nodded. "That voodoo backfire story makes a great argument, for a jury of Honduran citizens. Unfortunately, Honduras doesn't have juries. Possibly a judge would find the argument compelling. I certainly do. This is a breakthrough. I now feel convinced Carlos is innocent."

"You feel convinced? What about proof? Is this voodoo hex explanation enough for Jamboree Cruises?"

"Probably not, but it's a good start. I'm hopeful."

The video had had the opposite effect on me. She'd seen the same video I had and her client's totally murderous expression. Since when did she let superstition trump basic psychology? Carlos had used his resemblance to Slim to get into the Tower and gone to Blake's room to kill him. When he'd found the room empty he'd gotten pissed and thought of the rope swing. And, he'd had a box cutter to do the job. And, it was my fault for bringing the poor kid to the Tower.

"You're underestimating the power of superstition," she began, after I gave her my opinion. Then she stopped herself. "We don't have time to argue. Who's next? Scott Barnes? Bring him in."

Scott wore sloppy cargo shorts, rubber shower shoes, and one of his nerd T-shirts, but he'd combed his hair back after his swim, and he looked fresh and eager to help.

"I'm so relieved you were able to get Slim released," he told Lucy, seating himself across from her. "I felt terrible when I heard he'd been arrested."

"Why? Slim's arrest wasn't your fault. Was it?"

"I meant I felt terrible because I like Slim, and I know he wouldn't ever hurt anyone."

"Right. Tell me about your relationship with Blake Copland."

"What do you want to know?"

"You're an intelligent man. You know I'm going to find out, sooner or later, what Mr. Blake Copland was doing to torment you."

"Torment me? That's kind of strong. Blake liked to push people's buttons, that's all."

"You were offered a discount to come on this cruise, weren't you?"

Scott raised his eyebrows. "How'd you know that? Yeah, I'd been considering a cruise, and I got an email alert from Jamboree, offering seventy percent off an Epitome Tower cabin on this cruise, this week only. It was really last minute, which I figured was the reason for the discount. I was able to take a break from work, so I grabbed the deal."

"That's quite a discount. Do you go on many luxury cruises?"

"God, no. This isn't my style. I was looking at the more modest options. But with the seventy percent off, this ended up being almost the same price as the middle-range ones, and I liked the pictures of the pool, and there was a video gaming tournament on this voyage."

Lucy glanced at her notes. "Yes, I see you work in the computer game industry. Was Blake threatening your business?"

"Not in a real way," said Scott. "My company recently went public, and the price of shares has gone down about ten percent since the initial offering. That's not unusual, in a hot market, to have a high opening price and then a dip before the stock stabilizes. Blake told me he'd bought some stock in the offering, and he was considering bringing a shareholder suit against me.

"There's no basis for such a suit. I've never misrepresented anything about my company. Okay, a protracted high profile lawsuit would have been expensive, and not great for my company's reputation. So, yeah, Blake knew how to get to me. But his stupid threat, which I really doubt he would've carried out, wasn't a reason for me to kill him. I treated his threat as a joke. That kind of bugged him."

"How much money did Blake lose when the stock price dipped?" Lucy asked.

"Less than the full price of this cruise," said Scott, smiling. "So you see, his threats really were a joke. At least, the one against me. Maybe he made more serious threats against someone else."

"Like whom?"

Scott's smile disappeared. He clenched his expressive hands together in his lap.

"Blake had been scattershooting at everyone in sight. I don't want to put anyone under suspicion. It wouldn't be fair."

"What's unfair, Mr. Barnes, is my innocent client being accused of murder. I'm going to make a detailed investigation of everyone's dealings with Blake. Why not save me some time?"

After a little more prodding, Scott described Blake's threat to have Kronos fired for trying to keep Blake from scuba diving, his strange influence over Rick, and his plans to have charges brought against Dan.

"Charges?" Lucy asked. "You mean a lawsuit? For Dan's hiring away some of Jamboree's butlers?"

"I don't know anything about butlers. What Blake told me was, Dan was having cash flow problems and misrepresented the condition of some of his properties to get a loan. Listen, Blake threatened me and I haven't done anything wrong. Probably Dan hasn't either."

Scott said he'd brought on board a Swiss Army knife that he liked to have when he travelled. He agreed to get it from his cabin and bring it to her for examination.

When Scott left, Lucy said, "That's a cocky young man. Smart, immature. He's very attached to his company, and I can see him killing to protect it. And Blake must have something on Rick, too. Unless he enticed him on this cruise to use him sexually, as he apparently hoped to do with you. Armando, I'm afraid I'll need you to watch the video footage of Rick and Blake consorting in Blake's room. It would tell me nothing, but you may be able to glean some insight about the, uh, dynamics of their relationship."

"I'll get right on it, Boss." I grabbed the iPad and powered it on. "What was that date, again?"

"Not now, Armando. Put that down. Yes, now. Hand it to me. Thank you. Why don't you bring me Dan-Dan, our final guest. Bring Dan with him, too. I want to ask him about these new allegations Scott brought up."

"I could, Boss, but they're still asleep. And I'm starving. It's after one o'clock. How about we take a lunch break and then I get them? They're going to a cooking class onshore later, but I'll tell the butlers to bring them to you first."

"All right. I suppose we could all use some lunch. And I want to interview Carlos about Kenny's voodoo curse theory. You'll need to come down to the brig to translate. Wait, no, Kenny can do that. Go have your lunch. And don't let the Dans leave until I interview them."

When I got to the deck, the poolside had emptied out. People were probably in their rooms, getting ready to go ashore, or already disembarked. I hoped the Dans hadn't gotten off already, but Evans came out to see if I needed anything, and told me the Dans hadn't surfaced.

Scott came rushing out of his room.

"Armando! Someone took my jackknife. I'm sure it was in my room, on my dresser, and it's not. I checked all my pockets and my luggage. It's not there, and I haven't seen it for a couple days. I'll look some more when I get back tonight. Is that okay?"

"I'll let Lucy know."

"Thanks, buddy. Rick and I are gonna go swim with the dolphins. Too bad you can't come with us. It would be a lot more fun for me."

"Is he going to change out of that heinous shirt?"

Scott grinned and winked at me. "You're impressed I even noticed, right?"

"Yeah, I have some hope for your fashion sense."

"I give you and Slim credit for that."

I wanted lunch, but even more I needed to get my overheated body into that pool. From the pool, I'd be able to watch for the Dans, so they didn't take off before Lucy could interview them. I put on my suit and did half an hour of short, fast laps. Then I just floated. The sun warmed my face while the water cooled my body, and there was a faint familiar smell of chlorine and the feel of my fingers getting waterlogged. For a minute I thought I was in my pool at home in San Diego. But the air here was different, not just the salt sea smell or the soggy humidity that made my face sweat even while I was in the water. A dark energy had lingered on the *Adonis* ever since Blake had fallen to his death just a few feet from where I was floating.

I felt a sudden chill. My floating body got heavy and started to sink, filling my nose with water. Something was wrong, more than just Blake's recent death. I sputtered the water out of my nose and stood up in the pool. The deck felt too still, with no butlers or guests in sight.

A few minutes later, Slim walked out of the Tower elevator, backlit by the blinding sun behind him.

"I'm glad you're here, Slim-ster. I all of a sudden felt spooked. How's Carlos holding up?"

"He's kinda freaked out. Like you, he's not good with small spaces. You'd think he'd be used to it, staying in his tiny staff quarters on Deck Four. But in the brig, he knows he can't leave. I kept telling him Attorney Sanders is the best, and she's going to get him out. Then she came down with her bodyguard to talk to Carlos, so I left. Did you have lunch yet?"

Barron brought us lunch poolside. While we ate, I told Slim about Kenny's idea that Carlos had gone into Blake's room to deliver a "voodoo curse."

"Kenny's right," said Slim. "Carlos told me the same thing. He used the box cutter to rip the mattress to, like, symbolically let the bad spirits into Blake's bed. Carlos was going to just cut a nick in the door to Blake's cabin. When he found the door unlocked, and Blake not there, he went for the mattress instead 'cause that's more powerful. Is that explanation enough to prove Carlos didn't cut the rope swing?"

"No. Lucy's interviewing everyone and getting background checks. She's going to do the Dans next. We're just waiting for them to wake up."

Slim shifted his body, and we both turned to look towards the Dans' cabin. There was still no sign of life.

I checked my watch. It was after two o'clock. The sun was melting the blue of the sky into a blanket of white heat. The cement of the poolside was bone dry. Even the Infinity pool looked more like a pale blue eyeball than an oasis of coolness. I couldn't see the Lucky Star pool from where I was sitting, but the quiet murmur of voices from down below suggested few cruisers had chosen to be out in the sun at this hour.

"Isn't it getting kinda late?" Slim said. "I thought the Dans were going to a cooking class on shore."

"Guess they're not going to make it," I said. "Maybe I should wake them up."

"You better. Your boss only has a couple days to figure this out and get Carlos out of the brig."

I walked over to the Dans' cabin, but there was no answer to my knocks and calls. I knocked harder, and called loudly. "Dans! Open up! Time to get up, *amigos*!"

"Darn it!" I said. "I bet they snuck off the ship when I wasn't watching. Lucy's gonna kill me."

Evans appeared at my side. "They haven't left, sir. As I told you, we've been watching for them. Don't shout. I'll get the key."

He returned a minute later, with Barron. Barron tried his own discreet knock and call, with no result. The butlers looked at each other, and Evans took a key out of his apron and turned it in the lock.

23

Claude
Friday, San Diego

I go to Luce's law office early and put out a few fires. It's a piece of cake compared to yesterday, when I'd arrived to find nice Nancy, the temp Armando had hired, standing at the front door. She'd just found Mr. Arnold Snyder, the new attorney, upstairs in his office passed out cold.

"Thank God you're here, Mr. Washington," Nancy told me. "My son is at the emergency room, and I'm afraid Mr. Snyder may need medical attention. I just called 911, but I just can't wait around for someone to get here."

"I got this," I told her. "Go to your boy."

I ran upstairs to the windowless storage room where Lucy'd set up her new lawyer with a big oak desk and the many boxes of files that comprise the record in the death penalty appeal he's supposed to be working on. The strong sweet scent of alcohol poisoning in the room clued me in. I shook Attorney Snyder by his tweed-jacketed shoulder. He's a sorry looking specimen, jaundiced and bent, drooling on the blotter under his slack jaw. How could Lucy have hired him? He jerked his arm away, snarled, "lemme go," and put his head back on the desk. A few minutes later, the paramedics arrived and confirmed my diagnosis of EtOH overdose. An empty bottle of Nyquil suggested one of the sources of intoxication, and the Nyquil could have delivered a life-threatening amount of other substances. Attorney Snyder declined the paramedics' offer of an ambulance to the nearest hospital.

With the help of Mike, the attorney who has an office upstairs from Lucy's, I took Snyder to the sink in the small bathroom on the landing and ran his head under cold water. Having sobered him up, we sent him home, ignoring his stated desire to continue working. I picked up the crumpled mass of legal papers from the desk where his head had fallen, smoothed them out, and wiped off the sticky red smudges of Nyquil as best I could. Then I arranged for Mike and his highly competent secretary to contact the superior court to reschedule the court appearances Attorney Snyder had failed to attend that day.

So today, Friday morning, all I have to do is get Mike to cover one of Lucy's appearances, call the court to reschedule the other one, and cancel three appointments with clients who were to come in and sign paperwork Nancy has evidently not had time to prepare. Finally, I get a locksmith to install a padlock on the front door of the office, along with a sign saying the office is closed and giving my number to call in case of emergency. It's not pretty, but I don't want anyone, including and especially Lucy's problematical new employees, to get in and make any more messes for me to clean up.

I'm eager to get to the assignment Lucy's given me that morning, most of which I can get done on the computer. It turns out my brain is naturally wired to navigate cyberspace. I don't work cookbook-style. I like to explore possibilities, use trial and error, and think a few steps ahead of the other guy.

I find myself rubbing my hands together in anticipation of today's tasks, and smile as I think how Lucy does the same thing, rubs her hands or licks her lips, when presented with a tricky legal puzzle. Just as I'm back at my own office and sitting at my desk, I'm interrupted by a call.

"Claude, Sandy's mad at me, and I don't have time to hold her hand.... ...had to hang up on her... says her doctor told her to move her books to my house... incompetent fraud...

vindictive.... This investigation is going nowhere... Armando doesn't appreciate what I've done for him. Now he and his friend are cleared, he just wants me out of here so he can go back to his partying....

"Interesting class phenomenon, the butlers' cool and controlled demeanor under interrogation, while privileged guests nervous and vulnerable... role reversal.... little progress... have one idea.... Why can't I make Sandy understand the illogic of her behavior? Accumulation... lack of space... unchecked... disgusting... only a matter of time before my home, too, would become uninhabitable.... Doesn't it seem simple, to you? .... She has a PhD, for God's sake...."

As she starts to wind down, I say, "Where's your sister at?"

"Well, she was at home when I talked to her a couple hours ago. She's supposed to go to her program this morning. What time is it now, around eleven? No, it's an hour earlier where you are. She had time to make it. What if she's still bringing her stuff into my home? I can't allow it. Can you get her to take it away? If I lock her out, where will she go? Can you go talk to her?"

"I'm on it, Luce. Don't worry about Sandy. Just get this case solved so you can come home."

She finally relaxes. Before signing off, she tells me about her Honduran "consultant," an associate of the major cartel client she got released from prison last week. He's helping her understand the "cultural context" of the charges against her Honduran client. Maybe she'll visit Honduras some day, she says, to enjoy the rich and fascinating culture under more favorable circumstances. After I hang up, I think about this for about ten seconds. Then, I open up my notes on what Lucy wants me to investigate.

The list has eight names, with dates of birth, passport numbers, and states of residence, and some have special instructions attached. Seven of them are Armando's happy cruise mates, except they might not be too happy now seeing how they're suspects in a murder investigation. The eighth name is someone who's definitely not happy. Or maybe he is, but God only knows. It's Blake Copland, the murder victim.

Lucy wants background checks on everyone, and then has some more detailed questions on three of them.

Kidlat Cruz (a.k.a. Evans) is a common name, apparently, in the Philippines, but a man with that name and birthdate was deported from the United States five years earlier after being convicted of prostitution in Las Vegas, Nevada.

Robert Barron, from Cleveland, Ohio, yields only a website advertising modeling services. The site was last updated four years earlier, and I note that other than the home page, the linked pages are sketchy, like a project that never quite got off the ground. I wonder why it didn't, 'cause this dude is highly photogenic in the Western standard of classic beauty, and knows how to flirt with the camera. The cover page describes him as "a tall blond Adonis who can also be the 'boy next door.'" There are four fashion photos in different styles, with the locations superimposed: "Ohio Farm," "London," "Vegas," and "Manhattan."

Nikolaus Kronos is a common name also, but with his details I get a blank. That could be, in part, because he's a citizen and resident of Greece. I do find him listed as "Concierge Cruise Director" on the Jamboree Cruises website. I look at the picture of him in his white uniform and hat. There's a big square smile on his face but none in his eyes. I pity whoever has to work for him.

Daniel James Griffin, now age nineteen, was arrested for shoplifting in Los Angeles, California, when he was eighteen. The charges were dismissed a month later.

Next, I look at the victim, the Honorable Blake Copland, son of the Earl of Bath. I find no criminal or other records in the US, but he's gotten a lot of press and there's a bio on Wikipedia. British papers have reported his recent death as a shipboard accident, details pending. I skim through a few of the older news articles looking for anything Lucy might need to know. High society, expensive cars, yachts, art collection, extravagant parties, numerous arrests for "drink driving," and a few vague references to his family using influence to kill embarrassing stories about his "unconventional" romantic life and sketchy business ventures. He has a younger brother who, along with the father, runs the family business empire, and a younger sister, unmarried, active in society and charitable causes. His home is listed as London, England, although he owned residences in Southern France, Aruba, and San Francisco, California. It'll take some time to find out who inherits his fortune, especially as the family finances are a tangle of corporations and other business entities, entails, and trusts.

The remaining subjects are Rick Collins, Scott Barnes, and Dan Leone. Since we're in a time crunch and Lucy has some detailed questions on each of them, I delegate two of them to Tom, my teenaged consultant, a reformed hacker who's taught me a lot of my cyber skills. He tells me he'll have a report for me by the end of the day. One of the suspects, who looks the most promising, I keep for myself.

The next thing I know, it's after two o'clock. Lucy doesn't pick up her phone, so I send her a detailed email. Now I'm glad she's got a bodyguard, because at least one of her suspects appears to be a really bad dude.

I break for lunch at my go-to sushi place, just around the corner from my office. After a morning of intense brain work, it feels fine to enjoy my meal, slowly and mindfully. I eat in silence and then shoot the breeze with Haru, the sushi chef who also happens to be one of my classmates at the aikido class I take on Friday afternoons.

When I get up to go, I tell Haru, "Gotta go check on my friend's house. See you this afternoon in class."

"Better hurry," he says. "It's three-thirty. Class in half an hour."

"Awwww. I lost track of time."

"Go see your friend's house after," he suggests.

"Can't. Got a meetin' tonight, and then work. Dang. I hate to miss class."

"Choose class. House okay, house not like child or sick person or helpless animal. No worry."

I am tempted. Of course, it really is a sick person I'd promised to check on. I'd sort of promised Lucy to try to prevent Sandy from moving any more of her shit into Lucy's home. At heart, it was really a promise to check up on Sandy's welfare. Or is it? I know Sandy isn't in any danger. I also know Lucy's idea that I could talk some sense into her, or get her to clear her crap out of Lucy's home, is a non-starter. Lucy's dogs are being fed and walked by a neighbor, so they are safe and cared for. I said I'd handle Sandy so Lucy could focus on her work. What had I meant by that promise? And, was what I meant the same as what Lucy had understood me to be promising? By which side of the promise am I bound?

I decide I don't have to go to Luce's house. I luck out and reach Sandy on her cell.

"Oh, Claude! I'm so upset. Lucy hung up on me this morning; did she tell you? My therapist is helping me process the hurt. Did she ask you to apologize for her?"

"Sure, Sandy. Consider the apology made."

"Oh, thank you, Claude. Tell Lucy I forgive her. My therapist says that's important. Tell her I'm doing fine. Going to straighten up the house tonight."

"Of course you are. Good girl."

I get to aikido only five minutes late. I enter the room quietly, kneel on the edge of the mat and bow, and join the warm-ups.

After class I go straight back to my office. My email shows a message from Tom. Before I can open it, my phone rings.

"Oh, Claude, we're so glad you picked up. I'm Erica, Lucy Sanders's neighbor? Lucy gave us your number as an emergency contact. My husband and I just got back to her house after walking her dogs, and found her sister Sandy. She's in a...a situation."

The sound of dogs barking comes over the line. Then I hear the familiar soft whine Lucy's older poodle, Thurgood, lets out on the infrequent occasions when he's real dissatisfied with something.

The neighbor's husband, Carl, is waiting for me in front of the side gate that leads to the backyard. He's an elderly dude with a long scholarly face. One of his legs is bent at an odd angle, and he's resting his weight on a metal cane. We walk together, slowly on account of his lame leg, through the open side gate and along the side of the house to the backyard. Erica, a regal woman with thick grey hair styled high on her head, is seated in a patio chair she's moved next to the back door. She appears quite a bit younger than her husband, and her arms and legs are crossed in an attitude suggesting boredom or impatience. The dogs' leashes are wrapped around her left wrist and gripped tightly in one hand.

Thurgood and Ruth start wagging their tails and pulling at their leashes to get to me. I walk over to them and give them their favorite back scratch.

"Good dogs," I say. "Let's see what's goin' on with your aunt Sandy."

"Claude? Is that you?"

The bottom half of Sandy Sanders is protruding from the dog door, which is cut into the bottom of the back door of Lucy's house. She's on her knees, and her backside is wedged halfway through the opening, straining at the seams of her plum-colored velour sweatpants, of which her sister owns an identical pair. Sandy is more thickly built, her legs forming a straight, column-like line down from her hips while Lucy's legs curve in towards her knees and then curve out again at her calves....

"Claude! Don't let them call an ambulance. Just get me out of here."

"All right," I say. "Hold your arms over your head. I'm gonna pull you towards me, bring you back outside."

"I can't do that, Claude. I'm holding my shopping bags."

"Right. Let go of the bags, Sandy."

"No, that won't work. Hold my legs and push me inside, okay?" She straightens her legs out, pointing the toes of her sneakers and positioning herself like a rocket, like she's gonna launch through the door.

"Girl, there's no way your hips will go through this space," I say. "We gotta get you out the way you got yourself in."

"I can't. I can't let go of my bags. It's my important stuff, Claude. From the store."

"So you let go of the bags, leave them in the house, then we get you out, open the door, and you'll be reunited with your stuff."

"No. It's part of me. I can't let go of it."

Ah. I turn away from her and find myself staring straight into the spark in the eyes of Erica, who's seated herself back down in the patio chair behind me. Her hubby has taken a load off, and is sitting at the patio table, leaning forward on his cane and staring at the scene with gentle curiosity.

"She doesn't want to let go of her shopping bags," Erica explains.

"Got it," I say.

Three hours later, after some emergency phone negotiation with Sandy's psychologist and a long wait at the hospital emergency room, I feel like I've been carrying around a fifty-pound rock. I've been unable to reach Lucy. At least I've kept my promise to her. Her sister is as safe as she can be, and from the psych ward at least she won't be able move any more of her possessions into Lucy's house. I just hope, before she went out to sea and out of service, that Lucy got my email about Dan Leone.

24

Armando

Friday on the Adonis, Cozumel

Evans stepped into the Dans' cabin, and I looked over his shoulder. On the bed there was one body, slender and unmoving, covered by a sheet except the top of his head.

"Dan-Dan!" I cried.

Dan-Dan turned over and gave a low groan.

Evans and Barron rushed to the bedside. Evans said, "Are you all right, sir?"

Dan-Dan sat up slowly. "What's wrong? Where's Dan? Where are we?"

"Docked in Cozumel, sir. You've slept very late."

"I'm...sleepy. Cozumel? We'll miss the cooking class. Why didn't Dan wake me up? Where is he?"

"Shit!" I said, looking at Evans and Barron. "How did Dan get away? Lucy's going to kill me."

Barron said, "Evans, check downstairs to see if Mr. Dan's on the disembarkation list. I'd better report this to Kronos."

"What can I do?" said Slim.

"Um, you'd better go down to the brig and get Lucy and Kenny, if they're still there," I told him.

Dan-Dan pulled off the sheet and sat on the edge of his bed.

"Dan wouldn't go to the cooking class without me," he said. "I don't know why I was so sleepy."

"Let me help you get dressed," I said. "I'm sure Dan will be back soon, and ready to go to your class. While we're waiting, you can come talk to Attorney Sanders. She's a very interesting person, and kind of a celebrity in her own way."

He looked down at his smooth all-over-tanned body and looked back up at me with a faint grin.

"Guys don't usually ask me to put my clothes back on," he said. "What's your hurry?"

The faint darkening on his unshaved chin, gave a rough touch to his girly cuteness. His sleep-swollen eyes looked odd, and I realized the pupils were like small black pinpoints in irises of hazel green. He put his hand on my crotch, and I looked down to see the signs of arousal coming up on his body.

"Um, this isn't exactly the time," I began.

I felt a machine-like grip on my shoulder, and turned to see Kenny standing behind me. He spoke to me in rapid Spanish.

"What the fuck are you doing, *maricón*? The boss is in her cabin, waiting. She just received a report from her investigator with important information. It's essential she see this witness, Señor Dan Leone, at once."

"Well, Kenny, didn't Slim tell you? We can't find Señor Dan Leone. He wasn't in his room when his partner woke up. The staff are searching for him now."

Dan-Dan grabbed my arm. "What's he saying, Armando? Does he know where Dan is?"

"No."

"If I may, sir," Barron said, appearing behind Kenny. "We are going to search for Mr. Dan. Is there any place he might have gone this morning?"

"The gym, maybe?" Dan-Dan said. "Yesterday he was saying he needed some exercise, after all this eating and drinking. He might have gone for a workout while I was sleeping in."

"Good idea, sir. We'll check the gym and the running track. Anywhere else?"

"He loves the view from the Tiki Lounge. He might've gone there for a drink."

"I'll go right now. Unless you want help dressing, sir?"

Dan-Dan's eyes rounded as he stared in turn at each of us: Barron, calm and gorgeous in his morning outfit of white spandex shorts and short apron; me, smiling involuntarily at Barron's echoing my own earlier offer of help; and Kenny, muscle bound and impassive. His face flushed red, and he pulled the sheet over his body.

"No! Just find Dan."

Kenny steered me towards Lucy's cabin. As we walked into the sun and crossed the deck towards the port side of the Tower, Evans came running towards us from the butlers' quarters.

"Has Mr. Dan come back?" he asked, panting slightly.

"Not yet," I said. "Barron went to look for him at the gym. Did he leave the ship?"

"No, there's no record of him leaving the ship this morning. If he disembarked, he didn't follow procedures," Evans said. There was a line between his eyes, creasing his smooth forehead as he looked up like he was expecting something from me.

"What is it, Evans?"

"Sir, I'm not sure I should tell you this."

"Tell me what? Is it about Dan?"

He nodded.

Kenny elbowed my arm and jerked his head towards Lucy's cabin.

"All right. Come on, Evans. Let's all go talk to Lucy," I said. "She'll know what to do."

"Armando, finally!" Lucy was seated facing the door, her blue eyes blazing with impatience. "Where's Mr. Leone?"

"He's not in the Tower. They're looking for him."

"Well, I need to talk to him. Let me tell you what Claude found out. Dan Leone has been engaging in some serious criminal activities to fund his recent business expansions."

I remembered the look on Dan's face when Blake made his late entrance to join the Epitome Tower group on the *Adonis.*

"Okay," I said. "Is there any evidence Blake had proof of what Dan was doing? Or did he just make a lucky guess?"

"Claude's looking into that. It's tricky, because he's trying to find out whether Blake's family owns any of the banks or other companies involved in Dan's transactions. That's often hard to trace...shell companies...sophistication.... Dan has mob connections on his father's side of the family, and there was a suspicious and deadly fire on one of the family's commercial properties a few years ago. Of course, if Claude found all this after a couple hours of research, Blake could've hired an investigator to do the same thing."

At the mention of Claude's name, Kenny made a sound like a growl. Lucy directed her blue gaze at him. When their eyes met, he took a step backwards, towards the door of his bedroom, but then stood his ground. What were they...?

"Sir?"

"Oh, Evans! Sorry, I forgot you were here." Evans was standing quietly behind me. "Lucy, Evans wants to tell us something about Dan."

Lucy fixed her eyes on him. "Yes, Evans?"

"I didn't want to say anything in front of Dan-D... Mr. Dan-Dan. Mr. Dan sometimes likes to go cruising on Deck Three. Mr. Dan-Dan doesn't know about it. Mr. Dan may have slipped off while Mr. Dan-Dan was asleep."

"Ah. But wouldn't he have been back here by now?"

Evans shrugged. "People lose track of time."

"True. Let's hope he's still there, working off his stress, and that he hasn't jumped ship. Armando, go with Mr. Evans and get Dan. Don't let him get away. You'd better take Kenny with you."

Kenny and I followed Evans down to Deck Nine and crossed the deck to another elevator that took us to Level Seven. From there, we walked along the patio of the Tropicana, covered with cane chairs, Hawaiian print pillows, and palapas shading hot guys sipping giant translucent orange-pink Mai-Tais. As we reached another bank of elevators, I almost bumped into Evans as he stopped in front of me. He gave me the same questioning look as earlier.

"What is it?" I asked.

"Well, sir, there are two ways to go from here. I'm not sure which one Mr. Dan would have taken. Most likely it's this way," he pointed at the elevators in front of us, "but there is a back way that's a little faster."

"We don't want to miss him," I said. "You and Kenny go ahead, and I'll take the back way."

Evans put his hands on his hips and frowned. "I'm not sure. Your boss told us to go together."

"I'll be fine. I can handle Dan, if I find him."

Evans's laughter came out in a sort of yelp. "You have no idea," he said.

"Oh, yeah? What don't I know?"

"Sorry, Mr. Armando. It's nothing. Yes, you can take the shorter way very easily. You see that door over there? It leads to a short spiral staircase. When you get to the bottom, there's a hallway. Turn left and just walk along the hallway. It's kind of a long walk, but just keep going. You'll go past a door on your right, marked 'Engine room.' There's a door right after it that takes you to another short set of stairs, and when you get down them you'll be in a big hallway. That's the cruising area. We'll meet you there."

I opened the narrow door he'd pointed to and went in.

I was in a cylinder on a well-lit spiral staircase. Someone had spray painted in tagger-style writing on the wall facing me:

"Cruisers This Way," with an arrow pointing down the staircase. It was like I'd left the *Adonis* and had ducked into an old warehouse in an inner city. A few steps down, on the wall facing the other way, there were some crudely drawn pornographic images in red spray paint.

The first staircase was short, and I reached the bottom in a few seconds. Someone had painted another red arrow, this one pointing left. The hallway was long, windowless, and dim. Every few yards I had to step through small oval doorways that I guessed could be shut off if there were a flood or something. I shivered, and my footsteps echoed as I walked quickly ahead.

Why was Lucy so desperate to find Dan? She was afraid he'd jumped ship. Even if Blake found out Dan was involved in some iffy property transaction, that wouldn't be enough of a motive for Dan to kill Blake. Dan was a solid, enterprising guy. Even if he did get busted for some shady dealing, he would just build his business back up again. He disliked Blake, but he wasn't afraid of him. It would have to be someone really unstable, like Rick, or someone with more at stake, someone at risk of losing everything. Right?

But scenes flashed into my mind: Dan and Dan-Dan, giggling together and juggling bags of purchases on their way back to the boat from a day of shopping; Dan's expression as he watched Dan-Dan laughing and dancing on the side of the deck during our long wait for Blake's dinner party. Would Dan-Dan stick with Dan if money got tight? I saw again Dan's frown, and his clenched fist knocking over his coffee when he saw Blake arriving on the *Adonis*. And then Scott, running out onto the pool deck with a look of alarm on his face, telling me his knife was missing. Evans saying, "You have no idea." I liked Dan, but how well did I know him?

My footsteps beat an echoing rhythm as I sped up. I felt like I'd walked the whole length of the ship already. So how much further could it be? Allowing for the curve of the ship, I'd been going pretty much straight. Hadn't I? Had I missed the door out? I broke into a slow jog, focusing on the wall to my right for the doorway. I saw no doorways. What I'd thought was the echoing of my footsteps now made a syncopated beat, like someone was following me.

A grinding, growling sound started to come from all around me. I thought I saw a shadow moving across one of the oval doorways ahead of me. Should I turn around? Where was the fastest way out? Just as I was considering going back, I saw another red arrow on the wall, pointing ahead. Maybe I was almost there. I stopped and strained my ears for the sound of footsteps other than my own. But the growling had gotten louder, preventing me from knowing whether I had company in this dim endless hallway.

I took a deep breath and kept my head. This growling sound must mean I was getting closer to the Engine Room, which Evans had said I would pass on the way out. Maybe it hadn't been footsteps I'd heard, but the sound of the *Adonis's* giant engine. I started walking again. A few seconds later, I saw the door on my right marked "Engine Room," the source of the now-painful roar of sound. I put my hands over my ears and moved on.

A few yards past the Engine Room door was another door. On it was a brass plate that read "Stair to Level 3," and just below the plate another red graffiti arrow, bigger than the others, pointed straight down. I put my hand on the brass doorknob and started to open it. As I pulled the door towards me, I felt a hand on my shoulder.

I screamed, used my free hand to shove away the person behind me, and rushed through the open door. I slammed the door and ran down a spiral staircase like the one I'd started on. At the bottom of the staircase was a door, which I opened and went through, without looking back to see if my attacker was following me. Leaning against the closed door for a moment, I looked both ways. There was no sign of Evans and Kenny. I was in a long wide hallway, with small portholes on the outer side showing a blurry view of blue that could be sea or sky, dimmed by glass that was scuffed and yellowed with age. About twenty yards ahead to my left, the hallway opened onto bright sunlight. I could see the outlines of an outdoor walkway continuing towards the back of the ship. I ran towards the light.

There was no one in sight at this low spot on the far end of the ship. From here, I'd have a long head start if someone came out of the tunnel after me. Also, I'd able to see Evans and Kenny when they got here and I could tell them Dan wasn't here and we could go back to the Epitome Tower together.

I finally felt safe in the open space, with the sunlight and the sea around me. After the shabbiness of the cruising hallway, I expected this lower deck to be less well kept. But, like the upper decks, it was all like-new white paint, shellacked wood plank floors, and shining brass deck rails. Then, I saw a piece of rope knotted to the bottom railing. Some kind of ladder? I walked over to see where it went.

***

I came to lying on the floor of the deck. The smooth face of Evans, curious more than concerned, blurred and then came in to focus. A foot kicked my hip, and I heard Kenny's voice grunting, "*Levántate, pendejo!* Get up! Let's go, there's nobody here."

"Evans, the rope!" I pointed towards what I'd seen.

The two men moved to the deck's edge. Kenny started to swear in Spanish, and half a second later, Evans gave a high shriek.

"Pull him up! Help me with the rope," Evans said.

"No!" said Kenny. "*Madre de Dios,* you're pulling his head off! Stop. I go down."

I imagined Scott saying to Rick, "That would be Deck Two to you, brother," but it sounded threatening and not at all funny. The bright, almost blinding sunlight was everywhere:

from the midday sun above, reflecting up off the water, radiating off the glossy deck to burn my hands and knees.

Kenny pulled his muscle-bound frame over the rail. He half climbed, half slid down a pole that led to the lower deck, swearing when the friction of the metal tore the flesh of his palms.

Even from the direct aerial view, the second I'd seen it, I'd known it was Dan. From above, before I passed out, I had seen just the thinning area on top of Dan's head, the garish fabric of one of his Hawaiian shirts tightened over the tops of his shoulders and flapping out over his belly, and the tips of his bare feet, thick and tufted with dark hair. His unique energy, passionate and heavy and funny, still radiated from his hanging body.

Kenny put his arms around the waist of the body and lifted it, loosening the noose enough to allow Evans to lean over the edge and remove it from around Dan's neck. Evans tossed the noose on the deck next to me and climbed gracefully down the pole to join Kenny on the lower deck.

Kenny had lowered Dan's body to the ground. Dan's eyes were open and staring up at the sky like he was looking a thousand miles away. The bright sun revealed purple blotches discoloring the skin of his face and chest, and the skin on his legs was tinted pale blue.

Kenny was doing something with his hand in Dan's mouth.

"Is he still alive?" Evans asked.

Kenny tilted Dan's head back, and started administering hard chest compressions. After less than a minute, he shook his head.

"I think dead," he said. "You check, too."

Evans put his hand on Dan's wrist, and then on his neck. "No pulse, and his body's already cold. He's dead, sir."

25
Lucy
Prime Suspect

After Kenny and Armando left with Evans to search for Dan Leone, I took the opportunity to read Claude's report more carefully. Mr. Leone's illegal activities had been creative and varied. After reading Claude's report, I got online and gave myself a crash course on real estate and lending fraud. Dan had taken out a "liar loan" on one of his resort properties, misrepresenting the net income generated by his business and providing inflated appraisals of his other properties. He'd also engaged in "shot-gunning," getting multiple loans on his new property from different lenders at the same time.

We now had a solid suspect. I looked forward to interviewing him. Even if Dan didn't actually confess, I could turn over a strong report to the cruise line, which should be enough to get my client released.

Armando clearly liked Dan. If anything, that fact militated in favor of Dan being Blake's killer. True, I rely on Armando's observations of witnesses in our day-to-day work. But I've learned to keep in mind how easily my assistant is influenced by the most superficial of qualities. He'll develop quite unprofessional affections for witnesses and suspects. His criteria are: good looks, expensive outfits and accessories, and, most of all, the ability to give flattering attention to one Armando Felan. As a con man, Dan probably had Armando's number the moment they met.

Furthermore, Armando's mental and emotional state appeared to have deteriorated since he'd booked this cruise.

The week before he left, he'd been too excited about the trip to do much work at all. More than once, I'd come out of my office to find him with his feet on his desk and his head in a shiny cruise brochure. His hiring and training of Nancy was another case in point. Nancy, while a lovely person, and blessedly knowledgeable about the intricacies of the mental health system in San Diego, was useless as an office assistant. And Armando certainly wasn't blameless in the hiring fiasco that was my new attorney, the Nyquil-addicted Arnold Snyder. True, I'd reviewed the resumés and interviewed the candidates myself, but he'd put the ads in. Then there was his mishandling of my poor sister....

I felt a sharp stab of pain in my ankle, and put my hand down to feel for swelling. It felt the same as it had for the last couple of days, not at all swollen. Why did it suddenly start to hurt for no reason? I went back to my thinking.

Now, finally living out his dream on the good ship *Adonis*, Armando was in a very odd state. I could only describe it as a combination of hypersexuality, manic sociability, and a bizarre sluggishness. Was he sex-drugged? What could I do to get him back on track? His ex-boyfriend Justin had been an excellent influence on him. Possibly I could find a way to nudge them back together. Then, I'd just have to help Sandy get *her* act together....

A wave of pain washed over my ankle, and I almost cried out. I wished Kenny were back to get me an ice pack. I stood up to hobble over to the little fridge to get one, when I heard the key turning in the lock, and Kenny walked in.

He looked especially dangerous, his breath coming fast and his dark eyes flashing. Our eyes met. Oh. What I needed, what I really wanted, was--.

I looked towards my bedroom, with its sun-splashed, fresh white counterpane made tight across the king-sized bed. A breeze stirred the sheer white curtains. The oversized porthole was a two-toned painting of turquoise water and pale blue sky.

Looking back into Kenny's eyes, I saw he was thinking along the same lines. But instead of coming to me, he spoke.

"The man you ask me to bring is dead." Kenny looked sorry, like he'd failed somehow in his mission on my behalf.

"Dan Leone is dead?"

"He...." Kenny made a gesture, lifting his fist over his head and tilting his head to his side. "He hunged? Hank?"

"He hanged himself?"

"*Sí.* Yes."

"Oh, my." I sank back down into my chair.

"Is better this way? He killer, yes?"

"Yes. I suppose so."

The pieces of the puzzle had come together nicely, if rather abruptly. Blake's scheme to lure elite cruisers on board so he could torment them, Dan Leone's criminal activities that would ruin his business and could send him to prison if revealed, and now Dan's suicide as he must have known we were close to discovering his motive for killing Blake.

Kenny smiled, bolted the door to our cabin, and gestured towards my bedroom.

"Yes," I said. "Let's...."

There was a loud knock on the cabin door. Kenny swore and unlocked it, admitting Mr. Kronos and two of his assistants.

Kronos walked up to where I was sitting and shook my hand.

"Congratulations on resolution of your investigation. Very sad for poor Mr. Leone, of course."

"Of course. But I can't take any credit. I didn't even get a chance to interview the man. I suppose there's no question he, ah, did this himself?"

"We have no reason to question that, Ms. Sanders. He cut a length of rope off of the rigging for the shade cloths on the pool deck. The knife he used to cut the rope was in the pocket of his shorts. Evans tells me you learned Mr. Blake Copland discovered Mr. Leone was stealing money from banks. Very serious. So he killed Mr. Copland. Excellent work."

"I didn't exactly...."

"You are a genius, madam. You will write your report now, and then I will release your client from the brig. Tonight you will have a five-star quality dinner at Captain's table. Jamboree Cruise Lines is very grateful."

"Well, I suppose I can do that. I'm rather exhausted after all my hard work. I'll take a short rest. Then, my assistant will help me put together the report. Please tell Mr. Felan to come to my cabin in one hour." I met Kenny's eyes. "Make that an hour and a half," I said.

"Very well, madam. I'll let him know. He should be fully recovered by then."

"Recovered? Was Armando injured?"

"Oh, no, madam. He stayed to watch over Mr. Dan Leone's body while Mr. Evans came to inform me. I believe the incident was, ah, upsetting to Mr. Armando." Mr. Kronos's tone was neutral. His eyes signaled contempt. "Mr. Armando was sick. He's lying down in his room."

26

Armando

Report

Evans said he would return to Deck Seven and notify Mr. Kronos and the ship's medics. Kenny insisted on leaving with him to tell Lucy. When they told me I was going to be left alone to guard the body, I said I wouldn't fucking stay there another second, and demanded they take me with them.

But they were already gone, sprinting, and my legs were too shaky to run after them. My stomach heaved. I knelt, and threw up. The sudden spasm drove the top of my head hard into one of the metal rails, and left a hideous cascade of puke along the wall below me, not far from the rope that was still tied to the rail, the noose coiled now like a snake on the deck next to me. After the retching stopped, I sat back on my knees, away from the rail. I took deep breaths and looked out at the horizon.

Before leaving, Kenny had instructed me to keep my eyes on the body and not let anything happen to it. He was like a dog who'd caught a rabbit and was determined to bring it to his master intact. Was he going to bring Lucy all the way down here to view it? I moved away from the pool of my own vomit, and sat with my legs hanging over the deck. How was I going to watch over Dan's corpse without looking at it?

"Armando?"

I turned to see, backlit like a vision, the shining blonde figure of Barron.

"Hey. How'd you get here so fast?" I asked him.

"I'm sorry I startled you back there by the Engine Room," he said. "I just ran into Evans, and he told me what happened. I'm so sorry, Armando. Where is the...?"

I gestured to the deck below us. "I'm supposed to be watching him. But I can't look at him. It's too upsetting. It freaked me out when you came after me, Barron. And then I found Dan.... Why were you following me?"

Barron turned away from me to look over the deck railing. He stayed looking down at Dan as he slowly spoke to me. "My apologies, Armando. I wasn't... following you. I happened to be in the Engine Room. Mary thought she'd left her sunglasses there, so I went to look for them. When I came out, I saw you in the hallway. Somehow, I didn't think you'd come down for the, ah, cruising, so I thought you might be lost."

He turned back to me then, his beautiful face a mask of tragedy. "Poor Mr. Dan. And you. You shouldn't have had to find him. Why don't you lie down?" He moved gracefully to the wall behind him and pulled off a life preserver. "Rest your head on this." Then he took off his small apron and put it over my eyes. "This will shade your eyes from the sun."

I opened my eyes a few minutes later, when Evans returned with a group that included Kronos himself, and various medics and minions. Barron somehow got me back to the Epitome Tower, into the shower, and into bed with a hot cup of herbal tea.

As I lay in bed, I kept seeing the back of Dan's thick iron-grey hair, with the edges of his bright Hawaiian shirt floating out beneath it like the wavering body of a jellyfish. I remembered how his masculinity had seemed even more pronounced when he'd worn heavy makeup and that red feather boa, the night of Blake's Epitome Tower dinner. Dan, Dan-Dan, and Mary in their full drag, the trays of sunset-colored Beachside Bonfires, Blake playing on his rope swing and then talking to me about the stars and the constellations, the butlers discreetly putting finishing touches on the shining silver-and-china table settings, Slim wearing his pearls and Guatemalan pants and dancing to Pit Bull.... I turned my head towards the wall, curled up into a ball, and slept.

An hour later, I awakened to find Barron slipping into my cabin with his usual perfect timing.

"Where is everybody, Barron?"

"Mr. Dan-Dan is resting in his cabin. The rest of your friends are still ashore for the day."

"At least they're getting in another day of fun, before they find out about Dan."

"Yes. It's the last day ashore. Tomorrow is a day at sea, and the next morning we arrive in Miami. I'm sorry you missed Cozumel, Armando. I'm sorry this cruise has been so... difficult."

"Why should you be sorry? Anyway, I guess it's a lot worse for poor Dan-Dan. Do you think I should go see if he wants company?"

"I'd wait on that, Armando. He's been sedated, I believe. And you don't have much time. Mr. Kronos told me Attorney Sanders wants to see you as soon as she's finished with her nap. That will be in about twenty minutes."

"Oh. Right. She's still here. I thought.... I don't know what I thought. She could have gotten off the boat and flown home, since her investigation is pretty much over."

"She certainly could." Barron adjusted the curtain over the porthole, blocking off a sliver of blinding sunlight that had crept across my chest. "There are a lot of flights out of Cozumel."

Half an hour later I heard the metal-on-metal of a sliding bolt, and Kenny opened the door a crack before letting me in to Lucy's cabin. I was struck again by its size and luxury. My *jefa* sipped a martini and scrolled through the iPad that was placed on a pillow on her lap. There was an ice pack in a towel on the footrest in front of her, but her slippered feet were resting on the floor, neatly crossed at the ankles. She wore a fluffy white terry-cloth robe. I saw no sign of packed luggage in the room. She looked up at me with eyes the same color as the sea that filled the bottom half of the oversized porthole behind her.

"Are you feeling better, Armando?"

"What do you mean? I'm totally fine. What did they tell you?"

"Relax. I'm certainly not in a position to criticize anyone's reaction to finding a dead body. That last case of ours...." She shuddered. "Well. It appears our investigation has resolved itself. Jamboree Cruises wants me to write up the information I found about Dan Leone."

"So it was Dan who killed Blake?" I asked.

"It appears so."

We'd better get on it," I said. "The *Adonis* leaves the dock soon. You'll need some time to get packed to catch a flight."

"No. I'll be staying on the boat until we reach Miami on Sunday. The Captain has invited me to dine with him tonight, and it would really be rude to refuse. It's comfortable enough here. And it's Friday-- my work week is over."

"Okay." I picked up her briefcase and took out the laptop. "Have they let Carlos out of the brig yet?"

"He's still locked up. They want my signed report first. I'm not going to fight them over that. We'll get him out soon enough."

It ended up taking a long time to complete the report to Lucy's satisfaction. She insisted on including unnecessary and exhaustive explanations of Dan's financial misdeeds, complete with citations to the laws he had violated.

By the time I got out of Lucy's cabin, bleary-eyed from staring at the computer screen and head-achy from jumping to her orders, the sun was lowering in the sky. The white midday light was diffusing into unnameable colors that embraced you and gave you the golden promise of a warm sultry evening. The horror of Dan's death and the thought of how Dan-Dan must be suffering seemed like part of an alternate reality. Yet that dark alternate reality carried with it a relief. The investigation, the mystery of Blake's murder, the accusation against Carlos, were over.

Cruisers were lining up to get back on the *Adonis* after the day in Cozumel. I was leaning over the rail facing the dock, checking out the crowd and looking for what remained of my Tribe, when I felt a familiar hand on my shoulder.

"Slim-ster!"

"Hey, 'Mando."

I could tell from his hug and his voice and his expression he'd heard the news about Dan. We talked for a few minutes about what had happened. Dan had left Dan-Dan sleeping in their cabin early this morning, probably just after dawn, unseen by the butlers. He'd had a Swiss Army knife in his pocket, probably the one Scott had reported missing, and the knife had fragments of rope on it. Dan had cut a length of rope from the rigging above the platform, gone down to Level Three, and hanged himself.

"He shouldn't have done it," Slim said. "Blake wasn't worth it. If Dan really broke the law, he should've just gotten a lawyer and faced the music. He would've come through it okay."

"Some guys define themselves by their financial status," I said. "He probably couldn't stand the thought of losing that. Dan cracked under the pressure. Blake picked the wrong guy to jerk around."

"Poor Dan-Dan," said Slim. "What about my twin, Carlos? Is he out yet?"

"Yeah, Kronos brought him to Lucy's cabin. She insisted on Carlos being released before she'd hand over her report. They're making him work tonight, I told him we'd go see him after his shift."

Slim and I put on our swimsuits and went into the pool. The rest of our now-seven-member Tribe trickled back up to the Tower from their various Cozumel outings. Kronos's minions had met them at the dock to tell them the news, and they all arrived with expressions of shock. When Scott arrived, they'd taken him to Kronos's office to show him the knife that had been found in Dan's pocket, and he'd identified it as his own Swiss Army knife.

"Dan must have taken it from my room the day before he killed Blake," said Scott. Out of all of us, he'd seemed the most shocked by Dan's death. "I was with Blake onshore all day. Dan probably found the knife on my dresser. I've had that knife since I was a kid. I wish I'd taken it onshore with me. Maybe none of this would've happened."

"I doubt that," said Rodrigo. "From what Armando told us about Dan's financial crimes, Dan must have been pretty desperate. He would've found a way to stop Blake."

"You look tired, 'Mando," Slim said, after a break in our discussion of the day's events. "Are you going to be up for the Lucky Charm party tonight? Do you think it would be, like, heartless to go? What if we take turns staying with Dan-Dan, so he feels supported?"

"I don't know," I said. "I'm kind of torn."

"Why is this even a question?" Rick said. "Two of our friends are dead. Optics aside, it's just morally wrong for us to go out partying at a time like this."

"Worrying about 'optics,' Rick, is the definition of hypocrisy," Scott said. "I'll go out if I want to." His face was pale and his clothes even more rumpled than usual.

"If Dan-Dan wants company," Rodrigo said, "I'll stay here with him. But I don't see any other reason to change plans when there's nothing we can do for Blake or Dan now." He was tanned and glowing, and sore from his day of extreme zip-lining with his new friend Marko.

"I miss Dan. It's hard to believe he did this." Mary's reddish hair, backlit by the setting sun, looked like golden thread surrounding her face. Even in the shadow of the backlight, you could see her eyes were rimmed red from crying. Barron, who had been hovering nearby, started to put out his arm to comfort her, before he remembered his place and retracted it. But Mary, sensing him behind her, reached back and took his hand, holding it against her cheek.

Our group was silent while we all watched them. Mary's simple gesture felt complicated and significant. Evans gave a muffled gasp, and his face took on an expression of defiant amusement. Rodrigo looked at me and grinned.

"You miss Dan? The murderer?" Rick was saying, oblivious to the shifting vibe. "What about Blake? Blake didn't deserve to be killed. He wasn't perfect, but he loved life and he was a generous person. Aren't any of you grateful for that incredible dinner he gave us? Do you have any idea what that cost?"

"Get real. Blake was a cruel bastard who got what he deserved," Rodrigo said. "He used his money to manipulate people for his own desires. I'm sorry about Dan, but he made his choices, too."

Slim touched the gold cross around his neck. "I'm gonna keep praying for both of them. They're in God's hands now, not ours."

Scott stood up and came to put an arm on Slim's shoulder. "You're a good guy, Slim. I'm glad your friend, what's his name? Carlos. I'm glad he's off the hook now. I'm gonna go check on Dan-Dan."

"At least someone here has a heart," said Rick, who stood up to join him. They walked together towards the Dans' cabin. Rick was, I saw now, the kind of person who needed someone to kiss up to. And, with Blake dead, Scott was probably the richest guest in the Tower.

Barron melted off towards the butlers' quarters, and a couple minutes later Mary discreetly made an exit in the same direction.

Slim swam to the far side of the pool, and pulled himself out to sit on the edge. "So, we're going out, right?" he whispered. "Grungy Scott and Orange Tan can stay here with Dan-Dan. Do you think Mary still wants to join us, or is she going to be with...?" He jerked his head towards the butlers' quarters.

"I'll ask her," I said. "I mean, she's part of our charm bracelet costume. It wouldn't be fair for her to bug out on us."

"Yeah, go ask her. We need a few hours to get dressed, especially 'cause of the body paint and everything."

"Okay, Slim-ster." The prospect of the night of partying in our eye-catching costumes brought my spirits up. "I'll go talk to her now. Wanna hit the Ice Bar for an early dinner before we dress?"

"Maybe. If we have time."

I walked towards the butlers' quarters. Barron and Evans were working in the small kitchen. I stood just outside the door, listening for the sound of Mary's voice and not hearing it. Had she gone back to her cabin? I was about to walk away, when there came an unbutlerish, crude-sounding burst of laughter from inside. I moved closer to the door.

"Get out of town, Evans." It was Barron's voice, stripped of his usual courteous veneer. "Our elite guests were really debating whether it was okay to keep partying, with their two friends dead? Well, to be fair, I guess they weren't exactly friends. None of them, except possibly Mr. Rick, even liked the Honorable Blake Copland."

"Hah! Right!" Kronos said in his deep, accented growl. "Mr. Dan, though, that's different. He was just the first in line to off Mr. Copland. The other guests should be grateful. "

"Absolutely!" It was Evans's high, insinuating tone. "Blake was going to nail that stuck-up Mr. Armando any which way he could, and I'm sure he had some business dirt on the others.

For sure, he did on Mr. Rick and Mr. Scott, and maybe more. And some of us staff, we might be grateful, too."

"Including you, Miss-ter Evans," said Kronos.

At almost the same time, Barron said, "Don't go there, Evans. It's over."

"Mr. Dan killed himself just in time," Evans continued. "That scary old lady isn't stupid. She was getting a lotta information."

"I hoped to God she'd be off the ship by now," Barron said. "At least she's wrapped it up. Her report is signed, sealed, and delivered. It's fortunate the gentlemen have the Lucky Charm party tonight, because they're getting on each other's nerves cooped up on this Tower together. At least that poor kid, Carlos, is out of the brig and back to his slave labor."

"And Ms. Lucy Sanders is busy, dining with the Captain tonight. Tomorrow, she and her so-called bodyguard will be busy screwing their brains out all day," said Evans.

"I'll be glad to get this lot of fairies unloaded on Sunday," said Kronos. "I'm tired of watching my back."

"And who might you be dining with tonight, my deah Mis-tah Barron?" It was Evans, in a scarily perfect imitation of Blake. There was another round of coarse laughter, and I slipped away.

27
Lucky Charm

It was almost ten-thirty by the time Mary, Rodrigo, Slim, and I were putting the finishing touches on our charm bracelet costume for the Lucky Charm party. The total costume was so phenomenally epic, in concept and in execution, that I really should describe it. But it would just hurt me too much, because it never even got seen outside of the Epitome Tower.

I was standing next to the door of my cabin, with Rodrigo and Mary at my side, as Slim attached the light plastic chain that would bind us together for at least the early part of the evening.

"This chain really looks like gold," Mary said. "Fantastic job on the costume, Slim."

We were all hooked together and talking about how to make our entrance, when there was a loud rap on the door behind me and the door opened, hitting me in the shoulder and knocking me into Rodrigo. The four of us fell like dominoes and landed together in a heap on my bed.

Mr. Kronos and several minions filled the doorway.

"Yes, this is the rest of them," he said to a minion I hadn't seen before, a tall man who wore what looked like a white doctor's coat over his uniform.

"Good evening, guests," said Kronos. "We regret the interruption. Jamboree Cruises requests your attendance in the Epitome Lounge to discuss a protocol."

I shuddered. The last time he'd mentioned a protocol, I'd ended up in the brig.

"What's this about?" Rodrigo asked, detaching himself from the golden chain.

"We will explain the situation when we join them in the Lounge. The other guests are waiting."

Two of the minions followed behind us like prison guards as we left my room. The man in the white jacket walked ahead with Kronos. As we entered the poolside area on the way to the Lounge, Barron joined us.

Mary, walking next to me, whispered to Barron, "What's happening?"

"They haven't told me," he said in a low voice. "But that man," he nodded his beautiful head towards the white jacket, "he's the ship's doctor."

Rick was sitting next to Scott, at a table at the far side of the Lounge. Rodrigo walked over to join them. Mary stayed by Barron, who took a station near the entrance.

Lucy and her bodyguard Kenny were seated at one of the tables in the center of the room. She looked up at me, brushing back a strand of hair that had escaped her up do. Slim and I stood near Lucy's table. Sitting down right now would ruin critical parts of our body paint.

"Where's Dan-Dan?" Slim's voice went high, a rare sign of stress for him.

Kronos cleared his throat. "I have with me our ship's physician, Dr. Anward. He's going to talk to you about some routine medical precautions we will be instituting."

After a long rambling discussion involving medical terms and statistics and a lot of useless information, Dr. Anward turned us back to Mr. Kronos. Kronos announced crisply that Dan-Dan had something called ILI, Influenza-Like-Illness, and the Epitome Tower had been put under quarantine until twenty-four hours after Dan-Dan's fever was gone. Since tomorrow was the last full day of the cruise, we'd pretty much be in quarantine until the cruise ended.

"The whole b-boat's under quarantine?" Slim asked.

"Oh, no, fortunately not, sir," Kronos said. "Just the Epitome Tower. Our patient has not left the Tower since he developed symptoms. In Dr. Anward's professional judgment, a full quarantine is not indicated."

"Is Dan-Dan going to be okay?" Rodrigo asked.

The doctor adjusted his white coat. "Privacy laws prevent me from discussing his condition. We're testing him for the norovirus, of course, and notification will be given as indicated."

Slim, forgetting his body paint, sank into a chair at Lucy's table. I sat down next to him.

"Poor Dan-Dan," said Mary.

"We regret this unfortunate event," Kronos said. "Our Concierge butlers will make the rest of your voyage as comfortable as possible here in the Epitome Tower. Our precautions do prevent use of the swimming pool and the Jacuzzi. You may, of course, order meals from any of our restaurants here on the *Adonis*."

I looked out the window to the lighted poolside, where Evans was putting covers on our pool and spa.

Kronos left with Dr. Anward and the minions. The rest of us sat in silence. There was none of the nervous shock and excitement that had crackled through this same room when we'd been gathered here after Blake's fall. From the silent room, I could now hear the thump of music and cries of partiers from the decks below.

"I know!" I said. "Let's join the party from up here. We can dance from the balcony. Everyone will see us. We'll be, like, the go-go dancers."

Rodrigo stood up. "I'll pass. I'm going to wash my hands really well, and stay in my cabin. I suggest everyone do the same. Maybe I should take a shower, too. Barron, can you bring us all a bunch of hand sanitizers?"

"Fresh air is better," Scott told him. "The germs will be more flushed out."

"I don't think so. Germs blow around in the air. Is it windy tonight?"

"Scott is right," said Rick. "I wouldn't take a shower right now. In this humidity, showers grow diseases."

Barron went to get the hand sanitizer, and Mary followed him.

"I told everyone it wasn't a good time to be partying," said Rick. "Hey, Scott, want to play that new video game you were showing me? The one where you've gotten to level one billion, or whatever it is?"

"Yeah, I could sell my points right now for a fortune. You can watch me rack up some more. I don't especially feel like dancing on the balcony right now. Later, guys. Goodbye, Attorney Sanders."

She'd been so quiet, I'd forgotten Lucy was still there, seated behind me. She was brushing back that same stray strand of hair, and watching Scott and Rick leave the room. Where the hell had she gotten that black-sequined gown with the giant fake magnolia at the waist and the low cut that exposed her bony chest? It looked like a costume. It probably was. They'd probably gotten one of the queens to lend it to her for her dinner with the captain. As I gaped, she shot me an icy blue glare and stood up to leave. Kenny jumped up and escorted her out.

Slim and I were still chained together. In spite of his glum expression, Slim looked super hot in his costume and makeup. I knew I looked hot, too, and as a pair we were totally magnetic. I stood up and felt the floor below me vibrating from the action below.

"Let's go light the place up, Slim-ster. We'll have 'em climbing up the balcony, right?"

"I dunno. The effect's not the same, with just the two of us. We still look pretty great, though. Okay, let's go touch up this body paint where we sat on it. We can go out on the balcony of your room. It's closest to the dance floor below. We'll be the Toxic Tower Two."

"Ri-i-i-ght? Let's do it," I said.

As we walked towards my cabin, the Epitome Tower elevator opened and two of Kronos's minions got out, with Slim's double, Carlos, between them. One of the minions handed Carlos a small cloth bag. The minons went back down the elevator, and Carlos stood staring at us and clutching the bag.

"Carlos! I thought you had to work! *Que pasa*?" Slim cried.

Carlos had been put under quarantine, because he'd spent some time in the Tower that afternoon with Lucy. He would spend the rest of the cruise in the butlers' quarters.

Slim took Carlos's hand. "Come hang out with us!"

I watched their matching profiles, close together, as symmetrical as that "a vase or two faces?" graphic, as they held hands and chattered in soft Spanish. Carlos said he'd been instructed to stay in the butlers' quarters, away from the Epitome Concierge guests. He could lose his job if he disobeyed.

"Do you really still want this horrible job after everything that's happened?" Slim asked him. "I'll tell you something, you won't ever see me on one of these boats again."

"I don't like this job," Carlos said, "but I need to support my mother and my sisters. Things are very bad in my country…."

"I know," I interrupted. "Carlos, we'll tell the butlers that your attorney wants me to interview you some more. For her case files, or something. Then you can hang with us, and they can't get mad at you."

We stopped at the butlers' quarters to drop off Carlos's small overnight bag and give the butlers our story, before heading to my cabin.

When we got to my cabin, Carlos said, "Armando, can you tell *La Abogada* what we are doing? If they find out she didn't really want you to talk to me, there will be trouble."

"From the butlers?" I asked. At first, I thought Carlos was being paranoid. Then I thought about Evans's spitefulness, and

I remembered the rough conversation I'd overheard earlier that afternoon from the butlers' quarters. "Right. I'll let her know."

I stood with my arms in the air while Slim unchained me. As I left the room, I heard Slim's voice, a note of shyness in it, asking Carlos, "Do you like to dance?"

It was almost midnight, and it was tempting to wait 'til morning to talk to Lucy about Carlos. Except I really didn't want to cause any more trouble for Carlos.

Kenny let me in. Then he planted himself, immobile, inside the locked cabin door, his legs apart and hands clasped behind him. I laughed.

"The President is in the building," I said to Kenny, in English.

"*Que?*"

"Nothing, *hermano*," I said. "Good to see you alert and on the job. There's probably a lot of people out in the big, cold world who would love to kill my boss. Of course, they'd have to sneak on board the *Adonis* and break the tight quarantine that's securing the perimeter of the Epitome Tower, but--"

"Stop it, Armando." Lucy was sitting in her chair, still wearing her up do, but she'd lost the black sequined costume and had on her thick fuzzy white robe with the Jamboree Cruises logo. Her face was contracted in pain, and her foot was up on a footstool under a big bag of ice.

"Oh, no!" I cried. "Did the Captain step on your foot at the dinner dance?"

"My ankle's acting up again. I'm worried about Sandy. I should've flown home tonight. I can't reach her or Claude. Thank God I got Claude's report on Dan Leone before we lost service. Otherwise, we'd still be hunting for answers."

I told her Carlos was going to hang out with Slim and me and we were going to use her as our cover story so Carlos wouldn't get in trouble. But when I got back to the cabin, there was a text on my phone from Slim. Carlos was tired, and he didn't want to go dancing. They were going to hang out in Slim's cabin.

I walked out on my balcony and looked at the bodies moving below. "Armando Felan, party of one," I thought. Screw everybody else. I kicked off my flip-flops and climbed up onto the balcony ledge, holding onto the corner pole that extended to the balcony roof. Here I was, on top of the world, I thought, as I moved to the sounds of Cardi B's "Money." People below started to notice and reach their arms up towards the glorious heights of my spot in the Epitome Tower.

But I felt like a stripper with a dead face in a sad club full of strangers, strangers who held no potential to be something more because they weren't of my world. Maybe if I got closer to the crowd. I held onto the pole and stepped around it onto the section of the ledge that was right in front of my doorway.

The ledge fell out from under me.

For a second, I was falling toward the deck that now looked so far away, almost two stories down. I grabbed the pole in both arms, slowing down the fall, and got a grip in both my hands. My feet were kicking for something to land on. Finally, I wrapped one leg, and then the other, around the vertical pole. My legs were slippery with body paint, but I managed to pull myself up, hand over hand, until my foot reached the floor of the balcony.

I paused to rest, letting some of the weight leave my arms but still gripping the pole with my hands. The sound of voices came from the party below.

"Hey! Are you okay?"

"I would've caught you, baby!"

From just above me, another voice. "Let me help you up, Armando."

As always, Barron was right there when I needed him.

28
Lucy
Saturday, Still At Sea

I woke up from an uneasy sleep into a pool of sunlight. Kenny was asleep next to me, the white sheets accordioned around his body like an artist's drape. I pulled the curtain off the porthole and looked outside at the blue sea and sky.

It was an "at sea" day. I was not only at sea, I was quarantined, confined to this Tower with an amusing companion and, a gift from the ship's Captain last night, a book of extra-challenging crossword puzzles from the Cruise Line's bookstore.

I'd laughed when Armando told me the butlers on this ship were like genies. This morning I had to wonder, though, how did Evans know exactly when to knock on my door, holding a tray with my coffee and breakfast? Had he been standing there waiting for the past hour until I finally woke up? No. The roll and coffee were piping hot, the cranberry juice icy cold. I ate breakfast, then took my coffee and puzzle book and crawled back into bed. The mental stimulation was welcome, as Dan Leone's suicide had left me with no more to do for my client. I dove into the world of cryptic crosswords, setting up all the fronts in my brain to search for anagrams, retrieve almost-forgotten knowledge, and enter the mind of each puzzle's diabolical creator. It feels like magic when it all comes together, and the solution appears. I suppose the human brain is as much like magic as any other natural phenomenon. I was so absorbed by the puzzles that it was an hour later before I realized Kenny was up, sitting next to me in bed, drinking coffee, and playing some kind of game on his cell phone.

"What are you playing?" I asked. "Solitaire?"

He looked insulted. "No. DarkKnight. See?" He showed me a small console, which was attached by a cord to his phone. Using his thumbs on the console, he manipulated a tiny figure on the screen of the phone, which he held between his bare knees. It was a miniature version of those war-like games played by teenagers on their big screen TVs.

"Internet strong here this morning. I play with other people, real time. I make a lot of points."

"Oh, my. Good for you."

He kicked my leg lightly with his foot, causing his phone to fall into his lap. "I'm better than you," he said, pointing at my puzzle book. "My points worth money."

"Really?"

His eyes got round and he nodded, looking, despite his rough exterior, extraordinarily like a naughty child sharing a secret. I laughed. His eyes crinkled at the edges. He took my puzzle book out of my hands, set it neatly on the bedside table, and took me in his arms.

***

At midday, the air was still and sticky hot, even in the shade of the patio umbrella where I sat. I was sorry I'd accepted Kronos's invitation to join the rest of the guests for lunch on the poolside patio. The only escape from this heat would be to return to my air-conditioned cabin or to take a swim. But the swimming pool and spa were covered with heavy grey rubber sheets, and signboards reading: QUARANTINE: NO ENTRY.

Armando was the last guest to arrive for lunch. Although he told me he'd slept in, he appeared tired. Then I saw the raw red streaks on cheek, ribs, and upper arms.

"Armando!" I cried. "What happened to you?"

"I don't want to talk about it."

"Tell me."

"I slipped and fell, okay?" He proceeded to tell me about his idiotic attempt to join the festivities below the night before, by dancing on the ledge of his balcony.

"Don't say anything," he said when he finished telling me. "Barron told me those rails aren't meant to stand on. I just wanted to get closer to the crowd last night. Everyone downstairs was having so much fun, and I wanted to be part of it. You don't have to tell me, I'm as stupid as dirt."

"Honestly. What has this cruise done to your brain, Armando? You're as bad as...."

My automatic response died on my lips. As I looked at Armando's pale face, my mind jolted into clarity. Pieces of the puzzle flew into place, and my mind started working at top speed. It took a few minutes before my attention came back to what was going on around me.

The Tribe was restless. Pent-up testosterone, and something else that felt like fear, was in the air. You'd think everyone would be relieved the mystery of Blake's death had been resolved with such finality. You'd think these fellows would be glad to have a day to relax after a week of strenuous activity and late nights, but they all seemed to be jumping out of their skins. Even the staff looked restless.

Slim and Carlos, really like identical twins, sat apart from the others on the railings on the port side of the Tower. Rodrigo was doing sets of sit-ups and pouring pitchers full of water over himself at the breaks. Mary removed her robe, under which she wore nothing but the smallest of thongs, which I believe is called a Brazilian-style swimsuit, and reclined on a lounge chair with a copy of *Modern Plumbing*. Barron knelt at her side and they read the magazine together, his golden hair reflecting the burning sun. Barron was looking especially handsome, even for Barron, and there was little question, watching him with Mary, where that glow came from.

Lunch was served buffet style, but the lavish spread was wasted on this group. They wolfed down the food in near silence, and then started to vent their irritation. A sample of this follows:

Scott: I really need a swim. Look at all that water down there. This is like torture.

Rodrigo: Water, water, everywhere, and not a goddamn drop to swim in.

Rick: Evans, can't you do something about this heat? Can we go swimming in the ocean or something? Why does it feel like this boat is hardly moving? Are we becalmed?

Armando: You can't get becalmed on a fucking motorboat, you moron....

Scott: Don't talk to him like that, bitch.

Rodrigo: Don't fucking call him a bitch.

Rick, sitting at the table next to me, was the only one who seemed apologetic for the crass banter in my presence. Showing more consideration than his cruise mates, he moved his chair to sit by me and said, "You sure resolved your investigation into Blake's death quickly, Ms. Sanders. Congratulations. It's a relief to know what happened."

"Thank you. I really can't take any credit, however. Dan Leone died before I even had a chance to interview him. My job was simply to exonerate my client. Dan must be given the credit for accomplishing that."

"True. It's one thing to kill a man, and quite another to let someone else be punished for your crime. Dan was a killer, but I guess he had a noble side."

"That's an interesting take, Rick. Do you really think that's why Dan killed himself? I would have thought...?"

He waited for me to finish, but I just waited to see if he had the gumption to defend his position.

"Obviously, Dan could've just turned himself in," Rick said. "He didn't have to kill himself just to save your client. Dan thought he'd gotten away with killing Blake. Then Slim was arrested, and then Carlos, and then you came on the scene to investigate. Dan realized he'd have to own up to it. He couldn't take the disgrace, so he did himself in."

"All right. That's a reasonable scenario, Rick, on the surface. But it's flawed. If Dan had been so conscientious about taking responsibility and protecting others from unjust accusations, why didn't he leave a note or tell somebody, before hanging himself? It doesn't make sense. I'm afraid you're wrong about Dan's motivations. Fortunately, my job wasn't to investigate the murder, so I can relax and stop thinking about it. If I were a prosecutor, though, I'd not be at all satisfied with the current resolution of Blake Copland's case."

I had raised my voice slightly. There was a sudden complete silence vibrating around the poolside deck of the Epitome Tower, and my last few words had fallen neatly into it.

"Really?" Rick moved his chair closer to me. "What do you think, Ms. Sanders? Do we still have a killer on board?"

"I have some theories. There are a few facts that are not consistent with Dan Leone being Blake Copland's killer."

"If Dan wasn't the murderer, why'd he kill himself?" asked Rodrigo.

I let the silence vibrate some more.

"Ms. Sanders, are you suggesting someone killed Dan, too?" Rick asked.

"Well, perhaps it's not the time or place to discuss this," I said. All eyes were on me now. Even the butlers had stopped clearing the lunch away and moved closer so they could hear me. "I think I'll return to my crossword puzzle, in my air-conditioned cabin." I started to gather up my sun hat and bag.

"Excuse me, ladies, gentlemen." Barron cleared his throat. "While you were having lunch, Mr. Kronos consulted with our Captain. The Epitome catamaran is available for an ocean outing. The *Adonis* is making very good time towards Miami. The Captain is willing to stop while we take the catamaran out for a couple of hours. In less than an hour, we'll reach an area of rock formations where we can take you to dive and snorkel. Or just come for the ride."

We took an elevator to one of the lower decks and were assisted down a rope ladder to the waiting catamaran. All the Epitome Tower guests and staff, and even my client Carlos, had taken advantage of this opportunity to escape from the stifling, pool-less, quarantined Tower. I'd pictured the catamaran being a rather small boat on which we'd be crowded, but it was a large craft with a spacious interior lounge and a deck space with comfortable seating areas on all sides.

Kenny and I went to stand outside, near the front of the boat, where Kronos told us we'd probably see some dolphins after we got underway. Armando and Slim, wearing matching tight racing-style bathing suits, came to stand next to us.

"Now we're the ones having more fun than the rest of the passengers," Armando was saying. "I bet they're all watching us now, hey Slim-ster?"

His words were cocky, but his face looked tired, his brow contracted like he was in pain, which he probably was.

"Anyway, now I'm gonna show everyone. I'm gonna have the best diving experience ever. Kronos says these rock formations have live coral, and we might see more eagle rays. Did you know we're not far off the coast of Cuba? Come on, Slim, let's go get our equipment."

I felt a wave of sympathy for my poor assistant, as I watched him and Slim walk back towards the cabin. Those scrapes on his body were going to hurt when he got into the water. I adjusted my sun visor so it was firmly anchored behind my ponytail, and leaned over the rail to look for dolphins.

After what seemed like a short moment, the rock formations loomed less than fifty yards ahead of us. I counted five lumpy grey and tan mounds. The largest one was really a small island, sheer cliffs topped by a cover of frilly green trees that made a yellowish reflection in the teal-colored sea below. The catamaran came to a stop, and people started coming outside with their equipment.

Barron stood next to the captain's chair. "All right, everybody, listen up! You all know the drill. Follow the buddy system, whether you're diving or snorkeling or even just swimming. Mr. Kronos and I will do a final check of everybody's equipment before you exit this boat. Who's diving?"

"Not I," I announced. "I can't swim a stroke."

Armando looked at me in surprise, but didn't say anything.

Rodrigo and Armando raised their hands. They were standing next to each other, already wearing diving tanks, face masks pushed up over their foreheads like sunglasses. The others were snorkeling, except for Carlos, who seemed to have a firm aversion to getting into the water.

Barron, Evans, Kenny, and I were also staying on the boat. I took off my shoes and rolled up my pants so I could dangle my feet off the diving platform once the swimmers were launched.

Rodrigo and Armando slid into the water. Rodrigo spit into his mask, rubbed it, rinsed it in the seawater, and placed it over his face. Armando, holding his mask, sank into the sea and resurfaced, throwing his head back so his hair streamed away from his face, and then put on his mask. The two men disappeared under the surprisingly opaque surface, after leaving a short trail of splashing fins pointing towards the rock island.

The snorkelers were clumsier, laughing and duck walking and adjusting their masks before finally swimming off in a slow-moving cluster. When they cleared the platform, I sat on the edge and dipped my bare feet into the sea. Kenny stood next to me, leaning on the rail, and my young client came to sit cross-legged at my side.

The water made little splashing sounds as it hit the boat. Carlos and Kenny started to converse in soft Spanish. I relaxed my body flat onto the sun-warmed deck, put my visor over my face, and did some hard thinking.

29

Armando

Saturday

After my humiliating public fall from the Epitome Tower balcony on Friday night, Barron got me to a hot shower, put salve on my scraped hands and arms, and brought me a strong drink that he called a "hot toddy." Whatever it was, it got me to fall into a deep sleep that lasted until almost midday Saturday. I pulled on my shorts and walked out onto the balcony. The *Adonis* was quiet after all the noise and action of the night before.

On the deck below me, a group of four guys slowly cruised by on scooters. One of them was slender and pale, with longish red hair like Justin's. He wore perfect-fitting Op trunks and flip-flops, and had tied his T-shirt around his neck so it looked like a small cape. I overheard him saying to his friends, "I'm glad we've decided to just chill out for our last day." I watched them until they disappeared around the back of the Lucky Star.

Sometime during the night, Barron had propped the broken ledge diagonally across the balcony's lower rail, and then tied a rope across the open area where the ledge had been. I flushed. Would Jamboree Cruises make me pay for the damage? How could I know the bar would come off like that? It had worked fine when we'd danced on it, less than a week ago. And now I was going to have to go back to work next week, broke from blowing all my money on this cruise. And with the Tower in quarantine, how was I going to have any more fun?

Barron materialized behind me with my morning café latte.

"Thanks for letting me sleep," I told him. "I might as well, since we can't do anything else today. How's Dan-Dan?"

"He's feeling ill, and there's still a fever. I'm afraid the quarantine won't be lifted before we dock in Miami tomorrow, Armando."

"Poor guy. He must be missing Dan, too."

"Yes. How are your scrapes this morning, Armando?"

I let Barron put more lotion on my ribs and arms where I'd burned my skin on last night's pole slide. Ugly red burns and bruises had also shown up on my legs this morning, where I'd wound them around the pole, and I had a scrape on my cheek. I sighed as Barron's beautiful hands worked the soothing aloe over my wounds.

Once I was dressed, it was time to join the rest of the quarantined Tribe for lunch, out by the covered Infinity pool.

Everyone was assembled already, including my boss, who sat alone at the only shaded table wearing her usual expression of disapproval. I joined her, only so I could keep my sore body out of the blazing sun.

After lunch we got a surprise. The butlers had negotiated for the *Adonis* to stop in the middle of the sea so the Tower guests could go diving. It was a perfect day with no wind. The ocean water sparked up into our faces as we motored towards the emerald-green-topped rock formations marking the reefs. As I looked back towards the *Adonis*, I saw men lined up on the rails watching us. Slim and Carlos and I waved at them, and they waved back. We were going to have an epic last day, after all.

Rodrigo agreed to be my diving buddy. Kronos made a big show of checking our equipment before we left the boat.

We decided to make our way towards the biggest rock formation and follow the reef around it. The water stung my scraped skin a little at first, but within a minute I was in the zone, following Rodrigo's easy pace towards the reef. Had it been Kronos's idea to ask the captain to stop so we could take this side trip? How thoughtful. Of course, he got to get off the ship too....

We reached the reef. There had been some fish on the way over, but here there was an explosion of life and color. Rodrigo pointed out a big field of bright coral, a school of parrotfish, and an unusually large barracuda with its mouth moving up and down to expose rows of sharp teeth. I got ready to lose myself in the magical undersea world. How could anyone not want to see this? Why hadn't Lucy agreed to try it? She'd said she couldn't swim, but....

What kind of a game was she playing? And why had she looked so shocked when I told her about my accident last night? Did she think it was no accident?

Oh, God. Of course, it wasn't! Slim and I had danced on that railing the first night of the cruise, and it had been solid. But why would anyone want to attack *me*? If there was still a killer on board, as Lucy had suggested, the only person who might be a threat to the killer was Lucy.

Suddenly the glorious fish were just objects darting in and out of my path. I surfaced just long enough to locate the catamaran behind us in the distance. Rodrigo followed me up. I pointed back towards the boat, and started swimming towards it.

Aided by my long diving fins, my legs pumped me forward like I was being chased from behind. But there was no shark or oversized barracuda after me. I had a strong feeling the danger was ahead of me, but was totally confused as to what that danger might be.

Lucy had Rottweiler Kenny with her. Would that be enough to protect her? I put my arms into high gear, in a sort of underwater crawl. Kenny had seemed to be sticking to Lucy closely, but he wasn't the brightest bulb. He probably didn't know she was in real danger.

I tried going up to the surface and executing my racing crawl stroke. My arms windmilled, and my legs splashed on the surface. This only made my progress slower. The tanks on my back weighed a lot more out of the water. I looked up and saw the front of the catamaran, with a small figure, probably Kronos, at the helm. My boss wasn't in sight.

Rodrigo surfaced to join me, and touched my arm."What's wrong?"

"Lucy... in danger. Have to get back."

I put my mouthpiece back in and dove. Rodrigo kept at my side until we reached the boat. We surfaced at the platform, and I looked straight into the bright blue eyes of my boss.

"You're back rather early, aren't you?" she said. She was sitting with her feet in the water, her pants rolled up to her knees, and her face turned to the sun. Kenny and Carlos sat at her side.

"Oh. I got... tired," I said.

I felt stupid for worrying, but I didn't want to leave Lucy. I urged Rodrigo to join the snorkelers, who had found a reef not far from our catamaran. The snorkelers and swimmers maximized their time in the water, coming in right before we had to leave to get back to the ship. People had exercised into a satisfied tiredness, moving slowly, content not to be talking as they took off their equipment and toweled off. Tired myself, I began to think my fears had been just another panic attack, triggered by the stress of the week's events. I'd stupidly ruined my chance to have a last bit of fun on this nightmare of a vacation.

Kronos turned the catamaran towards the tiny white dot that was the *Adonis.* Once we were underway, Barron and Evans served drinks in the cabin. Mary, Carlos, and Rick stayed with the butlers in the cabin, while the rest of us took our drinks outside to the front of the boat.

"Ladies and gentlemen, if you watch carefully," Kronos called out from the helm, "you may see a Magnificent Frigatebird. I caught sight of one high up in the sky a few minutes ago. It was in the direction of the *Adonis*. Look up into the clouds. The first thing you'll see is a black speck. Then you'll see the wings, like a glider. It's a beautiful sight. We have extra pairs of binoculars for you."

Barron went to stand by Kronos at the helm, and they took turns searching the sky with a pair of binoculars. The rest of us clustered together in the bow, eyes glued to the sky, in the hope of seeing the great bird.

I wanted so much to see this bird. My [ex?] boyfriend Justin is a birdwatcher. If I saw it, it would be a sign Justin and I would get back together, because I'd have to call and tell him about it when I got home. He'd realize I wasn't so stupid to go on this fucking dangerous toxic cruise, after all.

I could hear people around me moving, going to different areas of the boat to spot the Frigatebird. Slim, next to me, said, "I wanna see this big bird. I'm gonna go get some binoculars."

Then I heard Lucy's voice announcing, "I'm going to try the back of the boat. Maybe the bird has a nest on that island where we were." A moment later, "No, Kenny, don't come with me. For goodness' sake, you don't need to follow me around like a puppy. I'll be fine."

"Fine...." I thought absently, scouring the sky with my eyes. There were shreds of white cloud, high up in the air, and I waited for a black speck to come down through them. "Lucy will be fine...." After a minute, I was starting to get a crick in my neck, and bent my head forward to release it. Fine?

"Lucy!" I cried out. I ran towards the back of the boat. Lucy was halfway over the back railing, her wide hips jackknifed over the rail, her feet kicking in an effort to reach the deck. Her straw visor had been knocked off her head and was bobbing in the wake of the boat. Someone was pulling her legs up and pushing her body over the edge of the rail. I wasn't going to get there in time to save her. She was going to fall into the wake behind her, and get sucked into the motor below.

As I watched in horror, a figure jumped down from one of the lockers by the back of the boat and landed on top of the struggling figures. Kenny pulled Lucy back onto the deck by the seat of her pants. His other arm locked like a vice around the neck of a struggling Scott Barnes.

30
Happy Hour

As the *Adonis* headed east towards Miami, the Toxic Tower was in the crosshairs of the setting sun. The hot haze muted the blues of sky and sea.

Of the original nine guests, two, Blake and Dan, were dead, and one, Scott, was in the brig for their murders. Slim's twin, Carlos, was now one of us for the remaining fourteen hours of the cruise. The original contingent of butlers was intact. But they seemed different, somehow, too. Their masks had slipped, and in some ways they were more like fellow guests.

Mary, Barron, Slim, and Carlos, shared one small table. Rodrigo sat at another with Rick and a pale, blanket-wrapped Dan-Dan. I was at the third table with Lucy and Kenny. *La Abogada* was drinking a cold martini and holding forth on how she'd cracked the case.

"When Armando told me the rail on his balcony had broken, I suspected the killer was still at large and ready to kill again. Unfortunately, this meant my work wasn't over. I had to redirect the killer's focus from Armando to myself, so that I could, ah, better control the situation. I let it be known that I thought the case wasn't over, that I was still trying to find the truth. I announced I couldn't swim. As Armando knows, that's not true. Fortunately, Kenny here saved me before I was called upon to test my skills on the high seas.

"My efforts to flush out the killer were successful. For reasons I'll share in a minute, I already suspected Scott Barnes might be our culprit. But there were reasons to suspect others, as well, and I had to be sure.

"Dan Leone's apparent suicide seemed to resolve the mystery of Blake's death. Dan's death coincided with my discovery of Dan's illegal financial dealings. Dan's financial crimes were serious, and Blake almost certainly did know about them and was threatening to expose them. So there was a motive. Dan had the opportunity: he could have left Dan-Dan sleeping in their cabin and snuck out to cut Blake's rope swing that morning. As to the means, Dan's body was found with Scott's knife. Dan could have stolen it, used it to cut the rope swing, and hidden it somewhere until he used it again to cut the rope he used to hang himself. But that's not what happened."

"I could've told you that. Dan would never have killed himself," said Dan-Dan. "It was against his religion."

"Yes, Dan-Dan. But you were incommunicado, understandably, after your very sad loss. And then your apparent contagious illness...."

Lucy hesitated and looked at us as if we were her law students and she was trying to choose a victim to call on. Everybody was listening, and people got a look of expectation.

Finally, Mary spoke up. "Apparent? You mean Dan-Dan was faking it?"

"I was totally sick, Mary," Dan-Dan said. He started to stand up, coughed, and sat back in his seat, wrapping the blanket around him.

"I don't doubt you were sick," Lucy told him. "I believe you were given a dangerous overdose of powerful over-the-counter sleeping pills. Scott had a half-empty bottle in his room. He probably gave them to you the night he killed Dan. He didn't want you to wake up too soon and start a search for Dan. You had a strong reaction, which gave you flu-like symptoms."

"How did Scott and Dan leave the Tower without anyone knowing?" I asked. "Did they go together?"

"I believe so," said Lucy. "But Scott had to be careful. The butlers keep an eye on who comes and goes from the Tower through the guest elevator."

"True. That system isn't airtight, but it would be a risk to leave that way," Barron said. "Any guest can use a room key to access the deck below via the fire escape ladders on either side of the Tower."

"Possibly that's how the two men left the Tower that night," Lucy said. "But I picture it differently. From what I've heard about Dan, he had a taste for adventure and a sense of fun. I think Scott found out Dan liked to go to the cruising deck, and suggested they go together. I think Scott suggested they cut off a piece of the sail ropes and use the rope to reach the lower deck. After leaving the Tower, they could have doubled the rope over the railings to climb all the way down to Deck Three. Scott kept the rope with him, and used it to kill Dan when they arrived at the cruising deck."

Dan-Dan made a sound between a sigh and a groan, which sounded too deep to be coming from him. It was the same sound I'd heard Dan make, when he was disgusted about something.

"I'm sorry, dear," said Lucy. "These details must be terribly distressing for you."

"It's not that," he said, in his normal, higher voice. "Just...the way you described it. I can see it happening. Dan was a real man, but he loved to play like a kid. But why did Scott kill Dan? Was it just so Dan would be blamed for Blake's murder? Why Dan?"

"Blake told Scott about his plan to expose Dan's crimes. Unlike some of the threats Blake was making to others on the ship, these threats to expose Dan were real and specific. Scott knew Dan had a strong motive to get rid of Blake. He believed Blake's threats against Dan, because Blake was making similar threats to Scott. Scott may be a brilliant video game player and inventor, but he is also unscrupulous.

"When Scott and Rick were going to play a video game the other night, they mentioned selling the points Scott had won. This morning, I learned from Kenny that this practice, sale of points, is an underground practice, not legal, or at least not good sportsmanship, in the gaming world. That got me thinking about Scott's character and business practices. Blake must have uncovered some shady dealings that could seriously jeopardize Scott's business if they came to light. I'm sure my investigator will find them, if he hasn't already."

Claude better find something good, I thought. Scott was going to put up a fighting defense, and there wasn't a lot of hard evidence against him. After he'd been caught red-handed trying to push Lucy off the catamaran, Scott had backed off. He'd said the motion of the boat had caused him to fall onto Lucy. Kenny had overreacted. I'd seen it with my own eyes, and I could tell a jury that wasn't true. But would they believe me?

"I don't get how Scott could've overpowered Dan to get the rope around his neck and throw him over the railing," Rodrigo was saying. "Dan was a big muscular guy. Scott is, well, Scott."

Dan-Dan said, "Dan thought I didn't know he went cruising without me, but, of course, I did know. When he went, he was usually drunk and/or high. He would've done whatever Scott wanted."

"And Scott is stronger than he appears," Lucy said, rubbing the sides of her arms. "Kenny and I were anticipating his attack on me, and Kenny was watching us from just out of sight. We needed to catch Scott in the act. He was a lot faster and stronger than we expected. I should have known he would be. Armando pointed out Scott made a show of not caring what he ate, of living on junk food, yet he had the butlers bring him a healthful vegetable drink for breakfast every morning."

Slim said, "So Scott used his pocket knife to cut Blake's rope swing that morning, after Evans and Barron checked it? He didn't have much time. We didn't get back to the Tower from our video gaming until after six-thirty. I mean, was he planning this thing all night, all the time we were playing, and winning, the tournament? I thought he was totally focused on competition. Did something happen after he got back to make him do it?"

Lucy took a sip of her martini. "Blake may have intercepted Scott when he came back from the tournament, and started up with his threats. But I think it's more likely Scott went directly to cut the rope as soon as he got in from the tournament. He probably made his plan the night before. Everyone knew Blake's morning routine with the swing, and the butlers' time for checking it. By the time Blake came out, Scott had already cut the rope."

Rick had been looking almost as pale as Dan-Dan. His orange spray tan had faded, and his voice when he spoke was hoarse, like he was sick or tired or both.

"Blake was playing with fire, like he wanted someone to try to kill him. He tried it with me. It's not what... what you all think. Blake knew I was having trouble getting a new position after what happened at my last job. He offered me a dream job at one of his family's financial firms. Then, he started asking me to do things to other guests, like getting me to tell everyone about Dan's money troubles. The night before Blake fell, he asked me to help him frame Armando, to put my Hermés watch in Armando's room and then accuse him of stealing it. I refused, of course, and Blake said he wouldn't give me the job unless I did it. Blake had a lot of great qualities, but he had a mean streak, and I'm not surprised he got himself killed. But Scott? He seemed like a legit guy. If Scott hadn't attacked you, Ms. Sanders, I wouldn't have believed he did this."

Evans, standing behind me, had his arms crossed over his chest.

"I need this job to support my mother and my sisters in the Philippines. Earlier that night, Blake made me plant his Rolex watch in Mr. Armando's room. I couldn't say no to him. Sorry."

He didn't look that sorry, but I accepted his apology.

I said, "What I really don't understand is why Scott tried to kill me, or hurt me, by sabotaging the rail on my balcony. I was no threat to him. I never suspected him. He was such a harmless-acting geek."

It was weeks later, back home in San Diego, that I realized what I'd seen that had caused Scott to try to kill me. The whole picture flashed in front of my eyes one evening on my way home from work, when I entered the grocery store and faced a pyramid of bright-colored navel oranges arranged to tempt entering shoppers. I saw Scott, smiling, his messy strings of hair half-covering his eyes, using his pocketknife to peel an orange. In the background were Dan and Dan-Dan, planning their day in Grand Cayman. Scott had his pocketknife, the one that cut the rope that killed Blake, the day *after* Blake's death. Possibly Dan had noticed the same thing, giving Scott another reason to kill him, but we'd never know.

Now, instead of figuring out why Scott had tried to kill me, I realized something else. If Scott's sleeping pills were what had made Dan-Dan sick, then Dan-Dan didn't have a contagious disease. No norovirus, no quarantine, right? As I opened my mouth to say something, I caught sight of Slim, leaning towards Carlos and softly translating the group's conversation. If we were de-quarantined, Carlos would be sent back to work on the lower decks tonight. He and Slim wouldn't be able to spend the last night getting to know each other better. On the other hand, the rest of us would be free to hit the last night of partying on the lower decks. I looked at the people around me, wondering if anyone else had thought of asking the ship's doctor to lift the quarantine.

People were talking about other things. Only Lucy was watching me, looking disgusted like she knew what I was thinking about. Like I wasn't grateful to her for putting her own life at risk to save mine, like I didn't realize how stupid I'd been to blow all of my savings on this nightmare of a vacation, and how that choice had probably made my amazing, perfect, way-too-good-for-me boyfriend never want to see me again. But it wasn't because she was watching me that I made my decision. Yeah, I put Slim and Carlos's interests ahead of my own that night. Anyhow, fun seemed kind of impossible to me. For me, this cruise was fucking over.

31
Lucy
Coming Home

I landed in San Diego on Sunday night. It was a relief to get off the plane with my carry-on bag, walk straight to the taxi stand across solid land, and breathe the cool, dry salt air of home. I walked straight to the line of cabs, glowing yellow and white under the floodlights with the dark night behind them. When the driver asked me where I was going, I could have told him anywhere I wanted. The choices were infinite, but I'd narrowed it down to three: my home, my office, or the senior psychiatric ward where Sandy was currently housed. I gave the driver an address, leaned back in my seat, closed my eyes, and let out a sigh.

Kenny had stayed in Miami to join his boss, my enterprising ex-client, who was currently engaged in some business dealings there. I was too old for the whole tears-at-the-airport thing, but after parting from Kenny, I felt unmoored, to use a nautical image.

There had been a few other emotional goodbyes among our party, but the one I would remember was Slim and his "twin." Slim and Carlos had said goodbye at the dock, holding hands and chattering with the uninhibited affection of grade-school boys. They wore identical colorful string friendship bracelets—Slim's on his bare right wrist and Carlos's on his left, where he'd folded back the cuff of his white steward's uniform so Slim could put it on. Even the narcissistic crowd of cruisers had stopped to stare, drawn by something more than just the resemblance and the beauty of these young men. I knew what that something was. These two dead ringers, one born in a rich country and one born in a poor one, meeting on an enormous white floating institution of class division, had smashed that division by recognizing each other as brothers. I admit I felt a measure of pride at my role in saving this subversive pair.

The taxi pulled up onto the driveway in front of Mercy Hospital. I paid the driver and headed for the psychiatric ward. Sandy was in her room, finishing dinner, when I arrived. Like the last time, she had a look of not belonging in these surroundings. She was nicely made up, her hair was styled, and she wore a soft green cardigan over her hospital robe.

"Well, you look just fine," I told her, giving her a hug. "That does my heart good."

"Oh, sister," she said. "I can't believe I landed back in here again. Can you believe it? I get my butt stuck in a dog door and go into a panic. Ha! How dumb is that? I'm so sorry."

"Are you all fixed now, dear?"

She smiled. "All fixed. I don't know what came over me, Luce. The doctors say the medication they gave me might've set me off. I'm on a lower dose now, and I gotta say, I feel like a new person. Tomorrow I can come home. I really think the medication was the problem."

"Well, that's good, if that's all it was. Really, how they could be so careless--." I was shaking my head, but a wave of relief washed over me.

"I know! So careless! Maybe you should sue them. Ha! You know what? I'm just glad I'm getting the hell out of here tomorrow. And I'm so happy you're home. I missed you. I have a lot to do. I'm going to do some cleaning up, and get ready to start teaching again."

At Sandy's suggestion, we left the ward and found a pleasant seating area in the main lobby. I told Sandy about my trip. She was fascinated by my adventures on the *Adonis*, and even more so by my shipboard romance with Kenny. I got to hear, for the first time, about a fling she'd had with an Italian actor while she was studying abroad in Florence. It was like old times, talking sister talk and sharing memories.

When I got home it was late, but the dogs had sensed my impending arrival. They were waiting outside, with their fluffy, sharp-nosed heads stuck between the slats of the side fence, when my taxi pulled up. They greeted me with licks and vigorous tail wags. So far, it was a good homecoming.

***

Monday morning, Armando and I arrived at the office at the same time.

"*Jefa!* Back on the job! Let's get on it."

"You're here early."

"I got home and slept for twelve hours," he said. "Then I figured I might as well come in and start kicking some ass. Whoa! What's this giant lock on our door?"

"Claude had it put on, to keep our temporary staff from entering and causing any further damage. Here, he left me a key."

The office was dusty. The cleaners, who usually come on Friday evening, had been kept out by the padlock. And there was something else, a sharp sweet odor of medicine and decay.

"Yuck, what is that smell?" Armando walked into the office and set his bag next to his desk. He sniffed. "It's coming from the hallway." He ran up the half-flight of stairs to the small landing room where we'd placed Snyder, our contract attorney. I followed him up the stairs with a feeling of dread. I knew Claude had locked Mr. Arnold Snyder out of the office, so what could be up there?

"Oh, God, no!" Armando said.

Papers were scattered all over the desk and floor of the cramped room. Snyder had opened most of the twenty-two boxes of files he was supposed to review and emptied their contents into unlabeled piles, some of which had tipped (or been kicked?) over, spilling papers all over the floor. The smell was stronger in here. An empty bottle of Nyquil stood in the middle of the desk. There was a small pool of the red syrup on the blotter, and a stack of papers someone had tried to clean off but still stained lurid red on the edges. The sweet candy smell of cough syrup failed to mask the scent of something stronger.

Armando picked up my favorite coffee thermos, which belonged in the tea cabinet. Now it was on the return of Mr. Snyder's desk. Armando unscrewed the top. He held it under my nose so I could smell the pure vodka. I could also see Mr. Snyder had, God knows how, managed to crack the inner casing. A jacket draped over the office chair reeked of tobacco, and alcohol poisoning.

"Mr. Snyder is gone, but his presence lingers," I remarked. "Why does it seem, Armando, that some people are put here on earth to make messes, and the rest of us are put here to clean them up?"

"I'll get out the Lysol," Armando said, "and start on putting these files back together. We need to get some fans going."

Armando sprang into action. I hung up my suit jacket and installed myself at my desk to start the day. Two hours later, we were making some progress. Armando had updated my calendar, a feat that had been beyond poor Nancy's technical capabilities. I could now plan my week.

As I was getting ready to leave for an arraignment at the superior court, Nancy herself walked in.

"I'm so sorry, Ms. Sanders. Hi, Armando. I know my last workday was supposed to be Friday, but I just thought I'd come in and check. On Friday, there was a lock on the front door, and I couldn't get back in. Is everything okay? How was your trip?"

"Oh hello, Nancy. My trip was eventful and ultimately successful. I'll let Armando fill you in, as I have to leave for court. How is your son, dear?"

"Better. He's stabilized, for now, and back in his board and care. How's your sister? Is the day treatment program working for her?"

"I'm not so sure about that. She ended up back in the hospital. However, she's being released this morning. I saw her last night, and she really seemed quite well, back to her old self, really. She's been staying with me, and she promises she'll have my house all cleaned up by the time I get home. Apparently, they'd given her some medication that caused her to act out, and that's why she's had all these problems. Sandy may not need day treatment."

"Oh. What good news! But... wasn't Sandy hospitalized before she started the medication?"

"I've got to get to court. Lovely of you to stop by, Nancy. My best wishes for you and your son. You were a great help to me, with the hospital and the insurance and everything. Goodbye."

The rest of the workday was a blur of activity. It felt like I'd missed a lot more than just two workdays at the office. When I returned around noon, Armando had already gone through the voice mail, rescheduled my missed appointments and appearances, and cleaned the upper office. He was still reorganizing the files that had been torn apart in *P. v. Johnson,* our twenty-two-box albatross of a death penalty appeal.

I was deeply relieved to have my assistant back to his old energetic self. I'd feared the unpleasantness and disappointments of the disastrous cruise would make him sulky and contrary, but he actually seemed eager to please. We had a quick lunch of sandwiches at our desks, and by the end of the day the deadlines and catch-up that had loomed ominously now seemed almost manageable.

It was almost four o'clock when Armando suggested I take time for afternoon tea. I brought the file I was reviewing into the front room and sat in my chair.

After Armando served me my Golden Monkey tea, perfectly steeped with the right amount of space left for cream, I told him, "When I got back to my house last night, it was filled with junk Sandy had brought in while I was gone. Did you know those books and magazines you moved for her are full of these little wiggling insects?"

"Yeah, I did know. Why's she even staying with you?"

"I meant to tell you, while you were on the ship, Armando, but we were too preoccupied. Sandy was hospitalized after you left. Twice. I thought I could help her if she stayed with me. I spent most of last night cleaning my kitchen. It was... unspeakable. Maggots in the trash can.... I had to go buy rubber gloves."

"Gross. You shouldn't let her stay with you."

"What can I do? She's supposed to come home from the hospital today. Her house is.... Well, you've seen it. Ouch!" A sharp pain pierced my ankle. "What I want to know, Armando, is how can I fix Sandy?"

"Well, this situation really sucks, Boss. I'm sorry, especially with everything else you've had on your plate lately. Maybe there are some books she could read. My mom used to have a little clutter problem, and there was some book that really helped her. Now she's, like, made an art of de-cluttering. Our house is like a Japanese teahouse."

"A book. I wonder. No, I can't believe the solution is to bring another book into the house. When does Sandy even have time to read? She's too busy buying books, and putting them in stacks, and making me fall. Maybe I should get this book, and read it myself. Would that help? I could read it, and then explain it to her. I'm so tired. Would she listen? Damn! My foot hurts so much, I can't even think. I just ache. Well. I don't have time to deal with this right now. Let's get back to work."

Armando went upstairs and returned with the vacuum cleaner and got busy on the downstairs rugs.

"At least you're bouncing with energy today," I remarked.

He turned off the vacuum cleaner.

"Am I being annoyingly hyper? Is the noise bothering you?"

"Not at all. I'm just happy to.... Get on with your work." I turned back to the file in my lap, surprised at the wave of gratitude that had actually brought tears to my eyes.

Walking to my car an hour later, I caught a preview of fall in the crispness of the late-July afternoon. The heat radiating from the asphalt of the parking lot was tempered by the breeze rustling through the palm trees along the parkway. The lowering sun reflected orange, red, and yellow in the windows of the parked cars. After the stifling hotness of the tropics I was grateful for San Diego's temperate climate.

Another wave of emotion washed over me. Was I becoming what Sandy's doctors would term "emotionally labile?" If so, was this the onset of a mental illness, and was I going to join my sister in the hospital?

No. Damn it, I hadn't cried a drop in over ten years. I was due a good cry, and this time I let the tears flow. Where in the world was this coming from? True, there were reasons enough for my emotions to be overflowing. I was quite relieved to have my office put back together and Armando back in charge of running it. I'd narrowly escaped death in rescuing Armando and his friends. I missed Kenny. Now I'd think of him whenever I heard Sting's "Fields of Gold." Wednesday night, I'd have my time with Claude. I'd be gratefully back in our routine, and I could thank him properly for fighting my fires here at home while I was gone.

Still, I had a feeling something was stuck in my life. It was a feeling of longing, almost a nostalgia, for something that had never been and could never be yet seemed as real as if it were right in front of me. With a pain that almost doubled me over, I suddenly ached for my childhood: summer days swimming in the quarry, summer nights when Sandy and I snuck out of the house and rambled through the dry sweet-smelling Oklahoma hills. I longed to be back joyriding on our neighbors' horses and seeing Sandy's eyes laugh at me across the breakfast table the next day, my childhood co-conspirator.

I got into my car but didn't start it up. I was overcome with awareness of what I had lost. Sandy and I were grown up now. I was never going to have my old sister back. Our time in the hospital last night had made me think I could, but when I'd gotten home and seen the condition of my house, I'd known I was wrong.

My sobbing subsided, and I was left with a strange feeling of peace. There was nothing I could do to fix Sandy. All I could do was clear out my own life. I started my car and headed home.

32
Armando
Return to Work

I'd been pretty sure, since that moment on the *Adonis* when Lucy looked at me with such disgust, that I was going to be fired. How could she not fire me? She'd missed several days of work, incurred travel expenses I didn't have the money to repay, and oh, yeah, almost been killed saving my life. All I could think of was that she was gonna fire me and I wouldn't be able to keep up the mortgage payments and I'd be homeless again and Ma'd be homeless too and she wouldn't get to finish school and she'd have to go to work as a maid or, worse yet, go back to my dad. My only hope was to try and win Lucy back.

I got to work early Monday and got cranking on restoring the office to order. Nancy had done an okay job with the filing and writing down phone messages, but she'd somehow screwed up the formatting on every document she'd worked on, and there was a red error light blinking on our copier/printer/fax machine.

The worst snarl, though, was the *P. v. Johnson* file, totally blown apart, with no understandable method, by that attorney Lucy hired. At least Lucy couldn't blame me for that. But while we were surveying the room, Lucy started whining about how her whole life was just cleaning up other people's messes. Like mine, even though she didn't say it.

I survived Monday, probably because Lucy needed me to get things back in shape before she fired me. Still, I was feeling good enough after work to join my friends for a drink at the

Bar Bar, our dive-y but friendly hangout in Hillcrest, a hip gay neighborhood just north of downtown.

Slim, Rodrigo, and Mary were already at a booth when I got there, along with Slim's boyfriend, Raul di Marco.

Raul stood up to give me a hug. He's a famous artist, about twenty years older than Slim, with a wide, mobile actor's face, courtly manners, and hypnotic light blue eyes full of kindness.

"Slim told me about your adventures, Armando. Not altogether the vacation you were hoping for? I'm starting to think this kind of excitement follows you around."

"No shit. I'm a freaking disaster magnet. Now, I'm expecting my boss to fire me, 'cause she was so against my taking this cruise in the first place, and then she had to come rescue me."

"Dream on," Rodrigo said. "She'll never let you go. I bet she's just happy she was proven to be right about the cruise. Now she's saved your life, you'll be her slave forever."

"Really? I've been pretty much planning on having to take a job on a cruise ship, where I'll lose ten years of my life on Deck Two before finally moving up to Deck Three."

"That's not even funny, 'Mando," said Slim.

"I wasn't trying to be funny."

"Carlos is keeping his job on the *Adonis*, you know. His family needs the money. Doesn't your boss have some connections in Honduras, someone who could help him get a job there?"

"Lucy's connections are all through her client, a high-level drug dealer. Getting a job with him would be a good way for Carlos to get killed. Lucy's trying to get a settlement for Carlos and his family from Jamboree Cruises, though. Carlos's brother killed himself after being abused by Blake while working on the *Adonis*. If Jamboree doesn't come through, Lucy may have a talk with Blake's family. They'd probably pay a lot to avoid the publicity of a lawsuit."

"Carlos didn't tell me that."

"There's no deal yet. But if she says she'll do it, it'll get done."

"That's the truth," Mary said. "She's so fierce. Barron says the staff were afraid of her."

"You know what I don't get," Slim said, "is how they got such high-class butlers. Barron and Evans. All the other staff members on this ship are poor and desperate, from really poor countries. The pay is so low no one else will do it."

Rodrigo laughed. "Armando looks so shocked! What did you think, 'Mando? All those minions running around, their greatest dreams are to serve the rich and famous in the Epitome Tower for Jamboree Cruises?"

I had kind of thought that. I changed the subject. "Our butlers all had motives to kill Blake," I said. "Evans was basically Blake's sex slave. What about Barron? If it was really his dream to leave the *Adonis* and go work for the Dans, Blake would have found a way to sabotage it. I thought Kronos might've done in Blake, maybe even been paid to do it by Blake's family, to get rid of their embarrassing black sheep."

Mary said, "You're right about Barron having a motive. Blake threatened to tie him up in court for a huge amount of damages if he tried to break his contract. Barron's their poster-boy butler, and he was a big draw on the high-end cruises."

"Is he really going to quit and move here?"

"He agreed to renew his contract for another two years if they'd let him work just three months out of the year. The time apart should keep us from driving each other crazy." Mary twisted her hands in her lap and met my eyes with a pleading expression.

"I wish you well, Mary," I told her. "Really. My crush on Barron ended with our cruise."

"Didn't any of you suspect the real killer?" Raul asked. "Slim says he was completely taken in."

"Scott Barnes was definitely flying below the radar," I said. "He seemed so harmless, like the nerdy boy next door. Like...."

Without thinking, I started looking around the Bar Bar. Except, Scott was really nothing like Justin. Justin's a bit of a nerd, but he's a sweet, passionate, straight-up guy. Scott was a slick, greedy businessman masquerading as a grungy hipster. Justin, I suddenly realized, was not a cruiser and he never would be.

"Justin's not here," Rodrigo told me. "I ran into his friend Pete. Justin's gone to his parents in the Bay Area for the rest of the summer."

Yeah. I just might get to keep my job, but I'd definitely lost my boyfriend. It hadn't quite sunk in yet.

"Why wouldn't he go on the cruise with me?" I asked my friends, for the first time. "If he really loved me he would've done it. It would've been good for him, 'cause he needs to learn to have more fun."

There was a long silence while my friends exchanged uncomfortable glances. I was going to make them tell me what I already knew.

Finally, Raul said, "It may be for the best, Armando. If I may use a nautical term, Justin is like an anchor for you. That's not a bad thing, he's just got different needs than you do right now. Don't ask him to change, and don't try to change yourself. You can't cruise if you're anchored down."

As I let this sink in, Rodrigo changed the subject. "I still don't get why Blake's threats to sue Scott for the drop in stock prices, would be enough for him to kill Blake. I wonder if there was something else Blake had on him."

Slim shook his head. "Scott had me fooled. He was a real cutthroat when it came to video gaming, but I saw that as just, like, an amazing skill. Not a mindset. You know?"

"I didn't suspect Scott," said Rodrigo. "I kept thinking Blake had an accident, or maybe even cut the rope himself to fake a sabotage, and it ended up backfiring. Blake was malevolent. Then, I thought Rick might be good for it. He was so anxious and hard to like. Just the kind of person Blake would have picked on in some sick way, and driven to murder."

"Lucy thinks Blake never had anything on Rick. Blake liked having someone around to suck up to him," I said.

"How did Blake get all this dirt on people? And why?" Slim asked.

"Scott, Dan, and Rick, were all successful businessmen who started out middle class and worked their way up. Blake resented people who were self-made because he wasn't. When he read about people like that, he used his family newspapers to investigate them."

"Trying to prove they cheated to get where they were," Rodrigo said. "And, of course, he found some who had. Getting a bunch of his targets on the cruise was Blake's idea of fun."

"And we all had the fucking terrible luck to be caught in the middle," I said. "Here's to never again setting foot on a cruise ship."

I raised my drink in the air, and we drank a toast. And no, we were definitely not drinking Beachside Bonfires.

***

Tuesday morning, I woke up less worried I was going to be shitcanned. But I still went out of my way to get in early.

"Here you go, *Jefa*, all part of the service!" I sashayed into her office, half an hour before my start time of eight-thirty, and placed on her desk a decaf café latte made with half-and-half, in a new Starbucks thermos to replace the one the now-fired attorney Snyder had destroyed. The new tumbler was black, with a vibrant design of delicate straight lines that made a pattern of red and white camellias with green and yellow leaves. I served it with a small raspberry scone, on one of the china saucers from her tea set.

"Is there an occasion for this?" she asked, shooting me a blue gaze over her reading glasses.

"Just trying to put our office back together, boss. I'm off to start on those translations for you, unless there's something more you need right now."

She folded her hands on the desk in front of her, a gesture I call her ready position.

"Sit down," she said. "We need to talk."

This is it, I thought. After all the times in the last five years that I'd quit, all the times I'd walked out on her only to come back, I was finally being given the boot.

"Last night, Armando, I came to a realization."

"About what?" I tried to keep my voice from shaking.

"It's about my sister. I realized I can't fix her hoarding problem, and I can't have her in my home. Those stupid doctors tried to make me believe I'm part of her problem or part of some solution they have in mind for her. But this is something she has to do herself. I tried to help, even after Claude told me I couldn't fix her. When she leaves the hospital today, she's going back to her own house. Armando, call a moving company."

33
Recovery

Wednesday afternoon, Claude came to the office carrying a huge bouquet of white roses. Frankly, after her licentious behavior the preceding week, I thought Lucy should be the one bringing the flowers to him. But I kept my smart mouth shut. Things between me and Lucy were going pretty good, especially after I'd worked overtime the day before so Lucy could dislodge her sister and get her home back. However, the Sandy Sanders Moving Project was now over, and my job was by no means secure. So, I greeted Claude politely and made him a cup of his favorite Lapsang Souchong tea.

Lucy was in her alpha chair in the front room, waiting for her afternoon Golden Monkey tea to steep. When Claude came in, she remained in her teatime position, ankles primly crossed, and held out her hand like a queen. And, I swear to god, he actually took her hand and kissed it before handing her the flowers.

"Claude! How lovely! I'm so glad you came early. We've gotten Sandy out of my home. You were right, Claude! I can't help her. We've gone with Armando's original storage locker solution. Armando let the movers in yesterday, and all her stuff is out of my house and into her storage locker. Then they cleared out the bedroom and bathroom at her own house, so she can sleep there again. I've alerted her day treatment therapist to prepare her for the changes, and Armando's going to pick her up from her treatment this afternoon and take her home. I have my house back. What a relief!"

"Good call, Luce," Claude said. "Well. You've had quite a week."

"Yes, I've gotten a lot done. We've gotten a lot done: you, Armando, and I. Your investigation helped solve the murders on the *Adonis*."

"I don't know 'bout that. That Dan Leone seemed good for the murder of Blake Copland, based on all his shady criminal activities, but it wasn't him after all."

"Yes, but the information you just got me about Scott Barnes's company, GamezOn, will be crucial to showing Scott's motive for killing Blake."

"Scott was such a smart guy," I said. "If he was doing something really illegal, it's hard to believe Blake would have found it so easily. I mean, Dan left a paper trail Claude found right away. But Scott? He would be more careful. It would be like playing one of his video games, only in real life. And I don't exactly understand what Blake even had on him."

Lucy put down her teacup and smoothed her skirt around her knees.

"As Scott admitted," she said, "Blake was threatening legal action based on supposed misrepresentations of the company's value before the public offering. Scott wasn't worried about that, but he had something else to hide. Claude and his assistant just found out what it is. Scott did have a lucrative patent on gaming technology when he started GamezOn, but then he'd branched out and put a lot of money into developing a gaming system that he hoped to market in China. The system turned out to violate international restrictions on Internet gambling. Scott was resorting to bribery to get an exemption so he could capture the lucrative Chinese market."

"Wow, how'd you find that out?" I asked.

"It was Luce's idea to look into GamezOn's dealings in China," Claude answered, for her. "Fortunately, my assistant Tom has some contacts there."

Lucy said, "Armando, you told me Scott had been seeing a Chinese man on the cruise. I'd wondered what Scott was really doing on that cruise, because it didn't seem like his kind of thing. Why would a closeted gay start-up millionaire obsessed with his company and with video gaming go on a luxury cruise? He was looking for a covert way to meet with his Chinese associate, and when he got the offer for this cruise it was the perfect cover.

"The irony is, I doubt Blake even knew about this bribery scheme. When Scott didn't seem worried by Blake's initial threats, Blake probably bluffed. He hinted he knew something that could destroy Scott's business. An experienced gamer like Scott should have spotted the bluff. But this was real life, and his company was at stake. Scott became paranoid and overreacted. He had a need to take control."

"Why'd Scott kill Dan Leone, then?" Claude asked. "Seems to me he would've gotten away with the rope sabotage. Unless Dan saw or heard something?"

"There, I suspect Dan's sense of humor may have signed his death warrant. Armando, you told me Dan joked about what he'd do if he'd seen something, like someone throwing a knife overboard. In his paranoid state, and, if I may say, having gotten a taste for real violence and murder, Scott decided Dan had to go. And the beauty of framing Dan for Blake's death was that it would make Scott safe from further investigation of his own financial ties to Blake."

"How's anyone going to prove all this?" Claude asked.

"It'll be tough. Scott Barnes will get a good lawyer and the charges will be bargained down. Blake gave too many people on that ship a motive to kill him. And the forensic evidence as to the cause of Dan's death has likely been destroyed or compromised by the quick and messy removal of his body. An autopsy may or may not disprove suicide."

I thought of something. "Wait," I said. "One thing about this story doesn't fit, Boss. Blake must have threatened Scott the first day he was on the *Adonis,* not when they were on Grand Cayman. Because Scott tried to sabotage Blake's diving gear the very next day."

"I don't think it was Scott who sabotaged the diving gear. The butler Evans most likely did that. As we know, he had complicated feelings about Blake. I think he intended to punish Blake for defying Kronos's orders, and for threatening all the butlers. I don't think he intended to kill him. If not Evans, it may have been Kronos himself."

Lucy began to tell Claude about the cruise ship and her brush with death on the Concierge catamaran. I cleared off the tea things.

"Boss, I'm off to pick up your sister. It'll be four-thirty by the time I get to Hillcrest. Do you want me to come back here after?"

"No. Help Sandy take her bags in, and make sure she gets settled in her bedroom. If she flips out because we cleaned out her room, call the police and have her taken back to the hospital."

"No worries. I'll stay with her a while," Armando says. "I'll get her some dinner on the way home, and make sure she's got something to watch on TV tonight."

Before grabbing my jacket and messenger bag, I checked out my reflection in the big gilded mirror that hangs on the back wall above the tea cabinet. Uh-huh. My hair was stiff and high, and my cheeks glowed from my days in the sun and sea. After I unloaded Ms. Sandy Sanders, I'd hit the Bar Bar and pretend I was still on vacation. I admired the brightness of my eyes and how my lashes still looked ridiculously long, but even more exotic and healthy since they'd been sun-bleached at the tips. Behind me, I realized Lucy and Claude had lowered their voices. But I could still hear them.

"Pretty Boy's being awful solicitous," Claude was saying.

"He's going through a bad break-up with Justin, triggered by his poor choice in blowing his money on the cruise," Lucy whispered. "I've never felt so sorry for him."

"That high-end cruise wasn't exactly what he was expecting. What was he thinking? Ain't those excursions just for old people who can't travel the regular ways anymore, or people who want to spend their whole day goin' from one unwholesome buffet to another?"

"Well…." Lucy began. And stopped.

Claude gave a sort of sigh. Then he said, "Or people stay in their cabins and screw their brains out."

"I've learned these gay cruises are a special case," Lucy told him. "They're about getting attention, and spending time in an atmosphere of total acceptance. Armando got a little too much of the attention, from the wrong places, and he didn't know how to handle it. I was afraid he'd be useless at work until he got over all his disappointments. Fortunately, for some reason, he's stepping up."

"We'll see how long that lasts," Claude said.

"Yes, he'll be back to his pert, rebellious self soon enough. I wish it could have worked out between him and Justin. Perhaps there's something I can do...."

I cleared my throat and gathered my things.

"Good evening to you both," I called out. "See you tomorrow, Boss!"

On my way out, I heard Lucy say, "Before we go out to dinner tonight, Claude, we'll have a nice long walk with the dogs."

"I thought your ankle was too sore," he said.

"Ankle? What are you on about? I walked the ten blocks back from court today, and I could go on forever."

I closed the door behind me and walked out into the warm evening.

R.H. Bishop is a San Diego-based attorney and the author of the Lucy Sanders and Armando Felan mystery series.

If you liked ***Cruising to Death***, don't miss the other books in the series:

Errant Justice
In the first Armando and Lucy Mystery, Lucy must defend a charismatic immigrant suspected of poisoning his attorney girlfriend. Will Armando and Lucy be able to save him and find the real killer, or will they kill each other first?

Cheating Death
A wealthy young bride falls off the treacherous cliffs of Torrey Pines Park. Her sister says it was no accident, but the police don't see it that way. Do Lucy and Armando make a dangerous mistake in agreeing to take on the investigation?

The Missing Justice (coming in Spring, 2020)
It's 2021 and Lucy is called to Washington D.C. to investigate the disappearance of her old friend, a Supreme Court Justice. The new POTUS also faces danger from the same unknown source—will Lucy and her team be able to save her? And will Armando find a way to work with his old boyfriend Justin, now a Supreme Court law clerk?

Visit *rhbishopbooks.com* for more about R.H. Bishop and the Armando and Lucy Mystery series.

Made in the USA
Las Vegas, NV
22 December 2020

14607678R00155